Love in a
Lost Land

Love in a Lost Land

James MacManus

First published in Great Britain in 2023 by
whitefox publishing, in partnership with James MacManus

www.wearewhitefox.com

ISBN 978-1-915635-41-9
Also available as an eBook
ISBN 978-1-915635-42-6

Designed and typeset by Koki Design
Cover design by Simon Levy
Project management by whitefox
Printed and bound by CPI Group (UK) Ltd, Croydon CR0 4YY

For Sally

Et pour Marie-Aude, cette belle jeune femme que j'ai
laissée a Paris il y a toutes ces années

Prologue

'I knew a country once that closed like a book at night, folding its stories into secrets told only to a few. I knew that country by night, never by day. Daytime was what might have been, a never-never land of hopes and dreams.

Night-time was for the death of hope, the darkness of the soul and what little love one could find in the landscape of a lost country. But it was beautiful; not the beauty of parched plains fingered by wind-bent trees and thorny scrub that would tear the shirt off your back; nor the beauty found in the rumple of grey-green hills that beckoned from every horizon.

The beauty I found was in a people unforgiven by history; a people who faced their end like the Stoics of old. They had no choice, of course, any more than I did when I crossed the border that night. I did so out of duty, not by choice.'

I smiled when I read those words in an old notebook that had turned up in the back of a desk drawer. A little precious, pretentious perhaps, but I think I was trying to find poetry in a lost cause, the inevitable conflict between those who have power and those who wish to take it. What little history I knew taught me that power and privilege always yield to the tides of time. That sounds a bit grandiose to describe a short and sordid war. I say sordid because all the wars I have ever seen have been bloody, belittling affairs that deny those involved the worth of their sacrifice.

But I did find romance in that war. I mean romance in the old sense, the romance of men and women fighting against logic and history for a doomed cause. Only one end awaited them. Their anthems would fall silent. Their flags would fold. They would become the fallen and, cruellest of all, the forgotten. That was the romance I found among black and white in that strange country. The remembrance of those days still makes me shiver and reach for a glass of whisky. It was a long time ago, but then everything in the past, even yesterday, is a long time ago.

Chapter One

I t was getting dark as we drove along an old riverbed that cut through the mountains to the border. The last of the sun laid a rim of gold on the high ridges. It had been a three-hour drive up from the coast and a similar stretch lay ahead to the city. The frontier was a simple affair: a metal barrier across the road, a couple of huts, arc lights slung from poles and a tall radio mast. All borders held the same sense of pleasurable promise, the crossing from an end to a beginning. The police officer looked at my passport and handed it to a colleague, who took it into a hut. He returned after a few minutes, told me to report to the ministry in the morning and waved us on.

The driver, a stranger who had offered me a lift the night before, said nothing, but smoked steadily and drove faster than seemed sensible at night. I had been advised to drink whisky every evening to avoid malaria. I had a small flask in my pocket and took a quick pull.

The wash of our headlights occasionally picked out countryside that turned from forest to open grassland as we left the mountains. It was a good tarmac road and we made the city just after eight.

'Good luck,' said the stranger, leaving me outside a large hotel with a pillared entrance. 'Franklins Hotel' was picked out in large gilt lettering above the portico. Music drifted from the panorama windows of a restaurant. Men in suits and ties, women dressed as if they had stepped from the pages of an old fashion magazine, faced each other across white tablecloths. Somewhere a band was playing.

I went to the bar as arranged. There was a mirror on the back wall engraved with dancing girls kicking up petticoats to reveal shapely legs. There were blown-up photographs of old Paris on the walls, turn-of-the-century images of horse-drawn cabs on sunlit boulevards, women with parasols, men in stiff three-piece suits and top hats, children on small bicycles. It was called the Cancan Bar.

The illusion of Parisian glamour and the fake zebra-skin bar-stool seats were unexpected. A barman with a blue sash across his white jacket was preparing a cocktail with the care of a priest setting out sacraments for Mass. With hair greying at the temples, a salt-and-pepper pencil moustache and an impressive bulk, he exuded the avuncular air of someone prepared to listen to the woes of lonely drinkers while mixing yet another lethal drink. He looked at me without expression and nodded to a woman sitting alone in the corner.

She wore a simple knee-length black dress with a large amber brooch that held the soft light from a few table lamps. A small gold disc hung from a thin chain around her neck.

There was an inscription or maybe a line of numerals on the disc. In the mirror, I could see that her glossy black hair fell halfway down her back.

'You must be Richard,' she said, looking me in the eye as she spoke.

The voice was firm. Jade-green eyes. I tried to place the accent. I knew very little about her. Sara Jane Shannon had been born here. Her father had died in a car crash when she was a child. Her early years had been spent with her mother in New York. She had worked as a photographer in Vietnam and then the Middle East. I was told she had had a breakdown there. A friend had been killed and a love affair had turned bad. Something like that. Now she had come back to her beginning.

'You look tired. Have a drink.'

The barman with the blue sash appeared.

'Gin and tonic,' I said.

She shook her head.

'Local cane spirit. Have a whisky.'

I ordered a whisky and soda.

'A large one, please, half and half with soda.'

'I'll have the same,' she said.

The barman returned swiftly with the drinks. I thanked him. He nodded.

She smiled, fiddled in her handbag, produced a pack of cigarettes and offered me one.

'No, thank you.'

She smoked, inhaled deeply and formed her mouth into an O to expel a grey plume of smoke that refused to assume the required shape and drifted away to the fake chandelier on the ceiling.

'How shall we start,' she said, 'your story or mine?'

'Let's hear yours.'

She laughed.

'I'm sure you've been told all about me.'

'Not really.'

I repeated the brief details I had been given. She stubbed out the cigarette and lit another one.

'There's a bit more to it than that.'

'I am sure there is.'

'Maybe another time.'

She paused, drank her whisky and ordered us two more.

'So, you've come to see our little war, have you?'

'You make it sound like a spectator sport.'

She stopped smiling. 'Well, it isn't.'

We did not talk long. She took me briefly through the history of the country, telling me what I already knew. Then she moved on to the weather.

'Everything works around the weather,' she said. 'It's October, and in a few weeks the rains will start. So, the farmers have to plant now.'

She drank deeply from her glass and lit another cigarette. I started to say something when she said, 'Tobacco, maize, soy beans, winter wheat.'

'I was about to ask about the war, actually.'

'Oh, the war.' She laughed. 'Of course. Well, the war depends on the weather, too. Soon it will be the rainy season, when low cloud makes flying difficult. They have the added advantage of thick cover. That's when they come over in big numbers.'

'"They"?'

'Don't act the fool, and don't take me for one,' she said.

She spoke evenly, without raising her voice. The terms of our discussion were becoming clear. She would give me limited help and advice. She did not like my presence in the country and thought herself better able to cover the story – as she saw it. I was working for a big American magazine. She was a fixer being paid a fee to assist me.

'The terrs, terrorists, guerrillas, freedom fighters – take your pick. In the dry season we have the advantage: the bush dries up, tracking is easier and air strikes resume.'

I wanted to hear more, but she apologised and said she had to go. She stood up and smoothed her skirt. My face must have betrayed disappointment. I was a stranger in a strange country.

'All right,' I said, 'but tell me this, where do I begin?'

Her smile returned and, with it, a half-laugh.

'Another time,' she said. 'I'm sorry, but I have to meet friends.'

We shook hands. It was a gesture as fake as the Parisian past on the walls. She paused.

'Two things,' she said. 'First, don't trust anyone here, not even your mother. Second, hire a car and drive as far as you can out of town. The further you get, the more you will find out – but drive fast, don't stop!'

Then she was gone, allowing me a little hand-wave over her shoulder as she left.

•

I rented an old Peugeot the next morning and drove north. The choice was arbitrary. The map showed some small settlements about 80 miles away. I liked their names: Mrewa, Mtoko, Shamva. The car drove well.

The city quickly gave way to sweeping grasslands sliced by drainage ditches. The fields were scattered with cows and bordered by pinewoods that climbed gentle hills. It was not what I expected, cultivated English countryside in the middle of Africa.

I made good time on the tarmac road, which soon rose into brown, dry country broken by clusters of thatched mud rondavels and rust-coloured tin shacks. The leafy branches of the few trees cast shadows over the sandy soil. Goats and dogs wandered by the roadside. Smoke drifted over these places. The only people I could see were young boys playing football on dusty makeshift pitches.

At one such settlement, I saw a group of women burdened with bundles of food and washing, moving quietly across the foreground. There were plenty of cattle in the fields beyond, but mostly rib-thin. I stopped the car. More people came into view, old men sitting on what looked like abandoned car seats. The silence was ominous, as if something fierce and untameable was about to leap from the bush.

Heat and silence made me want to shout a greeting, walk over and introduce myself. I felt then, as I was to do many times in the months to come, both a stranger and an intruder. This was the Africa I had come to write about, the real Africa, not cancan girls kicking up their legs in a hotel bar. But I didn't. I got out and waved. Receiving no response, I got back in the car. She had said to drive fast without stopping. I drove on.

The road rose once more to irrigated land, but not as before. Strips of rough country clumped with towering anthills and thorn bush lay between the rich red-black earth of ploughed fields ready for planting.

I passed a road sign at speed and just caught the name 'Shamva' before cresting a hill. Below in a valley lay a group of whitewashed brick houses with red and green roofs. The country around had been coloured gold by the dry season, with emerald-green islands of watered land.

I drove slowly through the town, past a police station, a small chapel, a farmer's co-op and a sign to a gold mine. On the outskirts I found what I was looking for, a weathered wooden board with a barely visible inscription: 'The Shamva Country Club'. 'You will find your stories where drink is taken,' a wise old bird had said to me long ago. And I needed a drink.

'What are you having?' said a voice as I walked into a long gloomy room made darker by the sunlight outside.

A wooden bar top ran the length of one wall. The voice came from the far end. As my eyes adjusted, I saw a tall sunburnt figure wearing jeans and a bush jacket. Before I could reply, he had asked the barman for two beers. I joined him. He raised a glass and said welcome. I thanked him. We drank in silence until he nodded to the barman. Two whiskies appeared. He raised his glass. I did the same. We clinked and downed in one.

'Come and have some lunch,' he said.

'You don't know who I am.'

'You're a stranger; that's good enough.'

He collected a rifle at the door and headed towards an old truck. It was an FN rifle, standard issue to modern armies.

'Do you use that much?' I asked.

He looked at me with hazy eyes as if trying to remember who I was.

'Yes,' he said.

I followed him as he drove out of town for a while and then turned onto a dirt road. Green Creek Farm lay in a clutch of green trees overlooking an L-shaped single-storey house with a corrugated iron roof surrounded by a wire fence. The fence was twice the height of a man and strung with small silver objects that looked like Christmas decorations. A rope from a tree was slung low over a small swimming pool. Beyond the house in a dip lay a fenced compound of mud- or wattle-walled huts.

A woman wearing khaki trousers and a dark green shirt greeted us, seemingly unsurprised at the appearance of a stranger. I introduced myself and said I worked for an American magazine.

'A writer,' she said. 'So, you're one of those, are you?' She laughed. 'John's always bringing waifs and strays back from the club, but we haven't had a writer before. I'm Layla Milan. Come and eat something.'

She turned and shouted at no one I could see, 'Julia, tell cook there's one more for lunch.'

A young woman in shorts and T-shirt skipped out of the house and beckoned me. She was pale, freckle-faced and had the athletic look of a sports champion, tennis perhaps. I could see a hard-surface court at the side of the house. She took me inside to a long dining room.

'As you may have gathered, I'm Julia,' she said. 'I'll fetch the others.' She looked at me for a moment, the quizzical expression on her face seeming to ask what I was doing there, and then she left.

I looked around. Large windows at one end were covered by wire-mesh cages that projected several inches from the outer wall. Two small silver pheasants faced each other on a long well-polished table. They looked oddly out of place. The room was lined with hunting trophies: heads of antelope, buffalo and other creatures I could not identify. The centrepiece of this collection was a pair of elephant tusks mounted on a wooden base.

On the mantelpiece over the fireplace stood a collection of fading photographs of family ancestors standing stiffly to attention for the camera. They were dressed smartly, the men in suits with wing-collared shirts and ties, the women in long dresses and bonnets. It was as if they were going to church on a Sunday morning. There was a farmhouse in the background and beyond a ridge of mountains. The women held hands with small children who clutched closely to their sides. I supposed the photo had been taken in the early days of colonial rule. They would all be dead now, their lives trapped like flies on yellowing paper.

The door opened and a middle-aged couple walked in, she purposefully crossing the room to shake my hand, he greeting me with a small wave from the far side of the table.

Julia returned to introduce us. Arnold and Hazel Elphinstone were neighbours, she said, and farmed a short distance away, the last farm on the dirt road along the valley.

'Rising Moon Farm. It's a beautiful place,' said Julia, 'you should see their orchids, they've got thousands of them under glass, every variety, every colour.'

'You grow orchids?' I asked. Hazel Elphinstone frowned and shook her head as if an embarrassing secret had been revealed.

Her husband said, 'Silly really, it's the wrong climate, far too cold at night, but they do alright under glass with a heater.'

'We are ordinary farmers, we just do the orchids as a side line,' said Hazel.

'And make a lot of money out of it,' said Julia. 'Airfreight every week to Europe, isn't it?'

'Shh,' said Hazel Elphinstone, putting a finger to her lips.

I wanted to hear more of what promised to be a good sidebar piece. Orchids were an unusual crop in a heavily sanctioned country supposedly gripped by guerrilla war. It was a counter-intuitive story that would interest my readers.

But I was to hear no more of orchids at that lunch. John and Layla Milan joined us and we all sat down to plates of cold chicken and slices of thick-cut ham served with baked potatoes and salad. Water was served from a pewter jug. For a few minutes, we ate in silence. I had a feeling that my unexpected presence had stifled the usual talk between these people.

I gathered the Elphinstones had come to Africa to escape a socialist government in Britain after the Second World War My attempt to draw them out on the cultivation of orchids was politely rebuffed. Neither they nor the Milans seemed interested in the stranger who had been plucked from the country club.

'Julia is in the national swimming team,' her mother finally said.

'Got a lot of medals,' said John Milan.

'Congratulations,' I said. 'Where do you swim?'

'Pool in town,' said Julia.

She raised her forearm to show a tattooed dolphin on the

underside. She had pale, translucent skin that had been kept well away from the African sun.

'The Dolphin Club,' she said.

'That must have been painful,' I replied.

'Not really,' said Julia.

We went on eating. I broke another long silence and asked about the silver objects I had seen on the wire fence. I made a little joke, saying they looked like party decorations.

'They're bells,' said Layla Milan.

'So we can hear them when they climb the wire,' said Julia. She smiled sweetly at me. 'Are you married?'

Layla Milan looked up sharply from her plate.

'Julia, really! You can't ask that!'

'Just curious, Mum. Why not?'

'Because it's rude. Mr, erm . . . is a guest.'

'Brady. Richard Brady,' I said. 'And no, I'm not married.'

'What are you actually doing here?' said Julia.

'He's here to write stories about us.' Layla waved a fork at me. 'But I hope you'll tell the truth for once. We never get a decent word from the foreign press.'

We drank only water. Afterwards, I was taken onto the veranda and given a cup of coffee. The Elphinstones briefly said goodbye. Hazel said, 'Come and visit us sometime and we'll show you the orchids.'

'I'd love to,' I said and I meant it. I watched them taking their rifles out of a Land Rover and slipping the safety catches off before driving away. Guns and orchids. I would definitely visit them.

John Milan waved a farewell and, without being asked, gave me a version of the family story.

Grandfather Milan had come up in a pioneer column in the 1890s and bought land from the local African chief for a bottle of brandy and a blanket.

'It was good French brandy,' he said.

I slipped a notebook from my breast pocket and began to write. He didn't seem to mind. Generations of the family had built up the farm, he said.

'We worked this land with our boys down there.' He pointed to the huts I had seen. 'Our sweat was their sweat. It was a hard life but good.'

He stepped off the veranda, bent down and scooped up a handful of earth. He let it trickle away between his fingers.

'It's good land,' he said. 'Rich and strong.'

I decided to ask about the 'boys' later. The farming was very much as I had been told: a seasonal struggle against the weather to plant and harvest maize, soya beans and corn.

John Milan talked of the early days of the farm without emotion or apparent pride. The conversation slipped a gear and he began talking of the war as if this was an irritating seasonal occurrence. The family now lived a compound life, staying behind the wire after dark and watching the roads for landmines and ambushes by day.

'Ambushes?' I said.

'The first group will try to shoot out your tyres. Down the road, as you roll to a stop, the killer group will be waiting.'

'Does this happen often?' I said, trying to sound as casual as possible. I was going to drive back that afternoon. I had been in the country for barely twenty-four hours. It didn't seem possible that I was going to risk death in an ambush.

'Often enough,' he said. 'They're getting clever. The tarmac softens in the sun at this time of year. They use a serrated bin lid to lift out the surface, scoop out enough dirt to slip in a Chinese mine, then smooth the tar over with a trowel. It's very hard to see when you're doing 150 klix.'

'How about going faster?' It was a stupid question because my old hire car could barely do 100 kph.

John shook his head. 'Makes no difference. Once you trip the mine the engine turns to shrapnel and all you have left on this earth is bleeding time.'

Bleeding time. I underlined the words. He watched me writing, seemingly interested in the hieroglyphics of my shorthand. When I looked up from my notebook he offered me a brandy. I needed it.

'Local. We can't get the French stuff.'

'Fine by me,' I said, and took the drink. It gripped the back of my throat like strong cough mixture.

'You're not going back tonight,' he said. 'It's too late.'

I looked at my watch: four o'clock. Down on the coast, where I had spent a fruitless week, the sun went down at six as if a light had been turned off. I imagined it would be the same up here in the high country. I wanted to get back to town. I couldn't spend a night with these people. I made up a dinner engagement.

'You'll be OK,' Layla Milan said. 'Pick up the convoy at the Mtoko turn-off and don't stop for strangers. Thing to remember is that this is a small country if you're white.' She surprised me with a kiss on the cheek and waved me goodbye.

Julia jumped up and down beside the car as I moved off and motioned me to stop. I wound the window down.

'Come back soon,' she said. 'I'll show you our cave paintings. They are amazing. The bushmen did them. Over there.'

She pointed to a line of rock cliffs at the side of the valley about a mile way. I thanked her and wondered what life held for an attractive young woman driving on mined roads by day and living behind a fenced compound after dark.

•

I drove back faster than I had come that morning. The drink had made me sleepy, but the thought of my engine turning to shrapnel kept me awake. I squinted at the road ahead, trying to spot a slight lift in the tarmac or any other sign of danger. Pure paranoia. I had been in the country for less than a day. But the trip had been worth it.

My editor, Meredith Kaplan, would be pleased. In the Hollywood version of events, Meredith would be a tough, bespectacled chain-smoker with a line of well-rehearsed put-downs for any correspondent who dared question her orders. My Meredith was a quietly spoken middle-aged woman who had written a well-received book on the rise and fall of the Spanish empire and who had achieved her senior position on the magazine by good fortune.

Her popular predecessor had died of a heart attack while taking a balloon trip over the Aztec pyramids in Mexico, an irony that would not have been lost on Meredith. She said little to her colleagues, did not join the after-work drinks sessions and chewed gum all the time. Even on the phone you could hear the chewing sound.

She was an important part of my life because a relationship

between a writer in a distant and dangerous part of the world and a desk editor can be intense at times, to put it politely. But Meredith had never been in the field as a writer or reporter and it showed in her occasional disregard for the insecurities of her correspondents.

All writers fear failure, but Meredith Kaplan had never failed at anything. She had joined the magazine straight from college and quietly worked her way up, moving from the metropolitan desk to features and finally to foreign. She was impervious to the jealousy this aroused, or simply unaware of it. She was married to a lawyer but never spoke of her husband or any children.

I swayed in my seat as the road twisted and turned, trying to blot out thoughts of Chinese mines. I thought of Marie Claire. She would be back in the apartment now, throwing off her office clothes, pulling on jeans, a T-shirt, calling a friend on that ancient cradle phone, fixing drinks or dinner.

I knew it so well, 150 Rue de Rome. How often had I climbed every one of those steps, all 114, to that room under the eaves? I counted them every time. She would leave the door open at the top. There would be a glass of red wine on the table and always that scent, perfume mingled with whatever was cooking.

She had only a small stove and basin but produced better meals than any of the local restaurants. Breakfast would be fresh croissants from the bakery on the corner. She would come back bringing a waft of freshly baked bread into the apartment. She loved that place. And I loved her, or thought I did. Such memories had become unwanted companions. I pushed them away.

I did not even turn to look at the villages I had seen in the morning. The serenity of that scene vanished in blurred images of huts. The road divided shortly and I saw a line of mud-spattered cars waiting beside two camouflaged trucks mounted with machine guns. I did not stop. I had wondered whether the warnings about mines and ambushes were a jokey way of dealing with a member of the hated foreign press.

Looking back, I think that was when my innocence, naivety or perhaps wilful ignorance, whatever you call it, came to an end. I had thought this war was more fantasy than fact, a story of gallantry against the odds created to impress the western world with the need for recognition and support. The hideous decor of the Cancan Bar had suggested that the whole thing was a glorious fake.

But it wasn't. Bleeding time. The bells on the wire. The war was real enough.

Chapter Two

It was dark when I got back. I had missed my appointment with the ministry but I had a story of sorts. 'This is a small country if you're white.' It was a good quote, a pointer to racial exclusion, or white paranoia.

I had the story of the farm, the sale of land for a bottle of brandy and a blanket, enough for a short colour piece introducing my readers to this faraway war in Africa. I only needed to be here for a week, no more. That would give me two decent spreads inside and maybe a cover article if I was lucky.

I should have gone back to the hotel, made notes for the story and settled in for an early night. Instead, I walked across the central square, beneath flowering jacaranda trees. The city was silent except for the cicadas. The sound was like a million musicians sawing away at broken violins. It was the musical tapestry of every night I spent in that country. After a while it became comforting.

The Pen and Ink Club, known to all as Pinks, had been described to me as a meeting place for foreign correspondents, a gracious refuge from the world where weary writers could relax in peace and discuss the day's events over tall glasses of cold beer, or better still iced gin. The club was based in the Diplomat Hotel, which I later learnt was one of the few multiracial venues in the city.

I imagined there would be copies of international papers and bookshelves of African geography and history. The food would be simple but filling, slices of game pie, sausages or ham with pickles. I was hungry. Lunch was a distant memory.

I found myself in a small, crowded room without chairs or tables and only a plastic-topped bar across one end, tended by an African barman wearing a black T-shirt carrying the image of a clenched fist. Cellophane-wrapped sandwiches were stacked in a pile at one side. The only concession to comfort was a small alcove with bookcase-lined walls and a table and chairs.

There were about a dozen people in the room, mostly men gathered along the bar. They glanced at me, then turned back to their drinks. A young man with greasy hair plastered onto his skull and the sweaty look of a drunk came over. He put his hands on his hips, looked at me and frowned, as if searching for words. He was unsteady on his feet and the words were slurred.

'So, you're the new Pom, are you?'

The use of the word told me he was from Australia or New Zealand.

'Yes,' I said, wondering how he knew who I was.

He smiled suddenly and put out a welcoming hand.

'Come and have a drink. They water the whisky, but at least it's real Scotch. Here is my new friend,' he said to no one in particular.

He handed me a whisky.

'You get all sorts in here,' he said, 'black, white, brown, yellow, pink and purple; hacks, spies, hangers-on and girls who will blow you for a bite at the curry house down the road.'

He was John Quigley, a New Zealander as it happened, working for an overseas agency. He swayed as he talked.

'Stay away from the white farms. The roads are not safe and they will only feed you bullshit.'

With that information, he sank slowly to the floor, knelt briefly as if in prayer, then toppled sideways and closed his eyes. Two men detached themselves from the bar, picked him up and laid him, still asleep, against a wall. It was done as if this was a nightly occurrence.

The door opened. Sara Jane Shannon wore the same amber brooch and gold medallion. The dress was different, red and revealingly low cut. The crowd at the bar turned to look and offered greetings.

'I thought I might see you here,' she said. 'Whisky, if you're offering.'

The assumption was irritating. We drank for a few moments in silence.

'So how was the farm?'

'What farm?'

'Out at Shamva.'

I looked surprised.

'Word gets round,' she said. 'It's a small country if you're white.'

'I've heard that before.'

'I'm not surprised. A quarter of a million of us and six million of them.'

Irritation slid into anger. She was so self-satisfied, so sure that the country was 'them' and 'us', a racial divide planted along with a flag a long time ago.

Them and us. I thought of Winkler, a new boy, as I was, on our first day at prep school in England. He was small, olive-skinned and French. He had arrived in a large black car. The next day, a Saturday, I joined a group of jeering boys to teach Frenchie a lesson. We covered our hands with handkerchiefs and gathered stinging nettles. We chased that poor French boy across the parkland, around the school, into the woods and out again until he turned to face us on a tree stump. We leapt forward in turn to lash his legs with the nettles. The masters soon broke up the shameful scene.

That night retribution came in the shape of a wooden butter pat wielded by the deputy head, an Anglican chaplain who took Bible classes. The guilty boys, me included, were hauled out of bath, bed, wherever they were found, and beaten. Winkler left the next day. I often wondered what happened to him. I am still ashamed to think of it. Him and us.

Sara Jane knew she had irritated me, just as she knew she stood out in this crowd, an attractive figure among a group of shabby drinkers.

'So, how did it go?'

'They tried to stop me driving back.'

'You were stupid. You should have had a swim and flirted with that pretty daughter of theirs.'

'I seem to remember you told me to drive as far as I could.'

'Not at that time of day.'

'I don't think you told me that.'

'I'm not here to baby-sit you.'

The drinkers at the bar had fallen silent, trying to listen to this promising conversation.

'Well, just what are you supposed to do for me? They told me you would be my guide and . . .'

'Your back-up woman,' she said, and put a hand on my arm. I could smell the scent.

'We have very thick skins here,' she went on. 'The world has put us in a box marked "rebel racist regime". A nice alliteration, isn't it? Makes it easy to say. You may not believe it, but we all get on better than you might think. If you don't believe me, ask yourself why we have a waiting list of them wanting to join the army and the police.'

'"Them"?'

'Africans.'

I didn't say anything.

'It's just the way it is,' she said. 'We are beyond the pale, isn't that what Cromwell said about the Irish?'

I am Irish by descent. With a name like mine it was easy to guess. She looked at me as if sharing a hidden truth.

'I think I understand that,' I said.

'I doubt it.'

'So what next?'

'Check in with the Information Ministry. They know you are here and where you've been.'

'If I don't?'

'They will deport you.'

'If I do?'

'They will give you a week.'

'Then what? Another drive over mined roads?'

She smiled, shook her head and handed me her glass.

'More ice this time. See the ministry people tomorrow. Then go into the township, but be careful.'

'Everyone tells me to be careful.'

'Everyone is right. Informers, bad beer and cheap dope. The only white faces they see down there are the police. So don't stay long.'

She made me feel like a schoolboy, which was the point, I suppose. I remembered poor old Winkler again.

At the frontier I had felt a prickle of anticipation, the same pleasurable expectation one has in unwrapping a gift, but it would hardly have mattered if they had turned me back. There were other stories, other countries. Then, I could take it or leave it; now, I wanted to stay. I counted myself a magazine writer, not a journalist tied to the spinning wheel of news. But this was a story I could not miss. A reckoning lay ahead for these people.

Chapter Three

I telexed a brief message to Meredith Kaplan in New York. I had the outline of a story but not enough for the 5,000–7,000-word piece she wanted. The next morning, I saw a copy of the telex in front me. It lay on the desk of a kindly-looking man with thinning grey hair, aged about sixty. He had the yellow parchment skin of one who has spent a lifetime in the sun. A nameplate on the desk said I was about to talk to Peter Fryer, Director of Information. He pushed the telex to one side and bade me welcome. He waved me to a chair and picked up the document.

'So, you're a writer.'

'Yes.'

'What do you write?'

I said I had written travel books, a novel and a little unpublished poetry. I now worked for an American magazine, which had commissioned a series of articles on Africa.

'What sort of articles do you write for your magazine?'

'Everything from wildlife to people profiles: peasants in

the fields, politicians, women at home working. It's the high-low approach.'

'*High-low approach*,' he said, repeating the words as if struck by their wisdom. 'Normally we don't issue work permits to journalists who arrive without prior notice.'

'I'm not a journalist.'

I said nothing more but wondered how my telex had arrived on his desk.

'However, this is unusual.' He twirled a pencil around in the fingers of one hand.

'I am glad you think so.'

He stopped twirling and stood up.

'I am going to give you the benefit of the doubt.'

A brief lecture about the history and tribal background of the country followed. I learnt nothing that Sara Jane had not told me. Then he surprised me.

'You have a week's permit. Talk to everyone you can. Print what they say. You may not like some things you hear, your magazine may not even print them, but you might find out what is happening that way. And you won't be lying, like most of the journalists here do.'

•

The Arcadia township lay five miles from the city centre. The name, implying rustic harmony, must have been someone's idea of a joke. A taxi drove me out the next evening as it was getting dark. We passed the shiny city centre with its high-rise buildings and shopping malls and headed into the wealthy suburbs where houses concealed themselves behind high hedges and security fences. I peered out of the grimy cab windows. Apart from the occasional sight of swimming pools and tennis courts, there was no sign of life.

In a poorer suburb, bungalows with small gardens and no pool gave way to the industrial zone, with factories, power plants and sewage farms. We passed a few cars and the occasional bus on the road. My attempts at conversation were met with a grunted reply or silence.

The township was laid out in a grid pattern of tarmac main streets with baked-earth and gravel side streets. Street lights were regularly spaced along the road. The housing was identical: all brick-and-tin single-storey shacks with small yards or gardens at the back.

There were plenty of people walking the streets, mostly colourfully dressed women towing small children. We passed water fountains, basketball courts and steepled clapboard churches. The driver stopped and asked me again where I was going. The Victoria Hotel, I said. An old guidebook had described it as a lively centre of township life, but that was long before the war. The driver shook his head, drove two blocks and stopped outside a two-storey building with a sign saying 'Hotel and Bar, Day and Night'.

As I paid him he said, 'You really want to go in there?' He did not wait for a reply and drove off.

I seemed to be spending all my time in the same bar. Where drink is taken, stories flow. A long wooden counter ran along one wall. Here the barman wore no sashed uniform, just a black T-shirt with a red clenched fist printed on the front above the legend 'A Luta Continua' picked out in silver. I knew enough Portuguese to know what that meant: the struggle continues. He was tall, skinny and gave me a look that was not welcoming.

'A beer, please.'

'Who are you looking for?' he said, making no effort to get my drink.

'No one. I'm just here for a drink.'

'No, you're not.'

'I just want a beer.'

'How about a girl?'

We stared at each other until a voice behind me said, 'Give the man a beer.'

The barman cracked open a bottle and pushed it across the bar.

'Four dollars,' he said.

'That's a lot of money for a beer.'

'And you're a lot of man coming down here.'

I paid, took the beer and sat with my back to the wall. A face thrust itself into my vision. A wispy moustache sparked with amber droplets. He had two prominent buck teeth.

'Jesus Amari. They call me Jeeze.'

He spoke in a husky whisper, as if afraid someone might overhear us. He swigged from a bottle of beer and put out a hand. I took it and nodded.

'What can I do for you?' he said.

I said nothing and looked around. A crowd of young men were laughing, smoking, drinking from bottles of beer labelled 'Castle'. They turned as one to look at me, then turned back into a huddle of talk.

In one corner, three women sat at a table. They wore uniforms: navy-blue slacks, with denim jackets and identity tags on tapes around their necks. Nurses or teachers, I guessed. They were drinking beer like everyone else and looked hard at me for a few seconds.

'You're a foreign journalist,' Jeeze said.

I nodded. He shook my hand again.

'I can get you whatever you want – interviews with the right people, money exchange.'

'Thanks. I'm OK.'

He sat back with a long, gurgling laugh and pointed to a young woman behind the bar.

'Fifty dollars, nice room.'

'No, thanks.'

Jeeze frowned and swigged his beer.

'Plenty of smoke if you want, cheap too, strong stuff.'

'How do you know I'm not a policeman?'

'No way.'

He gently pinched the skin of my hand.

'Where you come from the sun don't shine. I'd say you were looking for a little relaxation . . .'

'I've told you, I'm just looking around.'

He laughed.

'Your type don't come here to look around. See him over there?'

He pointed to a short young man with beringed hands and oiled hair slicked back into a ponytail.

'He can get you good stuff. Let me talk to him.'

'Maybe later. Let me buy you a beer.'

Jeeze told me he was a columnist on the local paper, the *Daily Herald*.

'It's run by whites, but to make themselves feel good and

27

show the world what a nice multiracial country this is, they throw us the odd bone.'

'And you're the bone?'

'Yeah. I write a weekly column.'

'And you can write what you like?'

Again the gurgling laugh that sounded like water running out of a bath.

'Listen up, I play the game, we all do. The whites play the tune and they think we dance to it. But we don't.'

'Is it safe out there?'

I nodded to the window.

'For now, yes. But it's coming. Yeah, it's coming, all right.'

I asked when he thought the war would lead to independence. Jeez shook his head and pointed to the three women sipping their drinks.

'You want to know what we think? Talk to the sisters.'

He went over, bent his head in brief conversation and came back.

'Buy them a beer and they will come,' he said.

I nodded. Jeeze ordered the beers and waved to the women.

Charity, Patience and Rosie were teachers. Introductions were made and then there was silence while we looked at each other.

Patience was in her early thirties, I guessed, the oldest of the three. She was a head taller than the others and had a large yellow butterfly clasp in her hair and big black diamanté disc earrings. Her nails were painted with yellow varnish. The effect seemed out of place with a teacher's uniform of white shirts and slacks. She smiled at me, a thin whisper of a smile. There was a flash of flint in her smoky grey eyes. Doubt and displeasure creased her face.

'Are you from the ministry?'

'What ministry?'

'They come here and inspect us. Bars, shops, hostels, schools – everything has to be inspected.'

'No, I am not an inspector.'

'What are you doing here?'

'I am a writer.'

'You write books?'

'No, I write for a magazine.'

She laughed and talked briefly in her own language to her companions, who laughed in turn.

'You come here to judge us?'

'I'm not here to judge anyone. I'm here to learn.'

Then she smiled properly and I saw her for the first time. She was beautiful, the beauty that comes with grace, the beauty of high cheekbones, dark doubting eyes, black hair scooped back into a bun. A frayed denim jacket turned up at the collar and left open over the school uniform shirt suggested both allure and arrogance.

'Learn what? What life is like being black in a white man's country – is that it?'

'Yes.'

'No, it's not. You are lying.'

Jeeze, who had been listening to this exchange with increasing alarm, jumped up and said something quickly in the local language.

He turned to me and said, 'I'm sorry.'

Patience swung round to him, raising one finger and holding it in the air like an admonitory schoolmistress.

'Don't apologise for me,' she said. 'He is like all the others.

29

They fly in from far away, stay in that smart hotel, write stories saying that white rule is terrible and it's not going to last. That makes them feel good because they say what the folks back home want to hear. Then they go to that fancy bar, drink cocktails and try to pick up a white girl. Sometimes they ask the barman if he can get a black girl for them. The next day they're gone.'

She turned to face me.

'Am I right?'

The anger was genuine. It was hard to think of a reply that wouldn't provoke her further.

'I'm sorry you feel that way.'

'Go home. You've no business here.'

'But I do.'

'No, you don't. You can't read our language, you can't speak our language, you know nothing about us. All you want to do is tell the world how many of our boys are dying in the bush. What's the ratio? Thirty of ours to one of yours, isn't it? That must make you feel good.'

'Not at all. I hate the killing. It's senseless that so many young men are dying.'

She ignored the remark.

'You sit around your steak barbecues, drink gin by the pool and have nothing to worry about. Thirty to one. That's a lot of dead terrorists. That's what you call them, isn't it – terrorists? What are they dying for?'

She pointed to the barman.

'See that man over there?'

I nodded.

'His name is Cephas Msika. He's eighteen years old. He is

the brightest student I ever had. He's my Shakespeare boy. Strong as a tree. He can recite from the sonnets.'

'Shakespeare?'

'Yeah, Shakespeare. It's what I teach.'

'Really?' I said. 'That's incredible.'

'Do you know how patronising that sounds?'

'I'm sorry, it wasn't meant that way.'

'Go up to Cephas and offer him freedom. He will spit in your face. It's just a word people throw around. Offer him a proper job where he's treated with respect, offer him a better life than waiting on tables or pouring beer in bars, offer him the chance to walk on the same pavement as a white man without being forced to step into the gutter when they pass and he will embrace you.'

Charity and Rosie were looking at the floor as she spoke.

'As for you whites, this is your war. You know you can't win it, but golly, you're going to enjoy it while you try.'

'Golly' struck me as such an odd word in the context that I wanted to write it down but thought the better of it. I sighed, drank and wished I had not given up smoking. The bar had fallen silent during this exchange. Everyone was looking at us.

'I think you should go,' said Jeeze. 'I'll call a cab.'

'No, don't,' I said.

Patience sat facing me, taking deep breaths that lifted her whole upper body against her uniform. I was angry too. Unprofessional, but I couldn't help it. This beautiful, infuriating woman with splashes of yellow on her hands and hair had lumped me together with every attitude, belief and prejudice of a minority-ruling white regime on the basis of my skin colour.

'Look, I am a stranger here,' I said. 'I've come to learn.'

She was about to say something but I raised a hand.

'I am here to find out what is happening. I have only been here two days but I know this. Truth is hard to find, but I am going to try.'

'You will only find the white man's truth. You will never find our truth.'

'At least I am going to keep my eyes and ears wide open and I'm going to learn.'

'Well, I'm a teacher, so learn from me. Go home.'

'What about your friends?' I said, gesturing to Charity and Rosie 'Do they want me to go home?'

The two women sat in uncomfortable silence, sipping their beers. They slowly nodded. Finally, Charity said, 'Our friend is a hard woman with a fast tongue.'

'Maybe too fast,' said Rosie.

Patience threw her head back and laughed. The diamanté earrings swung and glittered against her skin.

'Fast tongue yourself,' she said.

'But she is right,' said Charity.

'Let's go,' said Jeeze.

I shook hands with them, leaving Patience to the last. She gripped my hand hard and smiled that same cold smile.

I followed Jeeze to the door. There was a line of cabs outside. They were small Renaults dented and streaked with mud. 'Red Top Taxis' they said on the side.

He handed me a card. 'I'm sorry. Call me if you want.'

'Don't be sorry. She is an interesting woman. Just one question. What school does she teach at?'

'Don't do that,' he said, and faded into the night.

•

The desk clerk at the hotel handed me a cable. I read it and headed to the bar. New York had asked for 10,000 words by the following week. That was beyond my permit for a one-week stay. I would have to see the sallow-faced Mr Fryer again.

The same barman with the blue sash and white jacket was in charge. The Cancan was almost full. Everyone was hunched over their drinks, talking in whispers. The men were all in suits, the ladies in cocktail dresses. I looked in and turned away.

Across the square, Pinks was also busy that night. John Quigley was there with a group of friends. I just wanted a quiet drink, but this was not the place. John swayed over, taking small, slow steps in the struggle to keep upright, and introduced me to a tall man who had been leaning against the wall. He was well dressed in a suit and open-necked shirt. He did not fit in.

'Meet Bram,' said Quigley. 'He's our not-so-secret secret policeman, aren't you, Bram?'

The tall man looked down at him.

'Fuck off, John.'

'Be nice to him and he'll see they don't deport you,' said Quigley, before staggering back to the bar.

'How has your trip been?'

'Fine. You're a secret policeman, are you?'

Bram gave a half-laugh. 'There's nothing secret about what I do. European desk of the Special Branch. I look after the foreign press, among other things.'

'What other things?'

Bram raised his eyebrows and shook his head. He bought a drink and guided me to a small table in an alcove.

'You've had a busy time,' he said. 'How are you finding it?'

I shrugged. 'It's early days.'

'Well, you've heard two sides of the story, which is not bad going.'

'I take that as a compliment.'

I never knew whether Bram was his first or last name. When I asked he said, 'Just call me Bram.'

A visit to a zoo in Amsterdam had brought Bram to Africa. He had been a young man fresh from university. The sight of a grown giraffe bending its long neck to mother its offspring made him realise what he wanted to do with his life. He worked first in a zoo and then came to Africa as a wildlife conservationist, working in one of the big-game parks. He told me this later, but refused to say how and when he had joined the police.

Apart from one frightening occasion in a country on the west coast, I had not encountered the regular police in Africa and made sure to stay away from them. Plain-clothes police working in intelligence were different, a potential source of information. Bram seemed friendly and possibly helpful.

'Why don't you write about the game parks here? They are being destroyed. They used to bring in a lot of money. We will need that cash when this is over.'

'And when will that be?'

'You tell me. You people are supposed to know, aren't you?'

'Isn't that your job?' I said.

'My job is to make sure that none of you are working for a foreign intel service or looking a little too closely at the way we trade abroad.'

'What does that mean?'

'Sanctions.'

'You're being very open.'

'Everyone knows what I do. But it's got very busy. After Vietnam a lot of freelance hacks have turned up. War tourists.'

'Does that bother you?'

He laughed.

'They're a pain, but they bring in a lot of forex. So we keep them happy. Take them out on "facility trips" to talk to farmers, that sort of thing. But you've done that already.'

He smiled and drank his whisky. He knew I had been out to the Milan farm, just as he knew I had been to the township. I was quickly learning that concealment or privacy was impossible. I wondered if Sara Jane Shannon was one of his informers.

'I can arrange a facility trip for you if you like.'

'What would I see?'

'A lot of dead terrs, probably.'

●

Late that night I phoned Paris. She was half asleep. I had a vivid image of her leaning across the rumpled bedclothes, pulling the sheets around her, as if anyone was going to see her nakedness. She would reach for the phone on the polished mahogany bedside table left to her by her grandmother. Rue de Rome. Four flights of narrow stairs to that single room under the eaves.

'Where are you?'

'In Africa.'

'I'm asleep.'

The line went dead. The casual way in which we hurt people we love is hard to explain. Those thoughts followed me into a restless sleep. Such dreams as I had took me back to the Victoria Hotel and the hard woman with the fast tongue.

•

After breakfast, I walked a meandering mile or so, going nowhere in particular but trying to order my disordered mind. Thoughts think for themselves and can become a runaway train if one isn't careful. I pushed Meredith, Marie Claire and Patience away and concentrated on what was around me.

I found myself in the white suburbs, clearly an unusual sight given the looks I received from passing cars. On all sides the scene was the same: graceful jacaranda trees in full bloom with soft violet flowers, carefully tended lawns, gardens bordered by beds of flowers seen through mesh gates, and everywhere snarling dogs hurling themselves against the gated entrances with such force that I crossed the street in alarm. I walked in zigzag fashion down the street, a perfect metaphor for my progress in this country. The dogs were mostly on long chains but those that weren't showed every sign of being able to leap fences and gates and attack innocent strangers such as myself.

Even under the shade of the trees it was becoming too hot to walk. I waved down a cab and returned to the hotel.

Later that afternoon I went for a swim in the city pool. It was whites-only, but the signs that said so were small and easily missed. It was as if this comfortable community of mostly English stock did not want to admit to the original sin of racial segregation.

I absolved myself of complicity in this arrangement by pretending it was all part of research into city life. Moral transgression was hard to avoid in this city. In any case, smug self-righteousness had no place in a country at war.

The pool was 33 metres long. The water was chilly. A swimming team had two lanes on one side of the pool and I had the rest to myself. I swam ten lengths, then spread a towel on a bench to dry off. The heat of the sun was balm to a weary body. I had been in the country for three days. In my travels, I could usually make some sense of what was happening in a new place in that time. But not here. Nothing seemed to fit.

As I rose to return to the dressing room, I saw one of the team swimmers, a young woman, on the far side of the pool doing fast freestyle just ahead of two others. Her coach walked alongside her, stopwatch in hand. There was something faintly familiar about the swimmer. I stopped to watch as she tumble-turned and pushed off on the next length. She had a strong style, her white arms cleaving the water cleanly and her head turned slightly sideways to breathe on every other stroke.

I left to change and then I realised what I had seen in the pool. There had been a blue blurred image on the right arm of the swimmer, the image of a dolphin.

She came out with a bag slung over her shoulder, shaking a head of wet hair. Her face looked paler than when we had last met, a ghostly pallor that spoke of fear. She was frowning and her features were strained. She was more a grown woman than the teenager who had bounced around like a playful puppy at the Shamva farm.

'I thought you spotted me,' she said. 'Did you enjoy your swim?'

'I enjoyed watching you swim. But you look worried. Are you all right?'

She took my arm suddenly.

'Let's have something to eat.'

We sat in a small Italian restaurant called Sandro's. She asked for a glass of white wine. I watched her hands shake as she drank. She finished the glass quickly and began to cry, wiping away the tears with a handkerchief. I bought her another glass and waited.

The story came slowly through glasses of wine and a plate of spaghetti. In the late afternoon of the previous day she had been driving to town from the farm, followed by her mother in another vehicle. They had left slightly later than usual, but it was still light when they reached the area of the road along the reservation. She had pushed the old Renault to top speed up to the crest of a hill when the car swerved across the road and rocked from side to side. She heard a noise like a high-pitched drum roll. The windscreen shattered and the leather seat beside her burst into flames. She pulled the car back to the centre of the road, shrank low into her seat and pressed the accelerator to the floor.

This was the ambush they had been unconsciously waiting for. The instructions were simple: whatever you do – whether wounded, whether the tyres are shredded, whether the car is on fire – do not stop. Drive for as long as there is life left in the vehicle.

Her first thought was for her mother in the car behind. She saw her in the rear-view mirror weaving back and forth across the road.

'That was when I was most frightened,' she said. 'I thought her car was finished and she would be killed or, worse still, abducted. I almost screamed with relief when she came over the hill.'

They had driven to the first police station they came to in the city and reported the attack. Both cars had been taken away for examination. Later a police officer had noted down their story and told them how lucky they had been.

'He was so matter-of-fact about it. It was as if we had had a minor accident. But life goes on; that's the rule here. We had supper and watched television in a hotel room as if nothing had happened. Mum seemed to worry more about the dress she wanted to buy than the fact that we had almost been killed.'

'And you went swimming with the team as usual today?'

'What else can we do? We just pretend this is normal.' She waved at the windows and street outside.

By the time we had finished our pasta, we had also finished a bottle of the vinegary local wine. When the bill arrived she took it quickly, against my protest. She was a little drunk. She paid, then took my hand and looked at me.

'Will you do something for me?'

'Sure.'

'Take me to your hotel.'

•

I heard later that all but two of the eight guerrillas in the attack had been killed in the follow-up operation. Bram told me this quite casually the next day. He materialised like a wraith, giving the impression that he had been an invisible presence at my side for the last twenty-four hours.

He added that the ambush had been unusual only in the attackers' use of FN rifles firing tracer bullets. They had probably stolen the weapons from the Portuguese army across the border.

'Is that bad, I mean them using FNs?'

'Good and bad. The FN is more powerful and has longer and more accurate range, but it can jam if not kept clean, while the AK is lighter. It can be dropped in deep water, covered in mud and will still fire. For terrorists, the AK is much the better weapon.'

He said this as if he was discussing the weather. We were drinking a lunchtime beer.

'There is only one beer in the world,' he said. 'Amstel.'

'Because it's Dutch, like you?'

'Maybe.'

'What did you do with the bodies?'

'Photograph them, then distribute the prints to villagers in the area. Makes a point.'

'And then?'

'Burn them. Burial takes too long. The bones are usually dug up and used by spirit mediums to bring hellfire down on the whites – that includes you, by the way.'

It was a good story, but I knew neither whether it was true nor why I was being given the information. Was the story of the follow-up operation designed to burnish the image of the government forces, or was it to impress me and build a bond with a foreign correspondent he might find useful?

I had occasionally met these Special Branch characters on my travels. Their hospitable charm and easy way with privileged information concealed a brutal tradecraft. Behind the free drinks, the snippets of high-value information ('burial takes too long, we burn them'), lay bribery, blackmail and torture; these were the tools of the secret policeman's trade. Despite his innocent title of head of the European desk, I reminded myself that Bram was a secret policeman.

Chapter Four

The weather broke early that year. For days at the end of October, cumulus clouds had built up into towering castles in the sky, turning into deeper shades of grey. The rain finally fell in sheets, clattering off the corrugated iron roofs of the city and flooding the street gutters below. Baked earth turned to mud, leaving behind an often-impassable coating of sludge and slime on the roads. Distant bushfires that had cloaked the horizons in a haze of smoke vanished. Rivers flooded and livestock were moved to higher ground.

When the rains stopped, the sun emerged from the clouds and the land smouldered with steam, as if giving a huge sigh of relief. Mother Earth smiled again, as the old song said. Gardens and parks in towns burst into life and the bush beyond turned green and heavy with leaf. It was easy to see how the advantage swung towards those fighting to overthrow the regime at this time of the year.

I had a suspicion that Meredith Kaplan would be less interested in the shift in the tactical balance than in how the rains transformed the country. Our readers were largely metropolitan, but we sold well in the Midwest, where the weather really mattered to the farmers. I made a note to record the passing of the seasons. The rainy season would end in three months, bringing spring, leading to the long months of dry, cold weather of the African winter, when government forces and guerrillas tracked, attacked and killed each other.

The excuse I gave myself for what I did next was that travel out of town was becoming both more difficult and more dangerous. The true story of this country did not lie out in the endless miles of bush, in the white farms, in the villages where the guerrillas fleetingly found food and had their wounds treated. The war made that forbidden territory. In any case, the real story lay here in the city. I needed to dig deeper into the psyche of a people who both sustained the white government with their labour and also fought it with a growing militia of young men under arms.

That's what I told myself. It was a perfectly reasonable use of my time as the rain hammered down on the city. But it was a lie. I don't think I lie to myself any more than anyone else but, that said, we are all highly skilled in self-deception, both in its practice and in the way we deny it to ourselves.

I waited in my hire car outside the Frank Johnson school, named after a pioneer in the early days of the colony. It was the largest school in the township, a single-storey building with basketball courts at the back, and seemed a good place to start.

She came out with a satchel of books and a colourful umbrella. I could see the navy-blue uniform beneath a plastic see-through rain cape. I got out of the car and looked at her as she crossed the road. She didn't see me. I waved and called her name. She turned, squinted against the sun and stopped.

'What are you doing here?'

'I thought I might give you a lift.'

'I'm taking the bus.'

'Can I offer you a cup of tea?'

'Why?'

'You made me think. I would like to hear more.'

'I don't drink tea and I have had enough teaching for one day.'

With that she turned and headed towards the bus stop. I crossed the road and caught up with her.

'How about a beer this evening?'

She paused and frowned.

'You think they will let me into that fancy hotel?'

I hadn't told her where I was staying.

'You'll be with me.'

She said nothing and walked on to the bus stop, where a crowd of schoolchildren were milling around, pushing and shoving each other. They were smartly dressed in a uniform of grey shorts, shirts and blazers for the boys and white shirts and pleated skirts for the girls. I watched her for a minute, but she was talking to the children and paid no attention to me.

When an old grey coach appeared, mud-spattered from the rains, she vanished with the gaggle of kids. I got into my car and wound the window down to let in some air. The bus lumbered towards me, then stopped alongside. The driver leaned out.

'Leave her alone,' he said, and drove on.

•

I was summoned to the ministry the next day to discuss the extension of my work permit. I went only to say goodbye and to thank Mr Fryer for his advice. I had decided to leave. There was little point in trying to report a small bush war in a remote part of Africa, which did not seem to interest either my editor or our readers. I had heard nothing from the office since my last message. They would be fixated as usual on events in the Middle East, spiralling towards another regional war.

I could understand why a small war in Africa would have little interest to my readers, but I felt the magazine badly misjudged their interest in an oil-rich region of circular crises, which ended only so that all sides might draw breath, re-arm and start again.

I sent a brief telex to New York saying I would return to Paris and rebase wherever they chose. This allowed Meredith Kaplan to believe that my next assignment lay in her hands. As it was, I had no intention of leaving Paris in a hurry.

I rather liked Mr Fryer. He had the air of a benevolent grandfather puzzling over what to give his grandchildren for Christmas.

'How have you been getting on?' he asked, and without waiting for a reply added, 'I hear you have been sampling the hospitality at the Victoria.'

He gave a low chuckle at his own slight joke and began to twirl his pencil again. I decided this was a substitute for a much-loved moustache, which his harridan wife had ordered him to shave off. Or perhaps a childhood ambition to be a drummer in a band had been foiled by ambitious parents.

Fryer interrupted these agreeable flights of fancy.

'Why are you leaving us? You have only just arrived.'

I had no answer to this question. Or rather, the only answer I had was a lie. I could hardly tell Mr Fryer the story was not worth reporting when that was so obviously untrue. Nor could I tell him that I was leaving out of pique because a woman in whom I was professionally interested – or, let's be honest about this, to whom I was personally attracted – refused to talk to me. Yet that was the reason. A shameful childish tantrum.

'New York wants me to move on,' I said.

Fryer twirled his pencil more vigorously. He had received transcripts of my telex messages and phone calls. He knew I was aware of that. New York had told me nothing of the sort.

'A pity,' he said. 'I thought you were different.'

He handed me a small brown envelope. I opened it to find a typewritten note giving me a work permit.

'In case you change your mind,' he said.

•

I booked the next available flight to Europe, which had to be routed via the country to the south. The flight was in two days' time. I did little work beyond typing up my notes. I swam daily in the municipal pool but saw nothing of Julia. I avoided both the Cancan Bar and Pinks. I wanted to forget I had ever been to this place. The farm at Shamva, the afternoon in bed with Julia, Bram the Special Branch torturer – they were all to become distant memories.

Over tall glasses of iced lager in small bars on the outskirts of town I told myself yet again I had taken the right decision both for my readers and for myself. I pondered telling Sara Jane Shannon of my decision, but decided to say nothing until I had left. She had wanted the story for herself. Now she could have it.

On the day of departure, I checked out of the hotel and asked them to look after my luggage. I had several hours to kill before the flight. There was a close warmth in the air as I walked the streets. I felt strangely uncomfortable. I had nowhere to go and no one to say goodbye to.

That last thought stayed with me. The formality of a farewell would allow me to close this brief interlude in my life. I would say goodbye to the barman in the Cancan. If not exactly welcoming, he had been polite when serving our drinks that first evening with Sara Jane.

The Cancan was full of a noisy lunchtime crowd who looked as if they had settled in for the afternoon. I squeezed onto the last free seat at the bar and decided on a large whisky and soda. Despite a life of almost ceaseless travel, I am a nervous flyer and a stiff drink or two helps calm the nerves until take-off. The moment I hear the wheels slot into the undercarriage I relax.

I was forced onto the edge of the seat by a corpulent character on one side who was talking to a companion in a stage whisper about spare parts for street lights, runway lights, any sort of light as far as I could gather. On the other side, a middle-aged lady shifted sideways on her stool with a sharp sigh of irritation and slid her glass of wine on its mat away from me.

The barman had his back to me preparing drinks. He was wearing the same outfit as before, a gold-buttoned white jacket and blue sash. He turned with a soda siphon in one hand and placed a large whisky on a mat in front of me. I looked at him in surprise. He squirted the soda into the glass, exactly the right amount, smiled and turned away.

It was half an hour later, as I was about to leave, when he came over and handed me a folded piece of lined paper. He watched me open it. It was handwritten in the local language. Both surprised and puzzled, I looked at him.

'What is this?'

'It says she will be with friends out of town tomorrow and you may join them,' he said.

'Who?'

'I think you know who.'

'Where?'

'Kumati Dam. In the south of the city. She says take a taxi and make sure it is a four-wheel drive. They will know the way.'

Life is full of difficult decisions. This one was easy. I ordered another drink.

•

A range of low hills framed a wide expanse of bush and broken farmland dotted with small settlements. The visibility was good. The break in the rains was as if someone had pulled back a curtain, letting light into a darkened room. To the east, a drift of high cumulus clouds was assembling on the horizon. The heat was strong and steamy.

We pulled off the road, bumping along a dirt track that had dried out just enough to let the Renault cab make headway.

We slipped and skidded, wheels spinning and gears growling, along roads caked with dark, drying mud.

The road rose steeply and passed through a screen of trees. The Renault pointed its bonnet down and we slithered to a clearing beside a little reed-fringed river. Trees bowed leafed branches over its banks.

Water was foaming over a small dam into a large pool bordered by flat slabs of rock. I saw Patience almost immediately, standing head and shoulders above the same women I had seen in the Victoria Hotel. They were sitting on the rocks around a tablecloth laid with food, bottles of drink and vacuum flasks, all wearing long, colourful cotton wraps.

I paid the driver and walked down the slope. Patience waved, came over and greeted me in a language I did not understand. She turned to Charity, who explained, 'She said you are welcome and very privileged to join our picnic. Please take a seat.'

I thanked her, wondering what I was doing there. I felt as I had at the Milan's farm, an intruder.

Patience began talking in her own language. She gestured with her hands to emphasise whatever she was saying. The flash of yellow from her fingernails drew the eye to this strange woman. Charity and Rosie sat in a semi-circle, leaning back occasionally to laugh. Then she went down to the river and knelt down to wash her hands in the water. I was ignored.

Charity beckoned me and held out a plate of small baked cakes. I took one. She poured black tea from a flask into a plastic cup and handed it to me.

'This is beautiful,' I said. 'Do many people come here?'

'Not Europeans, because this is a reservation. Few of our

own people, because you need a four-wheel drive at this time of year. In the dry season more of our people come, but it's a long drive." She told me that she, Patience and Rosie came here every month to forget the long hours of poorly paid teaching and the grime of a dusty township.

'And do you swim?'

She laughed.

'Yes, even little dumplings like me. The water is so clean you can drink it, but very cold.'

I wondered how the office would react to a piece about a picnic in this surprising setting. It was beautiful: the rush of water over the rocks into a deep pool, a screen of assegai trees leaning over the river. In New York they wouldn't want an unlikely story about three African teachers having a riverside picnic. They wanted me to tell them of the nationalist force of arms that was bringing a bloody end to a regime that defied the principles of civilised nations. They wanted words to reflect the image of a white man with one foot on the throat of an African man with a gun pointed at his head. That did not quite fit this bucolic picnic on the rocky banks of a tumbling river.

'Can you ask Patience to join us?' I said to Charity.

She frowned, looking puzzled by the question.

'It was she who invited me here,' I said.

Patience came over and stood looking down at me. I was beginning to get up when she sat down.

'How are you enjoying our picnic?'

'It is a real surprise,' I said.

'You like our cakes?'

'Yes. Very nice. Thank you for asking me.'

'You seemed puzzled when you got my note.'

'How do you know that?'

'The barman is my uncle. George. That's his name. I know all about the Cancan.'

We began talking in the small ways one begins a conversation, mostly about the weather. At first, she did not appear comfortable. There was something distant and controlled about the way we talked. She avoided answering my questions, preferring to ask her own. What was I writing, where had I been and whom had I seen?

I replied as best I could and returned the questions. What was her life like as a township teacher in a secondary school full of presumably rebellious teenagers? We talked back and forth like two fencers.

There was one big question that had shaped itself in my few days in the country. The mystery became more apparent and more insoluble with every step I took. But this did not seem the place or time. In any case, there was an easier and more immediate question.

'Patience, why did you ask me here?'

'My uncle said you were . . . different from the others.'

'In what way?'

'He said you were polite. You said thank you to him.'

'That makes me different?'

She threw her head back with a full-throated laugh that lifted her whole body. The coloured wrap slipped slightly over bare shoulders.

'Yes,' she said. 'Different from almost everyone here.' She stood up. 'Are you coming for a swim?'

It was warm, the warmth that comes between tropical rains.

The water looked inviting.

'I don't have a costume.'

'You were supposed to bring one. He should have told you. Never mind. We don't mind, do we?'

She looked at Charity and Rosie. They all laughed.

With that, they stepped out of their wraps, revealing woollen costumes that stretched from neck to thigh. They carefully assumed the diving position, arms stretched out, heads bowed, and plunged into the water one by one.

It was a scene so far removed from the reality of a country at war that I knew no one would believe me back in New York if I turned it into a short feature, a 500-word panel that would run alongside the main article. I would call it 'The Swimming Pool Party'. It was a pity I didn't have a camera.

I would write that piece. I would tell Meredith Kaplan why I had changed my mind. I would stay in this strangely seductive place.

After much splashing and laughing, the women climbed out of the pool and scrambled up onto the rocks. Their clinging wet costumes denied them the intended modesty. They spread their towels on the hot rocks and lay face down. Patience was still in the water. She waved to me.

'We won't look,' she shouted.

The others were watching and laughing. I began to think this was a trap, a little sport at the expense of a white foreigner.

I shook my head and once again wished I had not stopped smoking. I slipped the hip flask from my pocket and poured a quick splash into the tea. Patience pulled herself out of the water and stood there for a few moments while Charity fetched her towel. She walked over and squatted beside me. I handed the flask to her.

'Mud in your eye,' I said.

She wiped the neck, took a swig and handed it back.

'What does that mean?'

'It's an old drinking toast.'

She repeated the phrase softly to herself and said, 'How long are you staying?'

'I don't know; as long as New York wants me to stay.'

'Have you found your story yet?'

'No, but I have an idea.'

'Which is?'

'There's no point to this war. You must know that.'

'That's not a story, that's just an opinion.'

'My story lies in the answer to this question: why are the young men of this country killing each other?'

'Because the whites will never give up until we drive them off their farms and out of their houses.'

'That's just a slogan.'

'OK, answer your own question.'

I lay back and shaded my eyes against the sun. The conversation was leading towards an argument I did not want. It seemed absurd in such a setting. I wanted to enjoy the moment, lying in the sun with three teachers at a swimming picnic in the heart of Africa just a few miles from a city whose hotels, shops and high-rise buildings stood as a testament to the economic power of a privileged few.

I sat up. 'I don't have the answer. Maybe you do.'

She moved towards me, lying with her head propped on her elbowed hand. Her swimming costume clung to her damp skin. Her body measured itself against mine. I could smell whisky on her breath, as she could on mine, no doubt.

'You know nothing about us, do you?' she said 'Our young men – and some women too – are leaving every night to travel to the Eastern Highlands and cross the border. They risk mines, army patrols and dogs bred to kill. Some don't make it.'

Over her shoulder I saw the others watching us. Patience did not move but just looked at me. She was making me want her, hoping that my arousal would be evident when I rose. I was to be the object of fun for these women. I remembered Sara Jane's words. Don't even trust your mother in this town.

She leant over me.

'Put this in your paper: we don't know where lightning will strike, but we do know it will bring thunder and rain.'

'What does that mean?'

'Write it down and work it out; it's not difficult.'

I had neither pen nor notebook to hand.

'I'll remember it,' I said.

She smiled, a more engaging expression than the flinty look I had received at the Victoria.

'You're not a bad man, but I've told you before – go home.'

We both got up.

'I would like to see you again,' I said.

She looked at me with a whisper of a smile. For a moment, her eyes lit the smile and then they turned cold and dark as before.

'Why?' she said.

I didn't have an answer, or rather there was no answer I dared give to this unknowable woman. In all our time together, I was never able to read the mind behind those eyes. Her face masked a mysterious interior to which I was to remain a stranger. I sometimes thought she was as much a stranger to herself as to me.

'Why not?' was all I could say.

She shook her head and walked away.

Chapter Five

We all carry portraits of ourselves in our heads, carefully created images showing the charm and intelligence that we know we possess. That smiling, handsome, attractive person sits in our imagination like a houseguest who never leaves.

There are times when the image fades and we try to be honest and admit to many of the sins with which the Bible charges us: dishonesty, cruelty, forbidden lust.

I had left Marie Claire suddenly, late at night without explanation, taking the last plane from Charles de Gaulle airport to Lisbon and on to Africa the next morning. Days passed, then a week, then weeks.

When I finally called, she told me that I had no heart or soul. I told her I loved her. We met again in Lisbon. She flew in from Paris at her own expense to find the fire that had once burnt so brightly between us. Those were her very words. Marie Claire always had a romantic way with words.

She joined me for lunch with some of my colleagues. I hadn't planned it that way. At the end of the lunch, she threw a cup of hot coffee over me and went back to the airport.

I felt now the tidal undertow that takes a swimmer from the safety of the shallows to the danger of deeper waters. The attraction to the woman with the diamanté earrings was sexual; I could admit to that easily enough. But there was another attraction – the lure of what is forbidden, the oldest attraction of all.

Julia Milan had been a brief distraction, which I justified as a wartime indulgence for a young woman seeking release from the shock of a road ambush and life behind a barbed-wire fence. We had spent a loveless afternoon in my hotel room with drawn curtains, a half-finished bottle of red wine and an ashtray filled with stubs of her Stuyvesant cigarettes, a rare treat in a sanctioned economy.

•

Bram was not in Pinks that night, which was odd. I had one whisky and was leaving when Jeeze appeared. I bought him a drink and steered him into the corner.

'Tell me about the boys crossing the border.'

He looked startled and then afraid, his eyes darting around the room.

'Not here,' he whispered.

'I thought you could talk about anything here.'

Jeeze beckoned me to follow him to the corridor.

'This place is full of ears. What do you want to know?'

'How many are crossing a week?'

'How would I know?'

'Because you seem to know a lot.'

'I will need paying.'

I gave him 100 dollars. The story he told me seemed as believable as anything else in this country. Young men had been crossing the border since the insurgency started two years earlier. Crossing first in couples, then scores, then hundreds, all making the journey from the city to the mountains some hundred miles to the east.

Catholic priests in mission stations along the border showed them how to avoid minefields and those stretches where half-starved tracker dogs had been let loose. St Saviour's, a major Catholic seminary close to the border post where I had entered, was a focal point for this dangerous operation.

'You make it sound easy.'

'The security forces can't stop it. They don't have the men. These kids are driven, or take a bus halfway and walk the rest at night. Local people feed them, let them sleep for an hour or so, and send them over.'

'Silly question: why do they go?'

'You are a young black kid, fresh out of school. There are no jobs unless you want to wash dishes or mow the lawn for a white man who calls you "boy". Someone promises you liberation, freedom, respect – and hey, if you go I'll give you a nice shiny AK-47 to shoot those people who pay you nothing to wash their dishes or cut the grass. It's not difficult, is it? They just want to fight. It's a young man's dream. And girls too. Anyone without a job goes. Though they always leave one young member of the family with a job behind to feed the old ones at home.'

'Young girls go as well?'

He nodded, looking from one end of the corridor to the other.

'The big men over there like them. They're good fighters. They don't get drunk and they know how to hold a gun straight.'

'How do you know all this?'

'How do you think?'

●

The air was cool and sweet after the sweat and smoke of the club. I crossed the square, past the fountains and the jacaranda trees bright with blossom. A few people were sitting on the benches enjoying the evening air. The tranquillity seemed a complete denial of what I had just heard. The beery crowd of journalists in Pinks inhabited a different world.

I climbed the curving staircase to the Cancan Bar and looked in. Patience's uncle was still at the bar polishing glasses. A late couple sat at the table arguing with soft hissed voices. I took a zebra-skin bar stool and ordered one last drink. I was drinking too much. Everyone was drinking too much. It seemed a requirement of the place.

'I had a nice day at the river,' I said as George moved a bar mat in front of me.

He nodded.

'Thanks for passing on the message.'

He placed my drink on the mat without a word.

'Can you give me some advice?'

He shrugged.

'What do you want to know?'

'Can you contact her for me?'

He shook his head.

The next morning the receptionist wrote a note for me in the local language. I knew the way now and drove to the Victoria. Cephas was behind the bar, smoking, reading a book. He gave me the same look as before and put the book away. He took the note, glanced at it and handed it back.

'She's gone,' he said.

'Gone? Where?'

Cephas shrugged.

•

I was suffocating in this country. It was like being in a small, windowless room. It was one of the joys of my job that I could go anywhere I wanted on the continent. There were always news stories around, which I could weave into the feature articles that Meredith Kaplan liked so much. That's what she wanted: nicely written pieces, with the caveat that they must be 'people-led'. 'Events do not make stories; people make stories.' Those were the words with which every correspondent was sent abroad. They were good words.

A few months ago, I had been in a West African country. I had only been there three days when I was arrested for revealing details of a drought up-country. Foreign aid to build dams had gone missing. I had toured the area with a young, ambitious politician who provided details of the corruption. He also gave me an anonymous but telling quote, which was used as a drop-in insert in bold in my piece: 'As a young man, I will fight corruption. When I'm a little older, I will be doing it myself.'

I was interrogated for two days by Inspector Mensah, who

wore an improbably creased uniform and carried a leather crop, which he swished back and forth. Mensah had seen too many Hollywood films and used a rusty anglepoise lamp to shine a bright light in my face during endless sessions in which one question was repeated. Who was the source for the story? When I told him everyone in town knew about the missing money, he merely repeated the question.

After the usual diplomatic flurry, I was released. Inspector Mensah took me to the airport, shook my hand and wished me luck. But it was he who needed the luck. Shortly afterwards, there was a coup and I heard he had been put against the wall of his own police station and shot.

I made Mensah the lead to the piece about my arrest. I had learnt a lot about him during our two days together. That was how I lived my life. Every country provided a different story. It suited me and it suited Meredith Kaplan.

Now I was stuck. I was weary of the crackpot politics and a futile war. Everything I wrote circled back on previous articles. The windowless room was getting smaller. I should have moved on, but I didn't want to leave. There was a story untold in this place, a mystery to be solved. That's what I told myself as I extended my stay at Franklins. The biggest lies are those one tells oneself.

•

To my surprise, game safaris were still being operated on the shores of a large lake to the north. The area had so far escaped the insurgency and was perfectly safe, or so I was told. It was part of the fantasy that the war was merely a police action against criminal elements among the local population. Thus tourism continued in a limited way and attracted mostly American visitors who enjoyed the risks as much as the scenic wonders described in the brochures.

Meredith would like the idea because it was exactly the sideshow story that would give her readers (they were always her readers, never mine) a different perspective on the recurring cycle of events in this distant conflict.

A bumpy plane ride to an island in the middle of the great lake and then a boat ride took me across to a tented camp on the foreshore. An old hunter presented himself as my guide, loaded up a Land Rover and drove us down a bush trail.

I made these notes about the following few days:

My guide is called Rob; looks as if he has been carved from one of the massive baobab trees here; long, bushy beard, grizzled face with a deep scar from chin to cheek; carries a vintage .303 rifle; makes me leave my trusty Remington typewriter behind; laughs when I ask if it's safe; says it is supposed to be and laughs again; a rumbling laugh that travels from his boots to his beard; I am nervous; no tent, sleep in a bag under stars as bright as diamonds; cliché but true; nothing like night sky in Africa; no fire; too dangerous, he says; makes me more nervous; supper is whisky, corn cob, beans and a plate of sausages; cooked on a Primus stove; the menu never varies.

Elephants come to drink every evening, walking single file past our camp; six, an old male, two females and three young; the large male watches, allowing the others to drink first; shambling creatures with their rumpled grey hides and yellow-white tusks carry with them time immemorial; been doing this before man even raised a spear against them; am told not to go too close to lake edge; crocodiles; Rob says elephants won't be here long; why? CTs, he says; CTs? – communist terrorists; they kill and eat them, he says; been here three days now; whisky finished; sick of sausages; time to go back.

Back at the base camp I tried to expand on these rough notes. I was pleased. There was a good piece there, but I needed more detail.

'Do people really eat elephant flesh?' I asked the hunter.

'Sure.'

'What does it taste like?'

'Like most bush meat,' he said, 'tough as teak and tasty, but only if you are hungry, which the CTs usually are.'

'They are not near here, are they?' I said, looking at the dense woodland that stretched down to the trampled grass of the foreshore.

'No. The elephants wouldn't be here if the terrs were close. They carry heavy packs and travel by day. It's hard, sweaty work and they give off a strong odour.'

'Aren't you afraid of being here on your own?'

'I can see them coming a mile off and I have a radio.'

'What is the point of you being here?'

'We still have tourists. They seem to like the danger, like being close to conflict. They're not always men, either. They bring their women with them sometimes; war groupies, we call them.'

I asked how he could possibly offer any realistic protection to such groups in a war zone. He told me that guerrillas crossing the border were mostly raw recruits from the big cities who had not been trained in the craft of moving without detection through the bush. They left tracks that were easy to follow and they were untrained in the art of anti-tracking. They ate their supplies of food too quickly and forced villagers, often with great brutality, to replenish their stocks.

'So, it is often easy for us to track them, and that way we can take them out.'

'I thought it was supposed to be safe here?'

'You believed that, did you?' he said, and laughed again.

I left the base camp and took the boat back across to the island. The water was peat-brown, a suitable colour for a lake full of crocodiles. I was the only passenger on the single-engine plane. A flight in clear skies over Africa is never forgotten. Even with a pilot beside you, the vastness of the land below and the sense of solitude in a cloudless sky make you feel like a rider in space.

In bed back at the hotel that night I thought back to the flight. It seemed a pitiful waste that such beauty below should have become a killing ground where men hunted each other and graceful animals were slaughtered for their meat.

I had a sudden urge to get closer to a war I was only hearing about. In that big-game reserve to the north, elephants were being killed for nothing more than the next meal. In the east, young men were crossing the border, threading their way through minefields to become fighters. Those young men were returning with their weapons to kill and be killed. It was all happening out of sight over the horizon. The reality of the conflict seemed as distant as Meredith chewing gum in New York.

•

After a week of persuading George at the Cancan to pass on a message, Patience agreed to meet. I invited her for dinner, but she refused.

'I will have a drink with you because my uncle likes you. But eating at a white man's table? No, thank you.'

Patience insisted that we sit on the zebra bar stools. George came over. She asked for a 'silver bullet'. George busied himself mixing the cocktail. He shook it with such noise and vigour that everyone turned to watch. Very clever. They would all want one now. He placed the drink in front of Patience.

'What's in it?' I asked.

'Gin, kümmel liqueur, freshly squeezed lemon juice and lemon zest with plenty of ice, finely strained.'

I must have looked surprised.

'A little sophisticated for a township teacher?' she said.

'It's not that. I have never heard of it before.'

'George got the recipe from an old American pilot here. He came from Albuquerque in New Mexico. You can't forget a name like that.'

We sipped our drinks, watching George making cocktails.

'I am surprised they haven't deported you yet.'

'Why?'

'You ask a lot of questions.'

'And I get answers.'

'Mostly lies.'

'Some, not all,' I said.

'Everything is a lie here.'

'The war isn't a lie.'

'It is and it isn't,' she said. 'Yes, it's getting worse, and no, you're not going to win.'

'Don't include me in this.'

She tapped the skin of my hand.

'You're in it whether you like it or not.'

It was the second time someone had done that to me. Skin and the colour of skin were important symbols here, more than elsewhere perhaps. I would work that into a piece. We drank, talked and nibbled, dipping our fingers in bowls of nuts and olives. After the second drink a familiar voice turned us on our stools.

'Well, hallo, Mr Magazine Writer.'

Sara Jane was with a handsome uniformed soldier whose chest was covered in military ribbons. This time she wore a different dress – black, short and lacy. She was looking at Patience.

'We haven't met,' she said, holding out her hand before I could introduce them.

'I'm Patience Matatu.'

'And I'm Sara Jane Shannon.'

They shook hands.

'Are you dining here?' said the big military man.

'Just a drink,' I said.

'And you're helping this struggling writer with his research, are you?' asked Sara Jane.

'The other way round,' said Patience. 'He's giving me background for my Shakespeare classes.'

'Shakespeare?' said Sara, framing the word to make her disbelief obvious. 'How interesting.'

Patience turned to the officer. She put out her hand.

'Patience,' she said. 'I teach at the Frank Johnson School.'

'André Lennox,' he said. 'Major.'

He gave a mock salute. We all shook hands.

'Are you with the army here?' Patience asked.

'Indeed I am,' he said. 'The African Rifles, a fine unit.'

'You must be busy.'

'It's full on, yes.'

'Where are you based?' asked Patience.

'Everywhere and nowhere,' said Sara Jane, taking his arm. 'Darling, we will be late for dinner.'

They said their farewells and left, her arm coiled around his waist. Heads turned. Whispered conversations told me they had seen someone important.

'Do you know who that man is?' asked Patience.

'No.'

'The most decorated soldier in the army. Former British SAS who won those decorations in Northern Ireland.'

'How do you know all this?'

'It's been in the local paper. Killed a lot of our fighters.'

'Maybe they were trying to kill him.'

'They'd love to, we all would, but he is said to be very good. And that's his girlfriend.'

'Obviously. Interesting.'

'How do you know her?'

'We . . . met once in the bar here.'

'Did you just?' she said, and finished her drink.

She and George spoke briefly in their language. She got up and I took her down to the taxi rank.

'I'm sorry we didn't have time to talk.'

'Let's walk,' she said.

We walked across the square to the fountains. Street lights filtered through the jacaranda trees. There was no one around. She leant against a tree and lit a cigarette.

'Do you work with that woman?'

'Yes, if you must know. She's just a stringer.'

'You won't learn anything worth knowing from her.'

'She seems pretty well informed.'

She lit another cigarette.

'When you drove out to join us by the river, what did you see?'

'Three beautiful women.'

'I'm being serious.'

'OK. A few settlements in the distance, huts made of tin.'

'Listen carefully. I can go into your world. I have a university degree. I did it by post. English Lit. I can get a PhD. I can travel abroad, start a business. I can do all those things in your world. You can go into those huts you saw, you can drink beer in the Victoria, you can see us swimming in the river – but you can never come into our world. You can listen to our music, eat our food, but never can you enter our world. Do you understand?'

'Not really.'

'My uncle was right, you are a decent man. But you don't understand. I can make love to you, but you can't make love to me. It's my choice, not yours.'

She blew another plume of smoke into the air. She took a few steps away and said with her back to me, 'Do you want me?'

I stood quite still and looked up at the trees. I tried to catch up with the sudden twist in the conversation. She was playing a game that I was going to lose. Of course I wanted her. I had wanted her since I had first seen her in that township bar. She knew that.

'Of course I do.'

She drew me to the tree and we kissed, slowly, breathlessly. She tasted of smoke and gin. I felt my hand around her back dropping lower, pulling her into me. She didn't resist.

'Let's go somewhere.'

'Not now,' she said.

She walked away, a night shadow visible only by the glowing tip of her cigarette. I watched the pinprick of light as it vanished into a taxi.

•

I tried to make sense of what had happened, except that nothing had happened. That brief moment under the trees, with street lights filtering through the branches, was just a kiss, or perhaps more an invitation to leave a white man's world and find lust and desire in a different, more dangerous place.

Or maybe she was just teasing, playing games so that she could tell Charity and Rosie what a fool she had made of me.

Marie Claire had teased me this way one Saturday afternoon in Paris. She had taken me to a floating pool on the Seine, a sought-after venue for which one had to book in advance. She had laughed at the innocent young Englishman trying not to look at the bare-breasted women around him lying half-naked in the sun.

That night I called her from my room. It was late. She answered without a word. She knew it was me. I began yet again to apologise, stumbling through jumbled phrases, trying hopelessly to make her understand. She cut me short.

'If you don't get yourself killed out there, you might at least learn to grow up.'

She hung up.

•

The mood in the country suddenly changed. A tragedy swung public opinion into a new and darker direction. The vignettes of the ordered life of white rule, nannies wheeling their prams past the fountains, a few tourists queuing up to buy tickets for township tours or even plane tickets to marvel at the mighty Falls, golf on the many courses, club cricket matches and cocktails in the Cancan Bar – it was as if this was a film and halfway through 'The End' had suddenly flashed on the screen. The blow that befell the regime was as savage as it was unexpected.

A Viscount airliner with more than fifty people on board had been shot down with a shoulder-fired missile. Worse still, the few survivors on the ground had been murdered by guerrillas who had tracked the fall of the plane. One or two had escaped the slaughter to report the words of the guerrilla leader before he opened fire: 'You stole our land.'

The wave of anger at this barbarity subsided into grim realisation that the tactic of fighting the war to a standstill, and thus a negotiated agreement, was now hopeless. There would be no quarter given by the victor to the vanquished.

I told myself that it was vital I see Patience to gain a sharper perspective on the mood of the African majority. Another lie.

I didn't need Patience in order to assess the mood in townships across the country. The barely concealed triumphalism was obvious. Servants in the big houses, the 'garden boys' and 'pool boys', the barmen, cooks, chauffeurs, even the township girls in the Red Top taxis off to deliver an evening of pleasure – all saw the anguish of the whites. They rejoiced secretly. They were winning.

Patience had vanished. I sat in the township bar night after night until Jeeze warned me to stay away. I was making people uncomfortable, he said. They didn't believe I was a writer. At the Frank Johnson School they said she had taken sabbatical leave. George in the Cancan shrugged and said he didn't know. I drank silver bullets every night, hoping that in that potent mix I might find at least memories of our evening together. I knew she would not come. I hoped George might have news. Every night he shook his head before I had even sat on the bar stool. It was always the bar stool, never a chair at a table. I just wanted to get closer to the night that we were there together.

Sara Jane found me there one evening. André was back with his unit in the bush. She slipped onto a bar stool beside me and ordered a drink for both of us. This was done casually, as if we had met by arrangement. We began talking, but no longer as staff writer and freelance fixer. Beyond the advice not to trust even my mother, she had not been much help to me. I didn't mind. I would rather go my own way. I liked Sara Jane.

Sara raised a glass and toasted 'Absent loved ones'. We clinked glasses but such an anodyne phrase did not describe what Patience had come to mean to me. The feeling of loss when she vanished had crept up on me by stealth. I knew from the worried look on George's face that she was doing something dangerous. She was in peril, far from friends. At night, I dreamt of the terrible things that might be happening to her, riddled with bullets on a darkened road, trampled by elephants, thrust into a tiny cell alive with killer ants or, worse still, crawling out of a crashed car, only to be . . .

By day, whether at the bar, in my room or walking the streets, I went over every detail, every expression on her face at the swimming picnic as she drank my whisky and lay in her wet woollen swimsuit in front of me. I saw her waving her arms as she talked, jabbing those yellow fingernail-painted hands at Charity and Rosie; I saw her in the dark of the square watching me as she smoked, waiting for me to kiss her; the kaleidoscope of images were as powerful as the sight of Marie Claire pulling on her stockings in the morning. I would watch her half asleep in the bed while she carefully chose between two skirts from a wardrobe, deciding on a pleated throwback to the thirties because that was the fashion. She would choose underwear, a blouse and neck scarf with equal care. She knew I was watching. Sometimes she would turn and smile.

Sara Jane pulled me out of this reverie. She wanted to talk about André. She wanted someone to hear her pain. She talked as if I was a friendly stranger rather than someone for whom she was supposed to be working. She didn't have many friends and was not the type for ladies' lunches. The confessional nature of our conversation suited me.

'I have never loved anyone like this,' she said. 'He is the kindest man I have ever known. He is always a surprise. He has fought in so many wars and yet comes to bed like a lamb.'

I didn't want to hear about that. She quizzed me about my 'good friend' Patience. She talked of the hypocrisy in a society where sex across the colour line was regarded as the ultimate taboo.

'Don't think many of those white farmers don't cross that line. They go into the servants' quarters after too much beer on a Saturday night. Plenty of bastard brown kids running around.'

I was hungry, but she just wanted to talk about André. She had met plenty of senior officers in Vietnam and had been on combat missions with them. They were just boys compared to André, she said.

Only then did I notice the slight twang of an American accent, more pronounced in some words than others. The way she said 'asked' and 'tomato' were giveaways. I asked about her early life in New York.

'I told you I was a photographer, but that's not how I made my money. I made enough to buy a small apartment in the Village. André is coming over when this is done. We are going to get married.'

She showed me a ring, a lustrous sapphire set in a circle of small diamonds.

She liked to shock. I think she had been doing that all her life, saying and doing things that jolted people into looking at her differently. She told me how she had started out as a penniless photographer in New York.

'Mother wasn't talking to me; don't ask why. I wasn't on the breadline, but I had to have dollars. I wanted to travel. I had to get out and get on. I could have slept with the magazine commissioning editors. That was the normal way up for a camera girl like me. I didn't do that, although there were plenty of offers. It wasn't pretty, what I did. I joined an agency and made a lot of money. Lonely rich men in hotels. Does that shock you?'

'It's a surprise.'

'Why? Half the women under fifty in New York would do that if they thought they could get away with it. Where have you been all your life?'

I had to laugh at that.

'You win,' I said.

'That paid for the cameras I needed for Nam. The real stuff. Nikon, Leica, top models. I had good commissions, sold a lot of pix and got great coverage in some big papers. So it was worth it. That's my story, or some of it. What brought you here?'

'Pure chance, really. I have a free hand to choose where I go.'

'That's unusual for a big magazine. You're lucky. But why here?'

'Same as the other guys who have pitched up here. Small war in a faraway place.'

'Don't be the same as the others.'

She spoke so loudly and with such asperity that most in the bar turned to look at us.

'You know why we're on the TV news every night in Europe and the US? Those handsome bastards pretend they are reporting a struggle for democracy in the heart of Africa, a downtrodden majority throwing off the yoke of colonialism.'

She was getting heated. She kept signalling for more drinks.

'But that's not what they're really telling their audience.

Watch those TV bulletins carefully and you will get the subtext. It's Custer's Last Stand all over again. A small, embattled group of right-on whites making a heroic stand against the native hordes. They wrap it up in the fight for civil rights, for majority rule, but that is a lie. They're selling a story that we're finished, that we've got nothing to offer.'

'I'm getting confused. That's true, isn't it? It's all over for the regime, surely?'

'No. What do you think André is fighting for out there? To be the last man alive in a massacre?'

'But you can't win.'

'We can fight on and force them to the table.'

She tapped my wrist just as Patience and Jeeze had done.

'This is what it's about, my friend.'

The missile attack on an aeroplane carrying civilian passengers had changed the fortunes of the war and placed this small country on the international stage. Even more American journalists began arriving. Sara Jane and Patience were both right. The world wanted the white side of the story. I would do the opposite: try to portray the conflicting loyalties of the African population. It was another act of self-deception.

•

In his own quiet way, George told me Patience was back. He was fixing the usual silver bullet when he looked at me and smiled, a rare occurrence on those granite features. I raised questioning eyebrows. He nodded. I finished the drink and took a taxi to the Victoria. Faces turned and looked away.

There was no sign of Patience, nor of Jeeze.

The next morning I left Franklins early and saw her arriving for the school day. She shook her head and pointed to her watch when she saw me. I drove back that afternoon.

'I've missed you.'

'I'm sorry.'

'Where have you been?'

She did not answer but got into the car. We drove to a ladies' clothes shop in the township. Women were crowded around racks of dresses. She walked me through to an office at the back. Everyone greeted her as she passed. The office was full of large cardboard boxes overflowing with clothing. Mugs of green tea were brought in with side plates of small cakes. I didn't ask why we were meeting in such a strange place.

She sipped her tea, took a cake and delicately bit into it. She positioned herself across the table from me.

'I wanted to get away, couldn't stand it any more.'

'Why didn't you tell me?'

'Why should I?'

'You might have told George.'

'Maybe he knew.'

'Where did you go? You have been away for weeks.'

'Is that your business?'

That's when I knew.

'You've been to the border, haven't you?'

'Supposing I have.'

'Supposing you've been smuggling the boys there.'

'What's it to you?'

'It's dangerous, for God's sake.'

'You're right. Very dangerous.'

'You could be arrested. Helping potential terrorists.'

'"*Potential terrorists*"! Whose fucking side are you on?'

She banged the tea cup down on the table. The swear word jolted me. It was so unlike her.

'I'm neutral. I have to be. You know that.'

'You can't be neutral in this war.'

She finished her tea, leant down and picked up her briefcase. She opened it and showed me a book. *Richard III* by William Shakespeare.

'Our next play. "Bottled spider",' she said. 'That's what his enemies called him.'

'And that's what the whites are here?'

She nodded.

'Why not? Make sure you're not in the bottle with them.'

'I want to see you again. Properly. Not in a place like this.'

'I don't think that would be wise.'

I kissed her quickly, leaning across the table. She pulled back at first and then allowed her lips to meet mine. She held me briefly, then walked round the table to me.

She told me everything that night. Hundreds of boys were crossing the border every month. Auxiliary troops, police patrols, minefields, electrified fences, dogs – nothing stopped them.

'It's a slaughterhouse over there,' she said.

A woman brought us more tea and cakes.

'The last thing many of those boys will see is a white man standing over them with a gun while their guts spill into the dust in shiny coils. Then *bang!* Or maybe if they are lucky an Alouette helicopter coming in low with a machine gun spitting tracer. They will see those bullets coming at them in a long white line and it'll be too late to do anything. They'll just lie there, squirming into the earth, waiting to be torn to pieces.'

'How do you know this?'

'Some, a few, far too few, come back. They're terrified and often badly wounded. They die quite quickly. We can't get them medical attention until they get back to the city.'

'You bring them back?'

She nodded.

'Why on earth help them cross the border? You're just getting them killed.'

'Many survive to fight. It's the only way.'

'You don't make it sound as if you're winning.'

'You go back to your farmer friends in Shamva and they'll tell you who is winning.'

It should have been no surprise. She was driving young men hidden under tarpaulins in a pick-up truck, using her teacher's identity pass stamped by the Department of Education to get through occasional roadblocks.

Her boys, as she called them, smeared themselves with a mix of herbs and cooking oil to put off tracker dogs trained to alert their handlers to human scent.

'But why send them to their deaths? What a waste!'

'If we don't fight for this country, we have no right to be here.'

•

We met whenever we could after that. She refused to let me pick her up from school and would not meet me at the Victoria. We met in small cafés in the township and cheap restaurants in the suburbs populated by Greeks, Lebanese and Syrians. They were mostly exiles who had drifted here to escape bankruptcy, the police or, as some complained loudly, the divorce demands of rapacious wives.

We became lovers, casually and without surprise, as foretold in every moment we had spent together since meeting by the river rock pool. Lust and laughter took us to bed, the laughter coming when she leant over me afterwards and whispered, 'Mud in your eye.' We were in her home, a house owned by the school and rented gratis to senior teachers. She loved the place, with its rug-covered cement floor, cane armchairs and a long wooden-framed sofa crowded with colourful cushions.

There were abstract paintings on the white-washed brick walls, all the work of her pupils – great splashes of colour to express rage and revolution; at least that's what Patience said. To me it looked more like someone throwing paint at a canvas for sheer fun.

A large desk piled with textbooks dominated one side of the room and more books lined every available space on the walls. The room spoke strongly of the person of who lived and worked there, a woman who drew strength from the anger of those she taught. Patience watched me as I looked around and then showed me her books, many on modern African writing; novels, poetry and history, which sat alongside the classics, Jane Austen, George Eliot, the Brontë sisters, Dickens and, of course, volumes on the plays and studies of Shakespeare. Then she showed me the bedroom

She became both a lover and counsellor, a cool counter to the increasingly frantic claims in the government media. She called herself a voice of the future and insisted on the righteousness of the violence that was sweeping the rural areas. She rejoiced in her role of helping young men cross the border to take up arms.

When she described her boys dying at the hands of the government forces, she was as emotionally disturbed as a mother at the death of a child. We argued. I demanded she recognise the sheer absurdity, the immorality, of sending unwitting young men to their death.

'We have the right to fight,' she said. 'You gave us that right.'

'The right to send men to die in their thousands when they don't need to?'

'This is our country. We have been here for thousands of years.'

'What's that got to do with it?'

'Everything.'

I thought back to the bushmen and their cave paintings.

'There was someone here before you.'

'And no doubt there will be someone here after us. What's your point?'

We talked about the extraordinary cave drawings, art created by a far-from-primitive people a few thousand years earlier.

'Where were your people then?'

'Up north. Then we came south.'

'So you were the colonisers?'

I thought she was going to throw her tea at me. We were sitting in her kitchen. She was wrapped in a loosely tied towelling gown.

'Are you still fucking that girl?'

The question was made more indelicate but somehow more exciting by the fact that only minutes earlier we had been lying in each other's arms, sweating, breathing hard, staring at the ceiling in silent wonder at such passing pleasure.

I was pleased. I had found a hidden side to this woman. She had taken care not to show any emotion in our meetings or lovemaking. More than once she repeated that I could not make love to her, only her to me.

She wanted control, the power to choose when and where we met. Now she was jealous. She enjoyed our arguments, but did so with precision rather than passion.

I recited a couple of lines from a poem I remembered from long ago: 'Love knows no limits; there are no frontiers to cross.'

'We're just lone travellers, mapless and lost,' she replied.

She had remembered the same lines but neither of us could name the poet.

She had reserved a part of herself, as if frightened of letting anyone see the whole. I had touched something within her. This woman might not love me, but she cared for me enough to resent my sexual transgression with another.

'Why?'

'Just tell me.'

The demand was made in the controlling manner that had been shaped by years of trying to enthuse unruly schoolchildren with the joys of Shakespeare.

'No.'

'But you have?'

'Why is this important to you? Does it matter?'

'Only a man would say that.'

She was angry.

'I slept with her once, that's all. It didn't mean anything.'

'Do I mean anything to you apart from that?' She nodded to the bedroom.

She meant much more than that to me. But I found it hard to tell her. Paris was far away. And yesterday.

'A lot of people tell me I shouldn't see you,' she said.

'Why?'

'You can work that out, can't you?'

'Who's saying this?'

She pointed to the window and the street outside.

'Never mind. Things are changing out there.'

She went to the bedroom to get dressed, closing the door behind her. When she emerged it was as the schoolteacher. The same uniform, the same yellow butterfly clasp as when I had first seen her. She picked up a briefcase. She told me to wait and then leave a little later. A taxi would come for me.

•

I now knew so much about what was happening on the border that the road to Shamva appeared more threatening than the last time. I passed a truckload of African troops and caught the insignia on the side of the vehicle: African Rifles Regiment.

They were standing on the open back of the truck holding guardrails, their rifles shouldered. It was a comforting sight. They had driven up the same road as I was travelling and had not been attacked.

Both Sara Jane and Bram had told me about their recruitment into the police and army. I had dismissed it as a classic bit of misinformation. Patience had tried to explain it, but her account did not make much sense. Here was some sort of proof. Beneath the racial divide lay a darker division between these people. How to explain that to my readers? I let the thought slide to the back of my mind, where I knew it would stay.

I made the farm in just over two hours. Speed cannot outrun a bullet, but I didn't care. Since every bend in the road held the threat of ambush, I held the needle at 100 kph all the way.

John Milan was away with his crops. Julia would arrive later from town. Layla Milan and I lunched on a salad and cold ham. She said little beyond small talk about her early days in the country.

That afternoon I swam in the pool, floating for a while on my back. The fencing had been strengthened and there were more silver bells on the wire. A mole had also been busy on the grassy lawn raising little hillocks. It was strange to find such an English creature embedded in the African landscape. It would be another question for Layla Milan if beer, or more likely a strong gin and tonic, made a longer conversation possible.

I lay briefly in the sun, took a nap and wrote some notes. Patience would be teaching her class now. They were on *Henry V*, a perfect sword-and-spears story for sixth-formers. She told me that it was never the story but the language that drew her students to Shakespeare.

'When you give a sixteen-year-old boy lines such as "Few die well that die in battle, for how can they when blood is their argument", you can hear him rolling the words around with his tongue,' she said.

'Where's that from?' I asked.

'You tell me. You're the expert.'

She waited a few moments, enjoying my ignorance, and then laughed.

'*Henry V*, you idiot.'

Chapter Six

The break in the rains had given the distant mountains a clarity of colour. Green bush and young pines climbed the lower slopes, giving way to brown rock that scaled the summit. Both terrorists and army used those hills to scan the plains below.

Down in the valley and out on the plains both sides fought brief engagements, usually at close quarters. The kill rate was as one-sided as Patience had suggested, trained troops against young men who had until a few weeks earlier been working as gardeners, waiters, barmen, road-sweepers.

In the mountains, those young men rested, watched and planned. Through binoculars, they would have a clear view of the dozen or so farms around Shamva.

I knew all this because in the short time I had been in the country no one talked of anything else, except perhaps the arrival of whisky, gin or vodka from the south. There was much resentment among the farmers that the Cancan and Pinks got first choice of these supplies. Most people had to make do with the locally made alternatives.

Julia arrived as the sun dipped into darkness. The landscape vanished, as did the fencing and the tree by the pool. A servant checked the mesh grenade screens over the windows.

We drank more than I wanted before dinner but it seemed churlish to refuse yet another large gin. Julia had little to say beyond talking to her mother about shopping and what was available in the department stores. They talked casually about security in the area: the road north-east to Mount Darwin had been mined twice, with damage to vehicles but only minor injuries to the passengers.

More seriously, and here their voices dropped to a whisper, a farm had been attacked on the slopes of the nearby mountains. The perimeter fence had been cut and big stones lobbed onto the lawns to detonate hidden explosives. A short but fierce firefight had followed. The attackers did not try to storm the house, defended as it was by the farmer, his wife and their eighteen-year-old son, home on leave from the army.

I tried not to look as if I was listening, but gathered that the attack had been repelled. The farm compound had been set on fire and several of the labourers had been killed. The guerrillas had changed tactics. Instead of a frontal assault, the aim had been to set the house alight, driving the occupants into the line of fire.

I began to feel like an unwelcome guest, although I had been warmly received when I'd phoned the day before to invite myself. I coughed quietly. Layla Milan apologised and rang a little bell to summon dinner.

We began to eat in silence, both women dwelling on their conversation. To change the subject, I asked about the moles in the garden. Were they indigenous? If not, when and how had they arrived from Europe? They looked at me in puzzlement.

'The lumps in the grass outside,' I explained.

They both began laughing.

'Moles?' Layla Milan exclaimed. 'Moles!'

She and Julia laughed again. I felt as if I had trespassed on some family secret. The truth was embarrassing. The little mole heaps were grenades that had been placed just beneath the turf and linked by wires to the kitchen. Layla Milan pointed to thin wires taped to the floor, leading to a box beside the bread bin.

'These are not contact explosives, but we can let them off if they break the wire fence.'

'What about the dogs?'

'No good,' said Julia. 'They throw poisoned meat over the fence. The dogs bark, but then they bark at anything that moves at night – including moles.' She and her mother laughed again.

I had planned to stay a few days, even if only to get away from the city. I changed my mind. I would leave in the morning. That night I woke from a deep whisky sleep as Julia slipped in beside me.

'Sorry we laughed at you,' she whispered. 'It's just that we don't get much to laugh at now, and moles – well, you understand.'

I did understand. The war was closing in on these people. The dangers folded into their nights forgave any behaviour. Afterwards, she lit a cigarette and lay there smoking for a few minutes, flicking the ash onto the floor.

'It's getting very close,' she said suddenly, echoing a remark I was hearing more and more often. She threw the glowing butt out of the window and turned to me again. I promised myself never to visit Green Creek Farm again.

•

I spent the morning talking to the labourers in the compound. Layla Milan was happy with that, which surprised me. Most of the men were out in the fields, but a few of the older folk remained with the women and children.

Julia came along, but not to translate, because the workers all spoke good English – another surprise. She held my hand briefly as we walked to the compound. The night had vanished into a memory that would soon fade. I suspected it would be the same for her.

If I was to believe the story that followed, the Milan workforce were content with their low wages. They were allowed to grow their own crops in small plots of land and were helped with illness by Layla Milan, who acted as doctor, midwife and teacher to the young children.

'They sprout up like popcorn,' said Julia, 'and Mum delivers them.'

On the drive back I reflected that nothing I had seen or heard so far fitted the received wisdom about this war.

The imperative of impartial reportage was an almost religious belief in the office and in most of the American press. As Sara Jane had so vividly noted, my editors might pay lip service to balanced reporting, but what they really wanted were reports of a winning war for the nationalists.

The editorial leaders justified the war by citing white-minority intransigence, which was fair enough. The idea that the white minority had any claim on the country was dismissed as whimsy. The nation was bound for African-majority rule, and the whites were bound for the history books.

That was true, and my writing had reflected this foregone conclusion. But truth wears a coat of many colours, a tiny bubble of quicksilver that eludes capture. I was becoming confused. Growing in my mind, I saw another side to the story.

I passed a burnt-out car and saw helicopters in the distance swooping like dragonflies over the bush. These were the Alouettes that Patience had talked about. I needed to see her. I felt like a ship that had broken from safe anchorage and been taken by the tide.

Last night I had not made love to Julia. Patience would use a much cruder expression. In the language of love, that was not the same at all.

I drove fast, tensing for what Julia had called a drum roll of bullets shattering the windscreen and punching into the bodywork of the car. I gripped the wheel so tightly that my knuckles cracked.

•

There was nowhere else to go when I got back. The familiar presence of George, with his pencil moustache and gravel voice, mixing cocktails with a slow and steady hand was a comforting sight. That was what I needed. Comfort, someone to talk to, someone I could trust, even if it was to discuss the latest cocktail in his book.

The bar was filled with the usual crowd of overdressed women and men wearing suits in various shades of brown. It was seven in the evening. The bar stools were full, as was every other seat in the room.

Seeing me, George whispered something to a young woman sitting alone at the bar. She finished her drink, looked around, gave me a long stare and then left, walking past without a sideways glance. George nodded to the seat.

'Thanks, but you didn't have to.'

'House detective. Off duty,' said George.

Without being asked, he mixed my drink and watched me finish it, which I did quickly. He leant forward.

'If I were you, I would take a drink across the square.'

I thanked him, signed a drink chit and left. The woman who had been at the bar was seated on a chair outside the door. She got up as I passed. 'Be careful,' she said.

I passed the fountain where I had kissed Patience, dipped my hands in the water and splashed my face. I had not even been to my room since the drive back. My back ached. I was tired. I asked myself a question to which, as so often these days, I knew the answer. I could have been anywhere else in the world by now.

One look at the crowded club room told me who was in that night: Quigley, who looked at me without recognition; a tall, smartly dressed woman of a certain age, smoking from a long cigarette-holder; and Chris Raymond, a man I had briefly met there before. He bowed in greeting from the bar. Raymond was interesting. He was dressed like a scarecrow. His wavy dark hair was greased with ointment. No one could dress that badly and use that amount of hair oil without having a secret to tell.

Patience was standing next to Jeeze, both with backs to the wall. He came over quickly and wrapped his arms around me in a hug.

'Good to see you, comrade,' he said. 'Let me get you a drink.'

He pulled out a wallet fat with notes and went to the bar.

Patience smiled a greeting. We both watched as Jeeze stopped for a brief word with almost everyone in the room.

'He knows a lot of people,' I said.

'He knows too much. How was the farm?'

'You were right. They are very worried. More mines on the roads. One of their neighbours was attacked.'

'What happened?'

'They survived, but it was close.'

She nodded. 'I told you.'

Jeeze was lost to sight in the bar crowd. We waited impatiently for our beers.

'How was your girlfriend?'

'I don't have a girlfriend.'

'Sorry. How was the girl you sleep with who isn't your girlfriend?'

Jeeze arrived with the drinks.

'Here's to happy hearts,' he said.

I have only a hazy recollection of the rest of the night. Jeeze clung to us, talking about the money he was making from the American TV crews for whom he arranged interviews with 'ordinary township residents'. These people were in fact his friends, who paid him for their fleeting moment of fame on American television. He told us of his plans to buy a house in the township for his parents. I remember him boasting about his career as a television producer when the war was over and Patience telling him sharply to shut up.

We ended the evening in a curry house. Most of the club drinkers had gathered there. The place was full, noisy and thick with smoke, steam and the clinging odour of curry. There was a group of troops in uniform eating, drinking and playing cards all at the same time.

A waiter seated us on three tables. Menus were handed out, beer was ordered. Quigley and Jeeze shouted over to the troops, offering beer. Their heads turned as they squinted at us through the murk.

'Let's not stay,' said Patience.

We were inching our way out when the fight started. A chair was thrown. Quigley was wrestling with one soldier while Jeeze danced around shouting encouragement. People scattered to the door. Waiters milled around, flapping their white tablecloths, trying to remove empty beer bottles from the tables. Several other fights broke out. We stood on the pavement outside listening to the fracas.

'Take me away from here,' she said. 'Out of this town.'

'Where?'

'Anywhere, somewhere far away. There are still places to go.'

•

The next morning the hotel produced a tourist brochure, which declared that a five-star hotel in the Eastern Highlands was 'as close to paradise as one gets on this earth'.

Photographs showed a fake castle with a long pool around

which couples in old-fashioned swimsuits lounged on reclining chairs; a grass tennis court featured two energetic-looking young men; women and children were pictured playing a game of croquet.

It looked ideal, but it was far too close to the border to be safe. I showed Patience the brochure and told her we had to look elsewhere.

'No,' she said, 'it's quite safe there. Let's book it.'

'How can you be so certain?'

'It will be fine. Just book it.'

I reserved a room with a reedy-voiced man who assured me of a warm welcome and high security. On the drive through the midland plains I again asked why she was sure it was safe to stay so close to the border.

She remained silent for a while and then said, 'I need to get away. The sight of those young men fighting made me sick. They are just like our boys – young, stupid, strong, brainless white boys – and all they want to do is fight. There's a gene in men, isn't there? An urge to fight.'

'That doesn't answer the question.'

'Don't worry. No one is going to bother us there.'

The hotel came into view long before we had emerged from a winding road through pine forests. We glimpsed the cone-shaped towers, castellated ramparts and the slate-grey roofing of a gothic folly through gaps in the trees. It was a bizarre sight in such a setting, a film set for a Victorian melodrama.

A barrel-chested man well into his middle years came out to meet us. He was wearing an old corduroy suit with a faded ribbon of service decorations on the lapel. His thinning head of grey hair was scooped back into a ponytail. With the same high-pitched, squeaky voice I had heard on the phone, he introduced himself as 'Colonel Horrel, owner and manager'. The voice suggested that someone small and thin lurked within his bulky persona.

He took our luggage and clumped into the hotel beneath a stone arch, which carried the motto '*Fidelis Ad Mortem*'. Two Dobermans sat chained in kennels by the front door. There was no sign of any staff.

We walked along a corridor and through a large lounge, trailing Colonel Horrel and our luggage. Patience looked at me, raised her eyebrows and wrinkled her nose. The carpets, furniture and curtains, indeed the whole place, had the mildewed air of decay and long closure.

Our room looked onto a drained swimming pool. There was no net on a distant tennis court. The room had the same odour of decay as the rest of the hotel. Once our host had left us, Patience stripped the damp sheets from the bed and marched out of a back door to find a clothes line. Eventually she hung them over the stone wall of a vegetable garden. The warming sun would soon dry them. No one minded, because there didn't seem to be anyone to mind.

We were the only guests. We felt like ghosts at a funeral. But the silence, the solitude and the air of desolation suited us. We lit a log fire, toasted ourselves with shots of whisky from tooth mugs and made love on the damp mattress. Afterwards we hauled the mattress off the bed and stood it close to the fire.

Patience disappeared into the bathroom. A minute later, she poked her head around the door and said, 'Hot water!'

I watched the mattress steaming slightly, threw another log

on the fire and drank more whisky. Patience returned with a towel around her and skipped to the window

She leant out looking at forests and mountains lit by a strong sun. She swung her hips and the towel dropped to the floor.

•

We wanted to walk in the woods that spilled over the hills towards the border, but Colonel Horrel said no. 'They can take me any time they want,' he said, 'because I am old and useless, but I don't want to lose a guest.'

Patience laughed and told him we were quite safe. We walked through the trees to the rim of the hill and looked down to the spreading plains of a foreign country beyond. The border was marked with a fence strung with barbed wire along a firebreak about a hundred metres wide on either side. The firebreak trailed off into the distance in both directions.

'Rebel country,' I said.

'Don't worry, no one will harm us.'

'You keep saying that. How do you know?'

'This is the area where our boys cross. We don't want to attract the security forces, so it's a no-go area for us.'

'"No-go"?'

'I mean our men are forbidden to operate here – we don't want to bring the army in.'

Us. We. Our. Every time she talked like this I was uncomfortably reminded that she was on one side of the war and I had effectively joined that side, forfeiting all pretence at impartiality. Bram and his friends would certainly see it that way.

We held hands and kissed by the drained swimming pool. Weeds were sprouting through the crumbled asphalt of the tennis court and the croquet lawn had lost its hoops.

There was only one member of staff, a handsome young African with gold rings on every finger and diamond piercings in his ears. That evening the colonel served drinks. He had never heard of a silver bullet but poured malt whisky in heavy cut-glass tumblers. He said there was plenty of wine into the cellar but no one to drink it. Dinner was curried goat served with rice and peas. Cheese with good red wine followed.

'So we get to eat a decent curry after all,' she said. The meal was a surprise in such surroundings.

The colonel joined us after dinner, pouring balloons of local brandy.

'Can't drink whisky after dinner,' he said, 'bad form.'

He called loudly to the chef to hear our compliments. The young African man appeared, thanked us and then sat down and accepted a glass of brandy. His name was Alfred – 'but I don't burn any cakes'.

We listened as the colonel told us that the hotel had been in his family for sixty years. His grandfather had made money in gold mining and had retired, seeking peace and quiet in the hills at the end of his life. He had designed his home himself. Subsequent family owners had turned the house into a favourite honeymoon destination. Young couples fresh from their church weddings flocked to the exotic retreat in the hills. A large staff was hired, including a tennis coach and a lifeguard for the pool at night. One drunken young bride had fallen in unseen by others guests and drowned.

'A short three-day marriage,' said Colonel Horrel. 'Her husband went down with that Viscount. Best thing, really. He never got over her death.'

I looked quickly at Patience. She frowned and breathed in deeply. I had deliberately avoided the subject of the Viscount. It was a war crime rather than an act of war, for which there was no justification, nor had one been offered.

I often try to remember the moment when I fell in love with her, as if locating the precise time and place might enshrine the memory in my mind. It was there and then in that ruined hotel. She never told me she felt the same and I never really knew.

She wouldn't say much about her past, especially where her love of Shakespeare came from. 'Women have their mysteries,' she said. 'Better to keep it that way.' The more she revealed her knowledge of the plays, the more curious I became.

I asked how she managed to convey the passionate love of *Romeo and Juliet* to township youngsters whose idea of love was probably masturbation rather than feelings for fellow human beings. She always gave the same answer: the language. And there was always a quotation to make the point:

Give me my Romeo: and, when he shall die,
Take him and cut him out in little stars,
And he will make the face of heaven so fine
That all the world will be in love with night.

'They get that?'

'Of course. Don't you?'

We lost ourselves in that place. The sense of abandonment in a crumbling folly built by some adventurer fifty years earlier was a perfect setting for love without limits.

Our room looked out over a rusty security fence towards the hills. The nights were cold and days warm under fleecy white clouds that drifted up from the coast. The border just two miles away. Patience's assurances were not convincing. Nationalist guerrillas were not part of a regular army. The idea that some central nationalist command could impose a no-go area on free-ranging young men bent on murder was ludicrous.

'I've told you. They won't bother with this place,' she said. 'There's nothing here for them. Besides, that young man knows them, I'm sure of it.'

'He knows the colonel pretty well too,' I said.

'They're lovers,' said Patience, laughing. 'Can't you see that? That's why Horrel is staying on here. It's nothing to do with that nonsense about "they can take me any time".'

Four lovers alone in the ruins of a great hotel, I thought. A perfect short story, perhaps a film script, but how would it end? The gothic folly aflame as rocket grenades burnt through the wooden walls? The young man killing his old lover in a drunken brawl after a surfeit of brandy and fleeing with as much liquor as he could carry to join his comrades in the hills?

And what of the two other lovers? They could hardly keep apart in the rotting remains of a grand hotel; black skin on white, white on black, bodies glistening with a sheen of sweat as they sought rapture in oblivion.

•

On the drive back we took a detour and visited the border town where I had crossed some months ago. It seemed like years. The frontier post was heavily fortified now with sandbags, more lights and a high wire fence on either side stretching up into the hills and the forest.

Patience got out of the car with me and stood on the roadside staring into the hills. I asked why she had wanted to come here. She shook her head, took my arm and guided me back to the car.

'Is that where they cross?' I said, pointing to the hills.

'No. Too many minefields and dogs at night. I told you, the crossing is usually near that funny hotel. They haven't worked that out yet.'

We sat in the car, she smoking, me chewing gum, desperate for a cigarette.

'There are tea estates in the valley over the hill,' she said. 'It's good tea, exported to the Middle East. Soft fruit farms as well – pineapples, avocados – all premium products grown for export.'

'Is that why we are here?'

'I thought you should know what a rich country this is. They could feed the whole of Africa.'

'"They"?'

'It's not our country yet.'

'I realise that.'

'I don't think you do.'

She opened the car door and leant out to scoop something from the roadside. She opened her hand to show me oozing mud.

'Take it,' she said, and squelched the mud into my hand. 'If you want to understand this country, look at what you're holding. That's rich earth, our land. That's the story for you. That's why you're here.' I opened the door and wiped the mud off on the rim.

She lit another cigarette, wound down the car window and pointed into the forest.

'See those trees? All pines planted by the settlers fifty years ago. Those are not our trees. Beyond you will find beeches, birch and elm that have been here for hundreds of years. Those are our trees.'

•

I had been in the country long enough to have collected background for the big article that New York wanted. It was not enough. I felt removed from the one thing that shaped everyone's life and the reason for my being there in the first place.

I had not come to write about the war. I had told myself when I crossed the border that I would stay only a few days to assess opposed opinions and try to understand the strength of those feelings.

Almost every conversation began with expressions of love for the land. The mud Patience had thrust into my hand was just that. Time and again I heard references to land, soil and earth, as if the dry dust of the bush, the rich, dark farmland, the thin topsoil in the reservations and the clay that carried the forest up and over the border mountains held some mythical property.

John Milan had scooped that handful of soil and told me the earth was rich and strong. That is what they were fighting for. That's what he had meant. Patience had pretty much said the same thing when she pressed mud into my hand.

I had come to understand that the roots of the war lay in myth and emotion, a longing to find a place in history. These emotions had sunk their roots deep in the well-watered soil and temperate climate of a country that lay several thousand feet above the oppressive heat of the coastal plain.

Everyone had a claim on the history of this land and could cite arguments about why one set of rights superseded all others. The arguments ranged from legal interpretation of ancient treaties to mad racial prejudice. The brutal certainty of these views allowed no compromise. The only language either side understood was that of the gun.

Patience refused to let me drive her back to the township. I left her at a bus stop with a brief kiss. I waited in the car. She turned as the bus approached, waved and with a nod of her head indicated that I should drive away. I had left my lover in the Eastern Highlands with the colonel and his gold-ringed boyfriend.

Chapter Seven

The helicopter took us low over scrub and bush, the pilot enjoying the terror on the faces of his three civilian passengers huddled on the back seats.

My vague notions of getting close to the war zone seemed less sensible now. The facility trip had been easy to arrange. Bram had made a few calls and I and a two-man Italian TV crew had been approved to fly to the north-east 'operational area' – a polite euphemism for a war zone – to visit a forward airfield. I saw this as the core of my next article: a look into the eyes of young soldiers who were doing the fighting.

The area had been the scene of a number of road mines and farm attacks. We were told that several guerrilla groups had infiltrated the region. Our pilot was not taking chances. He swirled around rocky outcrops, skimmed over hills and occasionally flung the aircraft almost on its side as he wheeled away from what he told us was a possible enemy sighting. The Italians shouted to me over the noise of the engine, saying this was pure bravado, as if they knew.

We landed on a dusty airstrip that was lined on all sides with earth revetments. Two more Alouettes and several fixed-wing aircraft were parked at the end of the dirt runway. Camouflaged gun emplacements had been dug in along the perimeter.

The camp consisted of two long tin-roofed shacks protected by sandbags. It was positioned on rising ground that gave a good view of the surrounding bush. There was no one to be seen. The place looked like a relic of a long-forgotten war fought against mutinous tribes in some distant corner of the British Empire.

On reflection, that was not far from the truth. We listened diligently to the detailed briefing that followed, but it was of little use to the TV crew or me. The number of kills in recent clashes, the name of a local guerrilla commander, the atrocities committed against innocent villagers, caches of captured weapons – this was the stuff of daily press conferences in town and offered us little reward for our flight.

The Italians wanted to go into action on a helicopter and film glittering arcs of shell cases ejecting from its 20-mm Browning machine gun as dark shadows flitted on the ground below seeking cover. This request was denied with a wry smile by the quietly spoken major who was to be our guide for the next two days. The Alouettes carried five, sometimes six, men into action and had no room for journalists, he said. There would be something to film the next day and a chance to interview the troops as they returned from operations.

I sat up drinking whisky with the major after the Italians had gone to bed. An Englishman in his thirties, he told me he had given up a career in the British Army after several tours of duty attached to NATO forces in Germany.

He stopped there. It was a semi-colon rather than a full stop. He looked at me to see if he had gained my attention. He refilled our glasses.

'Now you are going to ask me why I am fighting for an illegal regime in a losing war against a majority of the population who are destined for victory and independence in a few years' time,' he said.

'The question had occurred to me,' I said.

He tore open a new pack of cigarettes and lit one.

'A broken marriage to a perfectly decent woman. No prospect of quick promotion in the army. Above all, I was bored. Failure drives a man to do two things: blame everyone else or run away and hide from himself. That's what I did. I ran away. The coward's choice, I suppose.'

'But why here? There's no hope, is there?'

He leant back in his chair, searching the ceiling with eyes clouded by whisky.

'We could argue we are trying to fight them to a standstill and then get a deal, shared power and all that.'

'You're going to have to kill a lot of people to do that.'

'We have already killed a lot of people.'

'You too?'

'I don't kill people. I kill numbers. Five today, ten yesterday.'

He spoke softly, slightly slurring his words.

'It hasn't worked, has it?' I said.

I spoke harshly, spitting the words out. He watched me with what looked like a half-smile. I told myself to calm down and reached for the bottle. There wasn't much left.

'No, it hasn't.'

'And will it?'

'No, it will not.'

'So what's the point?'

He laughed then and tipped his chair back again, almost falling over.

'Maybe there isn't one. You ever read Camus?'

'A long time ago.'

'It's all there. Life is absurd. Roll a rock up a hill, lose control, watch it roll down and do it again.'

I told the major that I would take that thought to bed and got up. He pushed me back onto the chair. He wanted to explain himself, he said. He was a relatively young man, well trained as a soldier, seeking adventure and excitement. He was paid good money. What was wrong with that?

'So, you're a mercenary.'

'If you want to call me a gun for hire, so be it.'

'No belief in this war, no right or wrong?'

'They try to persuade people this is an anti-communist crusade, but that's nonsense.' He pointed outside. 'Out there the Russians and the Chinese are both helping, mostly arms, heavy weapons, even missiles we hear, but that doesn't make the terrs Marxist. They claim to be righting a terrible historic wrong, but actually it's the same old game.'

He raised his glass to me.

'This is what they want, the hard stuff. It's what we all want, isn't it?'

'I don't follow you.'

'Power. Everyone has been fighting for that since Adam bit the apple. Simple really.'

•

I lay on a sagging camp bed that night, regretting the whiskies and wondering what Patience would make of the major. She would hate me for being in a military camp, eating and drinking among men who were intent on killing her brethren.

I wouldn't tell her. I would let her read it. When the article finally came out weeks later, where would I be? Back in a tiny rented apartment in Levallois-Perret? It was a working-class district of Paris named after Monsieur Perret, a distant mayor of the city. As a journalist, you tend to pick up such useless detail.

No. I would be in Lisbon, waiting for the next assignment or possibly the damnation of a desk job in New York. But always with her. Yes, I was sure of that. I would read the piece to Patience and she would be proud of my skill as a writer, a man who could use words to shine light into the darkness. With that and other thoughts, I fell asleep.

I woke to the sound of helicopters thrashing the air as they came in to land. Except they didn't land. I pulled on some clothes and went outside, ducking my head against a dust storm whipped up by the rotors.

Two large nets bulging with dark cargo slung beneath the aircraft were being lowered slowly to the ground. They landed with a thump. The choppers swung up and away. A truck appeared. The nets were opened, revealing a dozen or so bodies in each net. From what I could see, they were all African. The bodies, covered in crusted blood and torn clothes, assumed grotesque shapes as they were loaded onto a truck and driven away.

The major approached.

'I was going to wake you. Have a coffee and come on over.'

He pointed behind the huts.

I drank the coffee quickly, swallowed two aspirins and walked around the back. The bodies had been laid side by side, almost touching. Men wearing gloves were going through pockets, pulling out bloody bits of paper and what remained of cigarette packs. A pile of weapons, mostly AK-47s, lay to one side.

I was too hungover to feel any shock. This was why we were here. The major had said it was a game of numbers; here were the numbers.

'Take a good look and photograph what you want,' said the major.

I began to feel shaky. I walked along the line of dead much as an officer might inspect his troops. It was only when I had passed the fourth body that I realised I was nodding to each one, a personal greeting to the dead. They were young, all with terrible wounds, mostly in the chest and abdomen.

These weren't bodies. They were corpses, dried blood around torn, blackened flesh, limbs lost. The expressions on their faces were those of terror and shock as if death had sprung from nowhere and caught them by surprise.

A few faces spoke of calm resignation, the expressions of men when getting out of bed to face a difficult day. On one face I saw a smile, as if at peace. They were dressed in what was left of their jeans, cheap denim shirts and bush boots. They were young, maybe early twenties at most, but many teenagers.

My hands were shaking as I took an offered cigarette from the major. It was the first in years. I smoked for a minute, began coughing and threw the cigarette away. Something bothered me about those dead young men laid out for inspection, faces frozen by rigor mortis. Somewhere among them a faint memory had stirred. I walked down the line again. I stopped at the fourth body. His legs lay apart. A bloody camouflage jacket had ripped open, revealing a torn black vest.

At first it was hard to see where he had been hit. The ripped black jeans around his groin had turned a darker colour. Two bullets had disembowelled him. Knocked backwards, he would have fainted with shock and pain and bled to death. I looked back at the black vest.

Through the dried blood I could just make out a red fist above the legend '*A Luta Continua*': Cephas, the barman at the Victoria, where I had first met Patience. Her Shakespeare boy, stronger than a tree, who could recite passages from the sonnets.

How had he ended up in the blood and shit of a military airfield? I tried to remember when I had last seen him. It was weeks ago. His hostility had not lessened; he had glared at me when I went in looking for Patience. He meant something special to her. He must have been driven to the border at night, climbed the hills, picked his way through the minefield, climbed the razor-sharp fence and crossed over to rebel country.

They would have taken him to a camp and given him a brief period of basic training in the use of his AK-47 and field craft. He would have been happy, exultant. He and his new comrades would have sung revolutionary songs and chanted slogans around the paraffin stoves at night. Never light a fire in the bush would have been one of the first lessons. Never stand or kneel when you fire; always lie flat. Then, with the camouflage clothing, rifle and new boots of a soldier, the barman would have climbed back over the border fence to die in his own country.

The major noticed my interest. 'Anyone you know?' he asked, looking down at Cephas.

I was about to answer, then silently shook my head. He looked at me oddly.

'What happened?' I asked.

'They were feeding from a village. An informer gave away the position of their camp. Then it was almost routine. A unit got into position on a track out of the village. Fire Force choppered in at sunrise. The terrs scattered down the track, where we nailed them.'

'"Fire Force"?'

'Rapid deployment of airborne infantry to the scene of a contact. A few terrs holed up in a gully where the K-car hit them with cannon fire. Rock splinters and shrapnel shredded them. It was all over in twenty minutes.'

'"K-car"?'

'Kill car. Chopper with a 20-mm Browning. Controls the action on the ground. Makes a hell of a mess.'

The major gave me these details with the bored air of someone who had said the same sort of things many times before. The dead terrorists, guerrillas, freedom fighters, whatever name suited the various political viewpoints of his audience, were laid out like meat on a butcher's slab and offered up to the cameras of the local press.

Their faces would be broadcast on that night's local TV news as evidence of a winning war. Occasionally, big TV stations in Europe or the US would pick up the footage and those faces would find a final life flickering onto news bulletins across the world.

The disgust I felt was not at my participation in this grisly performance. Nor did I feel shame. What I loathed about myself then, and still do when looking back, was that I felt nothing. The dead young men lying there had aroused no more than curiosity. I had never seen anything like it, unless one counts a startlingly blonde woman sprawling half out of her car after a crash on the motorway north of Paris.

I had become a voyeur looking at the private last moments of these young fighters. Perhaps that's why I had nodded to them as I passed.

What of Patience's star pupil Cephas? She had spoken of him not just with admiration but with love. Perhaps he had even been a boyfriend and had lain beside her, had kissed her, held her and, well . . . I stopped there. Jealousy can pluck fantastic thoughts from nowhere.

I could hardly be jealous of a dead man. But I was. Looking at him, I decided that he had indeed been her young lover, a pupil who could memorise passages from Shakespeare, and she the older woman, the teacher, the mother he may never have had, taking him into her arms after school, maybe with a fleeting kiss in the classroom after the pupils had gone and chalk dust was settling on the desks. They would have gone home on the bus, sitting separately, the forbidden lovers trying to hide from the world what they could not hide from themselves, then skittering from the bus stop into her house, the cheap local whisky and the bedroom.

And here was I, another useful idiot in the propaganda war. I wanted to get out of that camp. Patience and Cephas.

How was I going to tell her? She would have to know that I had seen him laid out as a corpse in that camp. She would hate me for it. She would not understand what I had been doing there.

'Are you sure you don't know that man?' said the major, pointing to Cephas.

'I thought I did but I don't,' I said. 'What happens now?'

'We try and ID them, then Special Branch take photos, then we burn them.'

'Where?'

'Down by the river. We let the locals see. Hope they learn a lesson.'

'And the war goes on.'

'Of course.'

•

Two of the ten troops who had taken part in the action were laid on for an interview. Behind the camouflage paint that streaked their faces they looked exhausted. One was clearly the older, but both were as young as those they had killed. They sat smoking and drinking beer from the bottle while the Italians tried to talk to them. How did it feel in combat? Were they frightened? What was it like to shoot and see the enemy fall to the ground?

I waited patiently until the Italians had left. The troops wanted to go too, but the major held them back for me.

'Do you know any young African people back at home?' I asked.

They looked surprised.

'Sure, we have a garden boy, and one in the kitchen, but he is an old man now.'

'Do you ever talk to them?'

'Sure, we're friends; the old man is called Tobias. We used to play with his kids, kicking balls around, running wild in the bush.'

'Any other contact with the ordinary people of this country?'

'Steady,' said the major.

'At the cricket club we sometimes played against their teams. Great bowlers they were. We would have a few beers together after. They were good guys.'

'What does it feel like to kill them?'

The major stood up and shouted, 'Out of order! Do not answer that question.'

'I don't mind,' said one. 'It feels good. They're just floppies.'

'"*Floppies*"?'

'When we shoot them they flop around on the ground.'

'But they are the same as those bowlers in the cricket team, aren't they?'

'They don't play cricket with AK-47s,' they said almost in unison and laughed.

'They bowl a neat grenade,' said the older one and they laughed again.

They were so young, barely out of school, so strong and possessed of such an unlikely innocence. I wanted to find out if they thought white-minority rule was worth fighting for and whether they thought there was any hope of victory or even a settlement; above all, I wanted to know whether, after all the killing, they thought black and white could ever live together in one country again. But the major cut the interview short.

In any case, it was stupid of me to think there was any value in such questions. These young men didn't think about the future of their country. They were sent to the bush to kill and they had become good at it. They tap-tapped out the copper-clad 7.62 bullets with their FN rifles held straight and steady.

They were not like Cephas, who would have panicked at the sound of the helicopters and fired blindly into the air, into the bush, at anything that he thought might be the enemy. His magazine would have run out and then, before he could reload, it was all over. Three bullets in the stomach and groin kicking him back into the dust of Mother Africa.

The men we had interviewed would not pay a price. They might have occasional nightmares about the screams of those flopping around on the ground, some begging for the final bullet. But they felt no guilt. They were doing their duty and obeying orders. They would tell their children and maybe even grandchildren of their bravery under fire. Some might admit they were as terrified as their enemy.

The guilt would not be theirs for the rest of their lives. I would not carry the burden of that guilt either. I had become complicit. I had surrendered my innocence; my supposed neutrality had been betrayed by the first stirrings of emotional attachment to a cause both immoral and utterly impractical. How could I have let a mercenary major, with his talk of Camus, and those two exhausted soldiers elicit sympathy for their deeds?

•

The major was not there to say goodbye when the aircraft came to pick us up. We flew back to base as dusk settled over the land. It was late when I got to the Victoria Hotel. I had decided to ask the magazine to take 15,000 words and build the piece around the short life and death of Cephas Msika. The remainder of the trip had given me the perfect counterpoint to his story.

It was probably my imagination, but that night the Victoria was quieter than when I had first been there. A new barman was pumping beer. He could have been Cephas's twin. The same strong features, the same surly confidence, but without the T-shirt.

There was no sign of Patience, but Charity and Rosie were in a corner. I joined them without invitation. They accepted glasses of lemonade and shyly waited for me to say something. We talked about their classes that day and agreed that the teaching of maths was a torment for teachers and pupils alike. The idea of getting an algebra coefficient into the heads of sixteen-year-olds was absurd. I hoped they might mention Patience, but it was left to me to ask whether they had seen her recently. They did not know where she was. Yes, they would give her a message.

I drove to the school, thinking she might still be there. She said she sometimes worked late at night, finding peace and quiet in the empty classrooms. There wasn't a light on in the building. I drove the narrow side streets of the township, trying to find the line of amaryllis trees that I had seen outside her house. It was nearly midnight when I gave up.

I knew the Cancan would be open for last orders. Opening hours had been extended to provide drink for those coming off duty in various ministries or even for officers back late from the bush. George nodded at me, turned and reached for the cocktail shaker. I asked for a beer instead. I hardly needed to ask the question. No, he had not heard from Patience. I left the same message as I had with Charity and Rosie.

I almost called Paris. The one-hour time difference made it only 11 p.m. there. I didn't. There was no point in provoking another slammed-down phone.

I sat in my bedroom looking at the phone, knowing the operator would put me through to Paris in seconds. I thought of what Marie Claire had said to me. Affairs have a beginning and an ending. Love from the heart lasts for ever, even after death.

She would speak in English when she said things like that, to make sure I understood. She was bilingual, with an English mother married to a Frenchman. They lived in Brest, where he did something with fish; canning sardines, I think. She had promised to take me there to meet them.

Chapter Eight

I could see from across the street that she was very tired. There was a ghostly pallor beneath the dark skin. She saw me, shook her head and walked quickly to the bus stop. I caught up with her.

'I can't talk now,' she said.

'I have something very important to tell you.'

'What's important to me now is sleep.'

The bus was approaching.

'It's about Cephas.'

'What about him?'

Her face set hard. I had planned this moment carefully, but when it came I could only tumble out the words.

'He is dead.'

Her face tautened into a grimace. She put an arm to the rusty bus-stop pole to steady herself.

'Take me home,' she said.

We sat facing each other, she on the sofa while I sat in an uncomfortable cane armchair. There had been no time for tea, a drink or even a glass of water. She had flung herself down and said, 'Tell me.'

I had intended to spare her the details but she insisted on hearing the full story. The colour had returned to her face. She closed her eyes.

I told her how I had been given a facility trip to a forward airfield – she groaned at this point – and how I had seen the helicopters coming in with cargo nets of dead bodies. She sat forward with a start and raised a hand. I stopped. Her eyes were still closed and every muscle in her face had tightened as if in pain.

'What did you think you were doing there?'

'I told you, it was a facility trip. I'm a writer, remember?'

'You were with the army, out in the bush. How could you?'

'Does that matter?' I said. 'Cephas is dead, that's what matters.'

'Not to you, it doesn't. He's just a paragraph in your piece. What will you say? Black barman who tried to sell me a girl gets slotted? That's the word they use, isn't it – "slotted"? Then you will throw in a few fake words of moral judgement: another life lost in a useless war. And your readers will be impressed with this observation because it will make them think their writer is above the filth and blood of this war, and that will make them feel good.

'They don't know, of course, that their writer is not sitting on the right hand of God deciding who is right and wrong, but down here fucking a farm girl one night, an African teacher the next, and in between strolling past the corpses of young men, making notes about the death masks of those who had the temerity to fight for justice.'

Everything stopped. There was nothing between us but silence.

'Have you got any whisky?' I said.

She got up and walked to the kitchen, speaking loudly over her shoulder with a voice that was like a thrown rock.

'Fuck you. How could you?'

She was exhausted, stricken with grief or remorse – I couldn't work out which. I was there to take the blame and accept the blows. I should have left then and walked away. But I didn't. I had to ask a question that would probably make her more angry.

'Did you take him to the border?'

She came back from the kitchen and thrust a mug of whisky into my hand, a splash of water, no ice.

'What if I did?'

'He was just eighteen, that's what.'

'How many times have I told you?' She hissed the spittle-flecked words at me. 'We have to fight.'

'But these boys aren't fighting. They are just dying, many of them before they fire a bullet. It's one-sided slaughter.'

'No, it's not. They're bleeding, the whites. They can't take the losses. They think the kill ratio will save them. It won't. I told you the ratio is thirty to one, twenty to one – what does it matter? We have the numbers.'

Numbers again. Patience and the major saw the war in the same way, a numbers game, a spin of a fixed wheel at the casino. I didn't know whether she wanted to hear this, but I told her anyway. I said that Cephas was lying among a line of the dead wearing the same T-shirt as when I first saw him.

'He loved that shirt,' she said quietly. 'Was he . . .?'

'Yes, none of them was a pretty sight.'

'And the body?'

I paused. There was no point in an evasive answer. I am sure most people knew what they did with the bodies.

'Burnt,' I said.

It was early evening. We were sitting in near darkness. I could see the harsh soda lighting from the street lights outside. She got up, turned on a light, then turned it off and went into the kitchen. I heard water splashing, cupboards opening and a voice saying 'fuck' repeatedly.

She returned with a bottle of whisky and a jug of water. She refilled our mugs. Black Label, I noted. She had splashed water on her face. It looked as if she had been crying. We sat in silence for a few minutes, me looking at the street lights, she lost in thoughts I could only imagine.

'I took him up with four others. It was a month ago. He begged me. I told him he was too young, but that just made him angry. He quoted Shakespeare at me. "Let loose the dogs of war." We were doing *Julius Caesar*. He called it *Julia Caesar*. I told him it was "Let slip the dogs of war." He said, "Whatever."

'I told him I would need money, a lot of money, and named a ridiculous price. He just laughed. He knew me too well.'

She threw her head back and drained the glass.

'I told him it would be months, maybe years, before he was properly trained and they sent him back. I said they had a rule about the age of people they sent into combat. He didn't believe me. He was right. I never thought the bastards would do this to him.'

I cannot remember how long we sat there, but I do remember thinking that her grief was more that of a lover for her beloved than a teacher for a pupil. Had there been anything more between them? Even if so, why would that matter? Such school liaisons happened; the world kept turning. Anyway, it was probably only a passing moment of passion, a flutter of the moth; she flattered, he curious.

We made love that evening, the silent coupling of two strangers.

Afterwards she lay beside me smoking. I thought of Sara Jane trying to blow smoke rings to the ceiling of that bar.

I wanted to make Patience promise to make no more trips to the border. It was not the moment. We made no arrangement to meet again. She said she would leave a message with George.

●

I spent the next day in my room working on the article. I had the characters: strong, stand-up people who would take readers by the arm and make them hear their story, like the Ancient Mariner; they were a colourful kaleidoscope of men and women at war with violently opposed views and every one certain of his or her truth.

They dug deep for those truths, unearthing nuggets of fact to suit their version of history. The Milan family, George in the Cancan, the moth-eaten circle in Pinks, Sara Jane and her hero/villain lover – these people provided vigour, variety and a splash of vinegar to my story.

Even with the profanity threaded through almost every remark, the quotes were good. I never took out the swear words. I let Meredith Kaplan do that. She let everything through except the 'fucks'.

I enjoyed the work but felt worried. There was no centre to the story, no narrative to carry the reader to the end. Above all, I could not give my readers the moral reassurance they required. I could not paint a black-and-white picture for them. The conventional nostrums and crowd-pleasing clichés did not quite fit the horrors unfolding in this beautiful country.

I envied the newspaper journalists or TV reporters, who spewed their words into a typewriter, telex machine or microphone every day and made room for next day's feast of hearsay, rumour and sometimes blatant fiction. They were lucky. They knew what their editors wanted. Meredith Kaplan left me to make up my own mind. And I couldn't.

I could say that the illegal declaration of independence and the break with the mother country Britain was a colossal hoax foisted on a young generation eager to believe a lie. The war that followed was the price for that lie. The drumbeat of propaganda gave young white men a cause and a reason to fight. 'No majority rule for a thousand years': the slogan was as senseless as it was surreal. But it worked. It put a gun in their hands and hatred in their hearts.

The nationalist side (although both sides presented themselves as nationalists) used crude propaganda to whip up the feelings of young kids in the townships, luring them across the border with promises of freedom and revenge for land stolen from their ancestors. Then they were given guns and pumped back, ill-trained to face the guns of professional soldiers.

Both sides believed their twisted versions of history because they wanted to.

I stopped at 5,000 words. I was writing on an old Remington plastered with stickers from every country I had been to in years of travelling. The machine was worn out but, like a much-loved old dog, limping and blind in one eye, I could not get rid of it. It had been a faithful companion for too long.

I was exhausted. A tray of old sandwiches and a pot of cold coffee lay on the bedside table. A maid knocked on the door, took the tray away and came back to turn down the bed. I said good evening and asked her name.

'Marion,' she said, 'like Maid Marion.'

She was a middle-aged woman who almost certainly lived in the township. I wondered if she knew Patience. Teachers were well-regarded figures there. I lay awake for a while watching beams of street light filter through the curtains, creating shadow patterns on the ceiling.

•

The hotel always did breakfast best. There were no lines of cold, congealed food lying in greasy dishes on a sideboard buffet. A waiter took my order. Black tea, scrambled eggs, toast and a dish of fresh fruit. The tea arrived at the same time as Bram.

'Mind if I join you?' he said and sat down.

I did mind but I had little choice.

'How was your trip?'

'You probably know better than I do.'

'It went well, I hear.'

'If by that you mean I got to see a lot of freshly killed

young men, then yes, it went well. The Italians weren't happy, though; they wanted to see some action.'

'Fuck the Italians. The major up there thinks you recognised one of the dead terrs.'

I shook my head.

'Was he helpful?' he asked.

'Not really. Everyone talks as if they are reading a part in a play.'

Bram smiled at this.

'Your girlfriend Patience . . .'

'She's not my girlfriend.'

It was an automatic reaction. This man had been spying on me.

'Very well. The woman who is not your girlfriend has been running terrorist recruits up to the border and helping them cross into a hostile country, where they are trained to return and murder innocent civilians, black and white, women and children.'

I took a long draw of tea.

'Why are you telling me this?'

'I thought you might like to know.'

'All I know is that Patience Matatu is a well-respected teacher who is enthusing her pupils with the works of Shakespeare by casting them in some of his great plays. A good story for my magazine, don't you think? If you know different, why don't you take it up with her?'

Bram looked at me with a slight smile, the look a mongoose might give a swaying cobra.

'We could arrest her but prefer not to.'

'Because . . .?'

'It wouldn't change anything. Those kids would still find

a way. It's much easier to track this sort of thing if we know who is doing it.'

Bram looked out of the window and tapped his fingers on the tablecloth.

'If we did arrest this woman who is not your girlfriend, we would charge her with aiding and abetting terrorism, possibly the kidnap of minors, that sort of thing.'

He looked at me again, smiling.

'Twenty years minimum.'

'I doubt this place will last two years, let alone twenty.'

Bram leant across the table so vigorously that the tablecloth rumpled and his coffee went onto the floor.

'Those young troops you talked to yesterday are fighting for their country. They were born here and may well die here, but they belong here.'

'And the Africans?'

'They are Africans, that's the whole point.'

'All right then, the majority black population? It's their country too, isn't it?'

'Yes, of course.'

'So what the fuck are you fighting for?'

'Power,' Bram said, and leant back, straightening the tablecloth.

A waiter bent down to pick up his cup and saucer.

'More coffee, boss?' he asked.

Bram shook his head and made to leave. I asked him to stay. Our brief exchange had raised a question.

'I see why whites who have been born here might have a case, especially young ill-educated men who are given a flag, a rifle, a cap badge and a cause. But you, Bram, why are you here? Why not a wildlife job somewhere, or else go back to the Netherlands?'

'I have family in Amsterdam,' said Bram. 'I could get a job there, but what did the Greeks say? Character is fate. I'm just one of those guys who like to stick it out. Besides, the weather is nice, isn't it?'

He left, threading his way through the tables. I saw him pause to thank the waiter who had picked up his coffee cup.

●

I walked to the central square and sat down by the fountains. The sound of running water and a shaded bench made me sleepy. I woke with a start as a street-sweeper brushed the ground around me. My watch told me I had slept for almost an hour.

When I was schoolboy I usually had toasted cheese sandwiches or a baked potato for high tea. When homework had been done, I was allowed to spend the best time of the day with my jigsaw puzzles. I was always given a new one for every birthday. My father and I spent hours putting them together.

Dad was a general practice doctor and had the sort of medical mind that could solve these puzzles, but he always let me try first. There were usually one or two pieces that refused to fit into the picture and were left towards the end. As I grew older, every birthday brought more and more difficult puzzles. I never got bored with these gifts, which made it easy for my parents when it came to Christmas.

The puzzles were boxed up and stored in the attic after I

left home. My parents died within days of each other, both in their late seventies, my father first and then my mother. They were like a pair of swans. They never knew how much they needed each other. The puzzles, and there must have been scores of them, went to a charity shop, which pleased me.

As I sat watching the sparrows flit through the falling fountain water I thought that here was the biggest puzzle of all. None of it fitted. It was like doing a jigsaw puzzle without the big picture.

The police knew Patience was smuggling young fighters to the border. Men like Bram and many others in the Special Branch knew the war was a losing proposition. The guerrilla commanders knew they were sending so many of their own to their deaths.

Neither side could win the war militarily, as far as I could see, although Patience had a romantically different view on that. The waiter who had called Bram boss and picked up his coffee cup knew that such deference was a shield against unemployment and poverty. He could afford to wait. But no one else could.

I summed up the war in my article as firepower against manpower. History shows that firepower almost always wins – look at the battle of Agincourt – but in this war I felt history was going to be proved wrong.

The only piece that did fit was Patience. Honesty and emotions of the heart are not easy companions. Lovers are always liars to themselves. Now I had found a truth. I had never met anyone like her. She would parade across the bedroom, moving softly, never looking at me. She made me wait while she undressed. When she turned to me it was without a smile.

She was flinty, striking sparks, setting fires. Patience knew what she wanted, but then so did everyone else in the country. She thought she had found a way to get it. She lived in a world without doubt. She broke the rules in a nation that had broken the biggest rule of all.

She knew what she was doing when she placed the great themes of Shakespeare before her pupils. Love, treachery and murder were easily understood by bored teenagers. She was telling them to love their country and avenge the betrayal of their birthright.

Subconsciously perhaps, she was preparing them for flight and fight. She ferociously denied this when I put it to her, but the eyes that flashed in fury at such a suggestion told a different story.

I shuddered at the thought that she might one day cross the border with the young volunteers. Bram had told me that women fighters were welcomed in the guerrilla camps, and not just as nurses and cooks. They trained as fighters and acquired respect and fear among the government forces. They all chose noms de guerre: Spill Blood, Die-Hard, Kill First, Stab Heart.

•

The city was small and I had nowhere else to go except my hotel or Pinks. Occasionally I would get in the car and drive wherever it took me. I would never go out of the city, but drove on long circular sweeps through the suburbs. I would stop somewhere, a café, bar or restaurant, have a beer and a sandwich and let the world go by.

Those occasions were never as calming as they should have been. Writers are cursed with an overactive imagination which denies them the privilege of immersing in the ordinary: the weather, a cloudy sky, a passing car, a curious cat. Instead, we imagine the best and worst that the day might bring.

The worst news was always about Patience. I had not heard from her for days. She might have been killed on the road to the border. Ambushes were becoming frequent, even on the main roads. The guerrillas would not know the difference between her vehicle and any other. Or maybe she had been arrested, beaten up and dumped in a cell somewhere. The police knew what she was doing. At the very least, she would have to answer awkward questions. I would warn her.

She knew perfectly well that I had contacts with the government and what were euphemistically called the security services. She would rightly ask why Bram had confided in me. Obviously to gain favour with me, I would say. To which she would reply – to what end?

The government paid close attention to visiting American journalists or those working for US media. They saw us as a conduit to the political opinion-makers in Washington, although I hardly thought my magazine fell into that category. That was one reason why Bram was paying me so much attention. There may have been another. Occasionally when he talked it sounded like the confession of a man unable to face his guilt as a collaborator with an outcast regime.

With that thought in mind, I changed my mind. I would not tell Patience that she was being watched. It would serve no purpose other than to brand me as a government lackey. She would accuse me of being a messenger boy for the regime.

Anger would trump love. A backstage change of costume and a new actor would appear on our stage. She would see me not as a lover but as an emissary of the enemy.

We had had these rows before, when I would argue that a search for the truth lies at the heart of all good writing. She would give me her flinty look and say that was liberal western moral bullshit (LWMB, she called it). There could be no neutrality in the fight for freedom. Usually I had managed, quite skilfully I might say, to end these rows in the bedroom.

Whether I was the man she made love to or whether she was in bed with a former lover summoned from memories of a pleasurable past, I do not know. I often felt a stranger in her arms.

As I walked the clean streets of the city centre, I wondered what I meant to her. I did once ask her whether she loved me. It was a mistake.

'What? Really, truly love you?'

'Yes,' I said.

'Love looks not with the eyes, but with the mind,' she said.

She loved quoting Shakespeare, partly to show she was much more familiar with his works than me, partly through love of the language, but mostly to show that a poor secondary school teacher in an impoverished African township could match any student of Shakespeare.

She said that if Shakespeare had been born black, the world would have been a different place. It was a vivid thought, expressed not so much to me but to the empty air. She would have said thin air, of course. She loved those phrases. I remembered her remark and used it in my next piece.

•

I walked back to the hotel and saw Sara Jane Shannon on the steps. I thought to avoid her but she saw me and gave a little wave. We sat in the lounge and ordered coffee. It was lunchtime and I didn't want to eat with her or listen to a lecture about the righteous cause of the government and its losing war.

She was supposed to be my fixer, but the only use she had been was to change some American dollars into local currency at the black-market rate. I didn't feel bad about doing this since my employers, although generous in terms of salary, took a view on expenses that would have pleased Scrooge.

It was just past noon. She was dressed in a khaki safari jacket with chest pockets, side pockets and trouser pockets, back and front. I was about to make a joke about a Dickens character called Pocket when she began to speak very quietly. I knew something was wrong. She asked how my writing was going. It was going well, I told her. I planned to send over an article that night.

'Can I read it?'

'Not until my editor has seen it. There will be many queries. Perhaps you could help with those.'

'Of course, but can you tell me roughly what viewpoint you have taken?'

'I have not been judgemental, if that is what you mean. I'm trying to get into people's heads, understand the thinking.'

'And have you?'

I thought of the bodies laid out behind the hut at the forward airfield and the way they had been searched, fingerprinted, trucked to the river and burnt. Cephas, who only a short while before had been serving beer in the Victoria, was now ashes. Aged eighteen.

'Not really,' I said.

'I just don't care any more,' she said. 'I thought this was my country. But we are going to lose it and I don't really care.'

'It's strange to hear you talk like that,' I said.

'Why? All I care about is André. Funny, isn't it? That's what this war has given me. But he frightens me.'

'Why?'

'Because he is a soldier and he loves it. He's out there somewhere now, fighting.'

'And killing?'

'I am not saying he loves killing. He just loves soldiering. He was born to it, he says. It's in the blood. An ancestor fought with Wellington at Waterloo, or some such story.'

'A lot of people have those ancestors.'

She smiled.

'I worry about him so much. Like all those men, he thinks it's never going to happen to him.'

She said this with her head down, gazing into an empty coffee cup. This was so different from the woman I had first met. It was difficult to leave her. I looked surreptitiously at my watch. A quick lunch and an afternoon at the typewriter had been the plan. Now I was being drawn into the role of a father figure.

'Do you mind if I have a drink?' she said.

We drank a beer apiece and then I took her up to lunch in the hotel restaurant. It was called La Fontaine, another pretence at Parisian glamour. We went up the circular staircase lined on one side with bearded pioneers from the early days of the colony.

Without asking, she ordered a bottle of wine, a 1968 Pauillac – a rare sight in a sanctioned country.

'I feel I've kidnapped you, so I'm paying,' she said.

We drank the wine, ordered steak and then another bottle, this time local. The Pauillac had been the last in the cellar.

Sara Jane told me she had arrived as a freelance photographer without a commission. She had been allowed to photograph a line-up of troops after a training exercise. André Lennox had been their commanding officer.

'It's a terrible cliché, and for most people it's not true, but it was love at first sight for us. I'm thirty-four and he's in his mid-forties. We were both lonely. I was born here, but this is not my country. I don't really have a country, although I could call myself American, I suppose.

'I have a past that would make an X-rated movie, as you know. On our first date, I told him all about those lonely rich men in their five-star hotel suites. He didn't mind at all. It excited him. He thought he had found a kindred spirit, a rebel. So in a way we found ourselves here. He had found a cause to fight for and I had found a man to love. It was easy to believe we were fighting against terrorists, evil Marxists who wanted to tear the place down.'

'And do you still?'

'I don't know. I just know I am worried sick. André is stupidly brave. I want him to leave, to take me somewhere where there is a war worth fighting.'

'Perhaps there isn't one.'

'Of course there is. You men never stop fighting, do you? Anywhere but here. Somewhere I might see more of him.

He's away all the time. They say he is good in the bush.'

'What does that mean?'

She laughed and drank the wine.

'Not what you think. He has learnt the local language. Tracking is easier if you get good intel from the villagers. He's in the bush all the time.'

That was what she wanted to talk about, a woman with loyalty only to the man she loved. Loyalty to country and cause had been surrendered to love for the solid shape of a mid-forties soldier who was good in the bush. I wondered if that made him good in bed as well.

She suddenly stood up, raised her glass to the restaurant with a sweep of her arm and proclaimed loudly:

'I love thee with a love I seemed to lose
With my lost saints. I love thee with the breath,
Smiles, tears of all my life.'

'Very nice,' I said.

'Elizabeth Barrett Browning. André used to recite it to me the night before he went back to his unit. I learnt it by heart.'

I tucked the information away. I knew the poem slightly too and made a mental note to look it up. 'Lost saints' was a good line. It suggested a metaphor for what the country, or at least the white community, was going through.

'I don't have much education, but that poem made me read more of Browning and others like her.'

'You don't need education to appreciate poetry.'

It occurred to me that the lettering on the small gold medallion around her neck might contain those lines. When

I suggested this, she shook her head happily.

'I'll tell you another time,' she said.

I drank more wine. I was getting bored. I needed help to place another piece in the jigsaw, an interview with a senior military commander, a politician. I needed someone from government to step aside from the propaganda and tell me what they really thought.

My mind drifted through the windows. I had to hear the other side of the story, not the crude justification for the regime offered by the old colonials. I wanted to hear an intelligent analysis of, and rationale for, the past and present in this bewildered nation.

History had collided here. The past was the present. The story was the same in 1919 as it was now in 1979. A short sixty years as the history hamster went endlessly round in his wheel.

I was thinking such thoughts when Sara Jane surprised me. She opened her bag and placed a small pearl-handled pistol on the table. It lay there between the wine glasses and the salt cellar. I had never seen a gun so close before. It was as if a tarantula had climbed onto the table.

Before I could say anything she spoke in staccato sentences.

'Beretta .22-calibre pocket gun. Kills at short range. Will bring a man down at five metres.'

'It's yours?' I asked stupidly, thinking of nothing else to say.

'He gave it to me for protection and asked me to carry it with me at all times. I've had training on a weapons range.'

She put it away and beckoned the waiter for the bill. She appeared unaffected by the bottle of wine apiece we had drunk. Lunch was over. The intimacy of our previous meeting had gone. Sara Jane had revealed herself briefly and now she resumed her former persona. It was as if a beautiful creature had emerged from the woods, looked around and bounded back into the darkness. I wanted to ask her advice about a government interview. But she left, giving me the same over-the-shoulder wave.

•

I slept off the wine that afternoon and made a late call to Rob, the white hunter who had shown me the wilderness along the big lake to the north. I needed that wilderness. I needed to get out of town, away from the raging complexities of a country at war with itself.

I wanted to see elephants and porcupines (for which I have an inexplicable affection) and hear the songbirds at dawn. Perhaps the shimmering waters of the lake where crocodiles lurked would provide a suitable metaphor for a piece on wildlife. My readers in New York, the Midwest or the West Coast weren't interested in a tribal squabble in the middle of Africa. But they loved elephants, especially those mothers with their young. Lions had long since been hunted almost to extinction, but the easier target, the shambling elephant, had survived. Hunted with rock, spear and gun from prehistoric times, they somehow lived and bred in an unchanged landscape. I yearned to see them again. 'The Future of the Elephant in a Troubled Land': I could see the headline.

A voice at the district commissioner's office told me that Rob had been called up and the game reserve had been placed off-limits to civilians. The war had spread to the lake. Patrol boats were sinking fast-moving enemy craft crossing at night.

I wondered about the elephants and went to the bar. It was the only way to deal with an afternoon hangover. George raised his eyebrows and nodded to the cocktail shaker. I nodded back in silent communion between drinker and barman. I sat on a stool.

'Can't get kümmel,' he said. 'We use a local spirit flavoured with wild herbs.'

He was repeating himself, getting old. He placed a bar mat and the drink in front of me. He had nicely manicured nails. I was drinking too much. It seemed a sensible precaution against the overwhelming desire to get on a plane and leave.

I hate the phrase 'move on' – 'Let's move on', 'I must move on' and so forth. It's a carthorse cliché that plods its way through language and conversation without meaning. Whenever I was on my travels, after a few weeks I always had the urge to move on (there you are, you see); another frontier beckoned, another border to be crossed. I had been there for what seemed like months. This seemed to be a good time to indulge such an errant impulse.

Patience had been a momentary infatuation, a sexual obsession, pleasure with a woman who had given me memories that would remain for ever. If one particular memory flickered like an old film in my head it was the way she had left the shower in a towel and crossed to the window in that crumbling hotel. She opened the window, bent over the sill and stayed there silently until the towel dropped to the floor, then merely gave a small sigh of pleasure as I crossed the room. I repeat this only because the memory is so clear, so arousing.

But that was not love. How could I love such a woman? Rather more to the point, how could she love me? Maybe she saw us as Romeo and Juliet – lovers divided by warring clans, black and white, English and African, man and woman.

I had not seen or heard from her for two weeks now. My worries had sharpened into barely suppressed panic. She had obviously driven to the border again. This time she had crossed over with those young men. The police had not stopped her. Why? So that she got killed with rest? And is that what had happened?

George came over, pulling me back to the Cancan. The dancers were still kicking their legs up on the walls, and no doubt those in the central square, the pram pushers, dog walkers and those strolling to lunch were staging their own seemingly timeless performance.

'She's back,' he said. 'Leave her be.'

Chapter Nine

There was an envelope placed under the door of my room when I finally went to bed. A telex from Marie Claire: '*TV news says big fighting where you are. Trust you safe.*' I didn't know what she was talking about and went to sleep remembering the sweet scent of wine and cooking on the top floor of 150 Rue de Rome.

The propaganda sheet that presented itself as a morning newspaper had its uses. There had been a huge raid into the neighbouring territory. A guerrilla base had been attacked by special and regular forces. The detail in the paper was shocking. Hundreds of young rebel fighters and accompanying civilians had been killed or wounded. Troops had swept into the camp at first light, backed by ground-attack aircraft. Surprise was complete.

One chill sentence made my heart stop. '*No quarter was given even to the many women fighters and support staff in the camp.*'

One soldier was quoted as saying that when combing the

camp kitchen he had tapped a large earthenware pot some six-feet high. The head of a woman had popped up. He had fired, the pot had shattered and the dying woman had fallen out amid clay shards. She was an unarmed civilian, the paper said, but 'those that support terrorists and their murderous operations in any capacity will be treated as terrorists'.

That's when I got into the car and drove north. Patience had not been in the camp. Yet some of those boys she had driven up to the border would have been there. She was back. George had said that. Leave her be, he'd said, pretty much the same words the bus driver and Bram had used. She would be hearing the reports of the raid and she would know what had happened to her boys. Woken before dawn by gunfire, they would have tumbled out of straw mattresses and reached for their weapons, but too late. Everything would have been too late. Aircraft had rained napalm down, troops had flooded the camp on three sides. There had been no time to use heavy weapons, the anti-aircraft guns and mortars. The raid was over in a couple of hours.

I could not bear to see her. There was no point in the inevitable bitter argument. The major had said character is fate. Her character was hewn from the hardwood trees she had admired so much in the Eastern Highlands.

She had looked at those trees as if she could feel their rough bark and said, 'The axe forgets but the tree remembers.'

'I don't think I get that.'

'It's an old African saying. The colonialists forget what they have done but we remember.'

I reached Green Creek in record time, just under two hours. I had not told them I was coming. I did not even know I was going to do so until I got into the car after breakfast. There was nowhere else to go except the township.

From the wire fence the farm was as I had seen it before. I waited at the front gate while the dogs howled. Layla Milan came out to see who the stranger was. She was alone and carrying a rifle. She unlocked the gate and greeted me without a smile or warmth. I noticed that she looked older. John had been called up and Julia had been told to stay in town. The road was no longer safe except in convoy.

We had tea inside. She leant the rifle in the corner and gently rebuked me for driving without joining the convoy and without warning her of my arrival. I asked whether she felt safe alone. She laughed and pointed to the rifle.

'I've got that and the dogs.'

She reminded me that the house was wire-fenced, with grenades buried in the garden and mesh windows shielded against rockets. We both knew it was not enough. What about the labourers in their compound? They're loyal but they're frightened, she told me.

I knew there was something that lay unspoken between us. I waited, drinking the tea while we talked in desultory fashion about Julia's work, the crops, the weather. It was midday when the conversation petered out. We sat in silence for a while, as if by common consent that there was nothing more to say.

I looked at her across the room and saw a middle-aged woman sitting back in a chair, hands crossed on her lap, eyes half closed. The smile, humour and love of life that had been so evident when I was last here had left this woman.

'Can I get you some more tea?' I asked.

She looked at me and shook her head.

'I want to tell you something,' she said. 'In fact, I had written it down to tell you because I knew you would be back.'

She fished in her handbag and took out a folded piece of fine paper.

'This is what I was going to say.'

She unfolded the paper, put on her spectacles and read.

'"The funny thing about this war is that it's told us who we are, and reminded us that this country is worth fighting for. Strange, isn't it? We had the sunshine, servants, swimming pools, weekend parties, but it always felt too good to be true. Something had to happen. And it has. The world has turned against us. War has come. We got used to the world being against us and being called racists and rebels. We believed we were right and we were happy to stand and fight for that belief."'

She folded the paper and tucked it away.

'That's what I was going to say, because I believed it. But everything has changed now. We can't fight on. It's madness. Listen to this and you will understand why. And please tell the world. You'll need a drink.'

She went to the kitchen and returned with two tumblers of whisky and water. She fiddled with the buttons on what looked like a tape recorder wired to a radio receiver in the corner.

'This is a tape from last week. Thursday, I think,' she said.

I find it hard to put into words what followed. I started to scribble some notes, then gave up because I wasn't going to forget what I heard.

The tape ran for about ten minutes. It was a recording of an exchange on a communal short-wave radio that linked the farming community in the area. In words of pure terror that rose to a screaming crescendo, it told of an attack on a farm some five miles to the north of Green Creek. Rising Moon Farm, the Elphinstone farm, the orchid growers, the couple who said so little at lunch that day. Apart from the orchids I had learnt little about them at lunch except that their home was a similar set-up to all such farms: barbed-wire fence, grenade-proof windows and a supposedly loyal labour force.

The tape began with the panicky voice of Hazel Elphinstone, who I recognised immediately, giving the call sign Romeo X-Ray and the address Rising Moon Farm. 'Terrs on the wire,' she kept saying. There was no reply. Then in a rising voice she began begging for help against a background of explosions and shouting.

The calm voice of a man designating himself call sign Delta Six finally replied, saying, 'Confirm sitrep,' as if the woman was having a panic attack after a nightmare.

Then a man came on, pleading for help. Again, I recognised the voice of Arnold Elphinstone. 'The bright light has been hit,' he shouted. 'Bastards are over perimeter fence, grenades coming in, the roof's on fire.'

Hazel Elphinstone came back on, screaming and pleading for help. There was more, of course, but I can't bear to think about it.

Layla Milan turned the machine off.

'That was last week, just up the valley.'

'Those were your neighbours, the ones who came to lunch?'

'Yes,' she said.

'You should have told me.'

She sat down again. She was breathing heavily and looking pale.

'Rising Moon. All gone.'

'What happened to them?' I asked. I didn't know what else to say.

'They were killed along with the bright light. You want to know how they died?'

'No, thank you. What's a "*bright light*"?'

'A reservist up from the city. They're just kids. They send them to help defend remote farms. I won't tell you what they did to him.'

There was another long pause. If she had not been alone on the farm, I would have driven straight back. As it was, there was nothing I could do. I had no words of comfort to offer. Weirdly I found myself wondering what had happened to the orchids. Thousands of expensive, beautiful flowers grown in long lines of hothouses to be freighted undercover to Europe to avoid sanctions. That was why they wouldn't talk to me at lunch.

Now the flowers lay uprooted among shattered glass. The attackers would surely have destroyed the hothouses. There was a metaphor somewhere in that mad savagery but I couldn't work it out. I had had enough. I had heard too much. I just wanted something to eat, a lot of whisky and an even longer sleep. That clearly wasn't going to be possible.

'I'm sorry I made you listen to that,' she said. 'You probably came out for some peace and quiet after all that nonsense in town. I just wanted you to see that this is hopeless. There's no peace and precious little quiet out here. We fooled ourselves. It's like waking from a lovely dream and finding it was just that, a dream. Worst of all it was our fault. We could have worked it out with them. Together.'

I didn't ask what she meant by that. I didn't have to.

Chapter Ten

There was a cable from New York waiting for me at the hotel the next morning. Meredith Kaplan liked the first article, especially the story of the elephants, and was anxious to see follow-up coverage. Diplomatic events were moving fast, she said. There was pressure on all sides for a peace conference.

I was walking across the main square towards Pinks when Jeeze appeared by chance, or so he said.

'You heard the news?'

'If you mean the peace talks, yes,' I replied.

'Don't believe a word of it. It's a trick, the old story. They want to impose a sell-out government on us. The boys won't stand for it.'

'So you know the boys, do you?'

We sat by the fountains, at his insistence. He said the sound of water prevented electronic eavesdropping. He looked around carefully.

'I have very good contacts,' he said.

'Tell me,' I said.

'No sell-out, no compromise. A fight to the finish. Put that in your magazine.'

This was where Patience and I had talked. It was only then I realised I missed her with a pang that almost hurt. I needed to find her. I wanted to hear her tell me that Jeeze was a liar, that peace negotiations were going to put an end to the savagery. Farmers slaughtered with senseless brutality, whispered talk of a fight to the finish and Meredith in New York telling me that peace talks were coming – it was pure madness, an outer circle in Dante's vision of hell. Patience would surely tell me it would soon be over. George would know where she was. He would not be at the bar until evening.

Jeeze got up, looking around carefully, and walked towards Pinks. There his inside information would be furtively passed on to the world's press as an exclusive story 'according to senior nationalist sources'.

I walked down the main street to Sandersons, a big department store. Air conditioning was a relief from the heat outside. I walked through the clothing department on the ground floor, noting the latest fashions: patterned shirts and thick socks for the men and long, billowy dresses for the women. The assistants were all women, the older ones white and the younger ones African.

I took the escalator to the coffee shop on the top floor. A panoramic vista stretched on three sides. It was the first time I had seen the city like this. A cluster of high-rise buildings and then glinting tin-roofed housing on every side, stretching into a palette of green, grey and ochre colours in the bush beyond.

A white man had planted a flag here some eighty years ago and built a fortified camp. Though why here was a mystery; there was neither a river nor sheltering mountains close by. European planners had been brought in to design the town. They had mapped out the street grid. Then African labourers had laid the streets with asphalt and built the houses brick by brick with corrugated tin roofs. A partnership had been created and later denied.

I drank bitter coffee and made notes in a little book whose pages had curled in the heat. A partnership created and then denied. That was too simple, but if a woman like Layla Milan felt that way, the end of this country was coming more quickly than I thought.

I drank more coffee and pondered the message from New York. They had as good as told me to stay until the bitter end. I should have been back in the hotel room, clicking away on the Remington. Instead, I was admiring a view on which so much history was written: a hundred years of white European history, thousands of years of black African history, the history of the bushmen and the Neanderthals before them. Before those waves of humanity, the cooling planet created life. The first recognisable forebears of modern man climbed down from the safety of trees and set foot on the soil of this continent.

It was a childish, simplistic summary that made one thing clear: it all began here. Somewhere out in the bush so invitingly seen from my coffee-shop window there had been a beginning. I would work up that thought and try it in the piece. There was a risk of sounding as if I knew my anthropology, which I didn't, and of coming across as both grandiose and mawkish.

Context, said Meredith Kaplan, is important. Don't just report the facts; report what they mean. Take the readers by the hand and walk them through the story. You know what they want. I did indeed know. They wanted the historic imperative of majority rule to be placed before the reader in the blinding light of the African sun while the brief years of white dominance were left in the shade of moral turpitude.

That had certainly been the tenor of my first big article. The body of Cephas Msika lying in a row of dead men, his tattered clothes being pulled apart, his fingers printed and his body finally thrown onto a truck. I knew who he was, but the military and police did not. Why should I tell them? I had posed that question in the piece. I knew both my readers and editor would feel satisfaction that their correspondent was not betraying the rebel cause.

The other side of the moral equation was not what my editors wanted to hear. Nor would Patience, I suspected. I reported it all the same. The first generation of Milans had come here when the town was just a fort. They had cleared the land, created a farm and paid a workforce. They were third-generation settlers.

The Elphinstones were different but they arrived here with the same intent: to find a new life and wealth in a foreign land serviced by people they would never know. Both of them, man and wife, had been tortured in their dying moments as their farm had burnt around them. Layla Milan had finally given me the details. I felt sick afterwards. The question was, why the savagery? Bloodlust or pent-up rage at decades of indignity and shame? I didn't have the answer.

As a narrator and writer, I had a duty to be honest with

myself and with my readers. The white minority did have a claim on the country they had helped build up. Did the failure to create a partnership with those who had built it with them mitigate that claim? Who was I to judge?

There was no conclusion to these thoughts except perhaps one: this was a nation without scar tissue, with no healed wounds to learn from, no long past to shape its present. It had been conjured up with a flag and a fort, creating a myth that had imprinted itself briefly on history. But we all shape our own history with myth, so who was I to blame the settlers for doing likewise?

I left a cold cup of coffee on the table, took one last look at the shimmering city and the blur of the landscape beyond and walked back to the hotel. The heat was beating up from the pavement, coming through my city shoes as if I was walking on the embers of a campfire – a suitable metaphor, I thought. I might even use it.

●

I arrived in the bar that evening at half past six, having made myself wait thirty minutes after the traditional time for an evening drink.

I slid onto the bar stool. George gave me a smile, an expression so unusual on that calm face that I knew something was wrong. He made no move to assemble the ingredients for my usual cocktail but merely nodded his head to somewhere behind me. I turned. Patience was sitting beside a glass-topped table with a tall glass of beer and a bowl of olives in front of her. She wore a simple black dress, which enriched the yellow of her nails and hair grip. She smiled and beckoned.

'I thought you wouldn't be seen dead in a place like this,' I said as I sat down.

'Shut up and give me a kiss.'

I kissed her firmly on the offered cheek and took a cautious look around. There were two other couples in the bar, both talking with lowered voices.

'Don't worry. No one has seen us,' she said.

'I don't care if they do,' I said, and kissed her again.

Over her shoulder, I could see that George's face had wrinkled into a deep frown.

'Where have you been?' I asked.

'I was about to ask you the same question.'

'I've been writing and researching.'

We fenced around in a similarly witless exchange until George arrived with my drink. She held up her glass.

'Another please, dear uncle.'

'Have a care,' said George.

She had not been to the border, it turned out, but had spent several days working with children of English missionary families in the east of the country. There were five families with sixteen children. She had arranged a stage reading in an old barn of *A Midsummer Night's Dream*, which had been a great success.

She disliked the religious role of the missionaries but praised the pastoral side of their work, helping with education and basic medical treatment. She had taken pictures and would write an article for the school magazine.

'Why didn't you tell me where you were? I was worried about you.'

'You talk too much to your policeman friend.'

'I talk to everybody. That's my job.'

'"Mud in your eye," she said and drank her beer, tipping the glass back so that it left a white foamy moustache on her upper lip.

'Why are we here?' I said. 'I thought you hated this place.'

'I wanted to see you. This was the only way. The township is getting dangerous.'

She dipped into her handbag, took out a tissue and wiped away the beer froth. I suddenly felt a fraud. She had come to this hated place to see me, having spent days deep in the operational area with missionaries. Travelling to such places was a high risk. She told me that the guerrillas had been ordered not to target mission stations. I knew she did not believe that any more than I did. The savagery on both sides had gone too far.

At that moment I decided to tell her everything. I offered dinner in the hotel. She refused, kissed George goodbye on the cheek, which caused ripples of interest among the other couples in the room, and took me to a small Italian two blocks away.

•

Looking back, I think that is really when our affair became more than the attraction of two strangers. We were both outsiders in an inside world, both happy to let loneliness and desire bridge the chasm of colour and class. We were aliens who had found each other in a hostile corner of the universe.

She looked at me without any expression as I told her that Bram and his Special Branch friends had long known of her trips to the border. They knew too that she had used her official school identity card to get through police road checks with a truck full of young men hidden under a tarpaulin.

I paused at this point to assess her reaction. She just shook her head. She did not respond when I went further – and this must have pained her deeply, although she never said – and explained Special Branch thinking. Why stop something that's going to happen anyway, was the police view. Why stop the conduit of young would-be freedom fighters into the gaping maw of a one-sided war against a superior enemy?

I remembered something she had told me once and tried to quote her words back to her: 'The last thing many of our boys will see is a helicopter coming in at low level with a machine gun spitting out a glittering stream of bullets. They'll just lie there, waiting to be torn to pieces.'

She said, 'Go on.'

I told her of the farm attack and how the Elphinstones had been murdered. I told her of the changed woman I found in Layla Milan and how the brutal truth had broken upon her: not just that the war was lost, but that all the years of colonial rule, illegal independence and the war that followed were just a tiny full stop in a thousand pages of history. That full stop marked the end.

I had told her this despite the fact that I knew she would accuse me of being a lackey, someone who had turned away from a moral imperative so clearly written in the history of a country ruthlessly dominated by a small, technically superior tribe insistent on their racial superiority.

I stopped then and poured two glasses from the bottle of cheap local wine that had been placed on the table without us asking. The restaurant was half full; the menus still lay between us.

'I'm hungry,' she said. 'Let's eat.'

I went on, trying to make her see that a writer with even a shred of responsibility to his editors and readers was obliged to talk to sources of information wherever he found them.

Finally, I said that I now knew for the first time where the whirlwind of her anger sprang from. Then, without any break and with the breathless self-importance that comes with such confession, I told her I loved her as I had loved no one before, that I had crossed some line in my life and that I hoped she had too. We should treasure what we had found.

I said that tornadoes in the Midwest of America begin with a small circular wind that picks up the dusty soil, then gathers pace and begins to move at speed, flattening grass and sending livestock fleeing. The whirlwind races across the plains, creating its own energy, until it flings people all over the place.

'That's what I feel now,' I said.

I stopped at that point because my tornado comparison had gone too far and was embarrassing, and such rambling declarations become meaningless with repetition.

We were the last in the place. A solitary waiter was putting chairs on tables. Patience got up. She stood there looking down at me, reached for her glass and finished it. She had hardly interrupted me except to pour more wine.

'I want to read what you've written for the magazine,' she said, and walked out.

When I got out onto the street she had vanished. I took a chance and ran one way. I found her in one of those dark little lanes that run between the buildings for garbage disposal. She was leaning against a wall amid rubbish bins, smoking and looking up at the sky. There was no light in the place except that given by the stars.

She had been crying. She brushed away her tears, drew the back of her hand across her face and nose, threw away the cigarette and hugged me so tightly that I feared that the flask of whisky in my chest pocket would hurt her. We held each other, lit by starlight, amid the sight and reek of garbage.

Arms linked, we walked back to Franklins. It was her choice. I let her take whatever direction she wanted.

The night porter handed me a key and glanced at Patience with a slight nod. We were both exhausted and we slept back to back until I awoke to the clatter of noise from the street below the window. She had gone, leaving only the imprint of her head on the pillow beside me.

•

To my surprise, George was helping serve breakfast in the dining room. Staff shortage, he explained. Over coffee and toast, I made notes for an article on the back of the menu.

I followed the approach I had adopted for the plays I had written (without success): bring the characters out early and let them slowly shape the narrative. Try to surprise the audience to gain their attention, but do not give too much away in the opening scene.

The what-happens-next question is as important for a reader as for an audience. Create atmosphere without trying to win a prize for melodramatic writing. Do not try to impress with your extensive knowledge of remote corners of the English dictionary. Let your major characters step forward and make bold decisions. The minor characters will find their own way in the story.

I stepped into my own story. I was a major character about to make the bold decision to reshape his future and leave this blighted part of the world. For weeks I had wanted to escape, regain my sanity and my health. I was drinking too much, taking no exercise and eating either rich hotel food or stale sandwiches in Pinks.

Now I had fallen in love. This is not an admission I ever expected to make. I thought that pangs of conscience about what had happened in Paris and late-night silver bullets with George had immunised me from such feelings. But I had found something magical well beyond the physical love we shared. Far from playing a bold part in my own story, I was going to take the coward's way out. I was going to stay to the bitter end of an unbearable conflict.

I scribbled notes until the menu was full and then ordered more coffee and asked George for another menu. He shook his head, vanished for a few moments, then brought me some of the hotel's headed notepaper. Below the name was the legend 'A Luxury Hotel for the Discerning Traveller'.

The waiters were trying to clear up in an empty dining room, waiting less than patiently for this discerning traveller to leave.

•

Jacaranda trees lined the square outside, sparrows flew through fountains, prams were pushed, dogs were walked, ordinary people leading ordinary lives did all the ordinary things that made up their day. The divorce from reality reflected my own. I was an exile from my own life.

I was not to know then what I do now. Bloody events began to pile up like the fires that burnt heretics at the stake. A second Viscount aircraft flying tourists from a weekend in the supposedly secure lakeside resort in the north of the country was brought down by a missile. All the passengers were killed outright. Further raids into the neighbouring country produced yet more security-force successes, as the local paper reported cheerfully. In the daily government communiqués, stories of gallant farmers fighting off attackers became commonplace.

The untold stories were of the farmers, their wives and families who met the same grisly fate as the Elphinstones. Sometimes these reports revealed that farm labourers who had been working for years, receiving food, basic medical treatment and crude schooling for their children, had turned on their masters and joined in the slaughter.

I sifted the more lurid details from the swirl of rumour, fact, intrigue and betrayal in Pinks. The place had come to fascinate me. It was like the scenes in the film *Casablanca* in which everyone in Rick's Café is drinking, spying and trying to bed the local women.

I drew Jeeze aside one night and asked him to spend a short time with me. We left the club, walked down the main street and took a table at a fast-food chicken-and-chips joint. He did not seem at all puzzled by this. He had been paid well by American TV crews for information and was used to the strange ways of the western press. Thinking I needed local gossip, Jeeze immediately told me that one of the barmen at Pinks was a police informant and that Paula, the receptionist at the Diplomat, was sleeping with a man from the BBC.

He was about to expand on the sexual antics of the press corps when I stopped him. I was as curious about the sexual idiosyncrasies of my colleagues as the next man, but the big question I wanted answered was why so many Africans had joined the white-dominated security forces fighting against their brothers across the border. The government press office made much of the regular influx of Africans who wished to train as police officers or to join the regular army.

Jeeze shrugged. 'They do so to become fully trained, thus able to support a new government in a free country.'

Although this was partially true, I knew as he did that it was not the real reason.

'In the south and north of the country there are two different peoples long and often violently opposed to each other,' I said. 'What does that say about the future?'

'What do you mean?'

'Civil war after independence?'

In all the articles I have written, mostly for American magazines where fact-checking, statistics and the source of all quotes are important, there comes a moment of clarity when a hidden truth emerges, a truth that cannot be checked.

Jeeze looked at me in triumph.

'It will be our civil war, not yours,' he said.

'What do you mean?'

'You English had the Wars of the Roses, America had its civil war, the Russians and the French had theirs. We will have ours. Print that.'

'Those were a long time ago.'

'When Romans arrived in Britain your people were running around half naked with faces painted in woad. That was a long time ago too. Print that. Quote me. By name. Jesus Amari.'

'Where did you learn all this?'

'You think I am just a fixer. I went to university down south on a scholarship. I think deeply about my country.' He tapped his forehead.

I scribbled a few lines in my notebook while Jeeze watched.

'That's a hundred dollars. I must go,' he said. I paid him. He paused at the door, came back and whispered, 'Remember. Our civil war, not yours.'

•

I went back to the club. Quigley told me in a beery whisper that Sara Jane had gone to join her lover, who was on operational duties in the bush. This was strictly against the rules, but Lennox was such a popular hero that a compromise had been reached. She had been allowed to take a room at a small hotel near the area of deployment. When Lennox returned to base, he joined his lover for romantic evenings overlooking the ruins of a once-great temple of stone built by an ancient African civilisation.

On my way out, I saw pinned to the door a handwritten flyer stating that a performance of *Love's Labour's Lost* would take place the following evening at the Frank Johnson School in the Arcadia township. The cast would be drawn from the pupils and the director would be Patience Matatu. The time was 5 p.m.

I decided to go but not to tell Patience. Immediately I changed my mind. I decided to send flowers on the first night with a note of apology saying I had an important meeting. I tore up that idea as the nonsense it was. I pushed the decision into the back of my mind. I was tired. I had been in the country far too long. Yet the desire to escape to some sort of normality elsewhere, especially the Middle East, where the world paid more attention to conflict than they did in Africa, had long since left me.

I had seen nothing of the war at first hand beyond the dead bodies at the bush airbase. I did not blame myself for that. There was little point in describing the rattle of rifle fire, the sight of tracer bullets or even the cries of wounded insurgents. The daily press and television broadcasts had given vivid detail of such combat operations.

The occasional French mercenary who came to the club spoke quite openly about the atrocities committed by government forces: badly wounded insurgents buried in open graves with their dead colleagues; field executions of those who surrendered or who were captured; civilians caught in cross fire, a deceitful euphemism.

They threw these stories out to impress their attentive listeners, especially the women among them. I used them in my writing without any proof. I had been in the country long enough to know them to be true. I was congratulated by Meredith for the painstaking research that had unearthed such atrocities.

I was commissioned to write a book with the title *The Rise and Bloody Fall of White Rule*, or some such. The publisher was part of the same conglomerate that owned the magazine along with newspapers and TV channels. I had thought myself an independent spirit roaming the continent with my Remington. But I was a company man.

•

I had managed to see more and more of Patience as the weeks passed. We usually met after school. She was always careful and made me park some distance away. She was not worried about her fellow teachers – theythey could think what they liked – but her pupils would be surprised and might ask uncomfortable questions: what was their teacher doing getting into a white man's car?

We would drive to small cafés or cheap restaurants in the poorer parts of town. The food was good if simple. Italian, Greek and above all Portuguese dishes were our favourites. Our talks were usually argumentative, but on one thing we agreed. Patience accepted that her part in smuggling young men to the border for onward transit to guerrilla training camps had to stop. It was not the danger that persuaded her but the fact that most of the raw recruits would end as Cephas Msika had done, laid out with their comrades to be photographed and then burnt or buried in a common grave.

Opinions spiced with questionable facts would fly back and forth across the table. She almost always used history to parry my comments about the failure of newly independent regimes on the continent. It had taken Europe five hundred years to recover from Roman rule, she said, and a further five hundred years to move forward from the tribal wars and savage religious repression of the early Middle Ages. Why expect Africa to be different?

She listened carefully and occasionally nodded her head in agreement when I tried to counter these views. Whenever I did, she would remind me that the supposedly civilised nations of Europe had conceived the most hideous torture for the impious.

'Can you imagine any government stretching a chained man until his joints cracked and his limbs snapped to force an admission of treachery? Or putting a man to death while disembowelling him alive?'

I could hardly argue with this, nor when Patience casually dropped Hitler into the conversation. How had the land of Goethe, Schiller and Beethoven given birth to the Nazis and the Holocaust? She mocked my replies, telling me I was beholden to the British idea of empire and would never understand the liberation demanded by so many people in the world.

I pointed out that western colonisation was slowly being replaced by eastern powers anxious to plunder Africa's mineral wealth. I also reminded her that Shakespeare had been equally beholden to the political powers of his day and that many of the timeless plays and sonnets had been written to curry favour with the Queen and her powerful courtiers. In today's terms, Shakespeare would be counted as a Conservative of the deepest hue.

She dismissed this as a convenient opinion. There was plenty of revolutionary writing in Shakespeare if one looked hard enough.

This allowed me to insist on an answer to a question I had put to her many times before. I was tired of brush-off answers. It was important that I knew, I told her. What was the source of this passion for the great playwright? How did she know so much about the man and his works? It was beyond belief that she had acquired such knowledge from a township education or even a correspondence course in English Lit. Her usual retort had been to describe my curiosity as patronising prejudice.

'Why shouldn't a poor township black girl love Shakespeare?' she threw back at me.

I told her that true lovers should not keep such secrets from each other, a feeble argument but one that seemed to work.

'How apt it is to learn. Any hard lesson may do thee good,' she said.

This slight corruption of lines from *Much Ado About Nothing*, as she later told me, came with a frisky smile, but it did not answer the question. Finally, and with the fast tongue that Charity had mentioned loosened by wine, she told me the story.

Her father had left home when she and her siblings were young, never to be seen again. Her mother, a devout churchgoer of the Protestant faith, had become a cleaner in a mission school. After much pleading Patience, the eldest child, had been admitted as a pupil, aged ten.

The mission teachers were of a fundamentalist faith and believed that the Bible should be the centre of all learning. At that young age children were made to learn by heart tracts of the Old Testament, especially the book of Ecclesiastes. The uniforms were blue smocks for the girls and shorts and blue shirts for the boys. They were housed in separate dormitories. The food was plain but plentiful.

As Patience grew older, the initial scolding for bad behaviour gave way to long periods of detention for those who could not repeat the sections they had been given to learn, or who had been talking after lights out or failed to finish their meals. For what were deemed more serious offences, such as stealing from the kitchen, the errant child was made to hold the Bible in one hand while he or she was strapped on the other.

When I expressed my horror at this regime, Patience said it was much better than other mission schools she could name.

Mrs Elizabeth Haworth was a commanding figure in the school, for which her late husband, an American evangelist, had raised the foundation funds. Thus Mrs Haworth was free to pursue her own ideas of teaching without interference from the rest of the Bible-minded staff. She believed that study of the English classics was more important than learning to recite dusty passages from the Old Testament. So it was that in her class, Patience and other girls were taught to learn about, and more importantly to enjoy, the plays of William Shakespeare.

The more Patience read, the more she realised that Shakespeare spoke to her and her generation. Love, betrayal and revolution were compelling themes for a young African girl growing up in a white man's world.

It was as if a curtain had been drawn back and a window opened on a new world, Patience said. At this point she was in her teenage years. She told Mrs Haworth that her ambition was to become a teacher and use her love for and knowledge of the great playwright to enliven the dreary school curriculum.

'And that is what I am doing,' she said to me. 'Does that help you?'

It helped a lot. I now understood how Shakespeare had come to grip the mind and imagination of this woman. But I had learnt little more about who she really was. She remained unknowable, a wearying enigma, a door closed and locked on her past.

Chapter Eleven

By now I had become quite well known to both sides or, as Patience would put it, the oppressor and the oppressed. While several well-known journalists had been declared prohibited immigrants for flagrantly one-sided reporting, I was allowed to stay and was even greeted with reasonable warmth by the Information Ministry officials who turned up at the club on Friday evenings.

I told myself that this was because I had managed to steer a middle course between the righteous nationalist cause on the one hand and the intransigent determination of the white community to fight to the death on the other. Yet there is little doubt that careful reading of my reports revealed growing sympathy for the reckless stand by the whites against impossible odds.

History presented several examples of suicidal stands by beleaguered minorities facing certain defeat. The Roman siege of the Jewish Masada fortress is one of the best known, but there have been others. I have always admired the purity of belief that leads to such sacrifices. I accept this is a romantic view, born of my studies of the great era in literature in the nineteenth century when poets such as Baudelaire and Rimbaud consciously sought an early demise. Grudgingly, and perhaps unforgivably, I began to see the tiny minority of settlers here in the middle of Africa in the same light.

Many fought on because there was nothing else to do and did so without recognising their folly. Layla Milan at the farm at Shamva was different. She remained there stoically, her husband on almost permanent call-up, knowing that inevitable defeat meant the end of a foolish dream.

I took such thoughts to the performance of *Love's Labour's Lost* that night and saw a chaotic performance by young pupils, none of whom could have been over the age of sixteen. Patience believed her class should follow her example and get to know the Bard and his works early in their young lives. She stood to one side of the makeshift stage, prompting her faltering cast with whispered words and using her hands as if conducting an orchestra.

Afterwards she briefly thanked me for coming and said she had to go to a meeting with the headmistress. It was 6.30 at night and already dark. The school day had long finished. The meeting sounded ominous, but I said nothing.

•

At Pinks that night after the play I was introduced to Stella Knight, a grand old lady I had seen there every night since my arrival. She was known as the Queen Mother of the local press corps and dressed accordingly. Irrespective of the weather, she always wore long, white or cream-coloured dresses with a satin scarf twisted around her neck. To complete the ensemble, she smoked from a tortoiseshell cigarette-holder. She had seen me on my visits to the club but never introduced herself. She peered at me myopically through thick-lensed glasses and said, 'Oh, that's who you are.'

I agreed that that's who I was and watched as she cleaved through the crowd to the bar like a ship in full sail. She returned with two glasses of whisky and a small bottle of water.

'Real Scotch. Have a splash, darling.'

I had wanted a beer but I did not like to refuse. I allowed myself to be steered to a small table in a corner. She bade me welcome and raised her glass. I raised mine in turn and we drank.

'How are you finding our little country, darling?'

I had noticed that she called everyone 'darling'. I replied in the usual way, with trivial remarks about the weather, the hospitality of local people and so forth. She made no response to these platitudes.

She let me finish and said, 'I gather you know Sara Jane Shannon and her boyfriend, that lovely man André Lennox.'

'I do.'

'Fine soldier. A real hero.'

She paused and drank her whisky.

'He's been killed,' she said. 'It happened last night up near the border.'

'I am so sorry.'

I wondered why I had been drawn aside to hear this information. Everyone in the bar must have known.

'How did it happen?'

'You'll find out soon enough. I'm telling you this because

Sara Jane wants to see you. She is devastated, beside herself.'

'Of course, but any idea why?'

'She wants you to write an article about André, his life and military career, the risks he took for this country and the way he loved the people – all the people. She wants an international paper to carry the story.'

This was crazy. I was not going to write the obituary of a man who had fought for the wrong side in a losing war. I did not wish to parade my discreet sympathy for his cause in front of Meredith Kaplan and my readers. Besides, his grieving lover would no doubt hang like a hawk over every word. I had no intention of putting myself in such jeopardy.

'Tell me exactly what happened,' I said.

The story was bizarre. Lennox had been in command of a unit of African troops in the eastern border area, always the most dangerous part of the country. They were camped near a stone-built conical tower, part of ancient ruins. A group of insurgents had approached at night using the ruins as cover. Lennox had led a section of his men around one side of the tower while the rest of his unit had gone round the other. In the confusion and darkness, a firefight broke out. Lennox was shot at close range. He died of his wounds several hours later, before he could be evacuated.

Sara Jane had been staying in the nearby guest house for tourists. Hearing the shooting, she had rushed to the scene to find Lennox lying in a tent, coughing blood and bleeding heavily from his chest. He was clearly dying.

She had flung herself upon him and no amount of persuasion could drag her away, even when it became clear that her lover was dead. She cradled him, talking in whimpering whispers as if he was alive. When dawn came, a helicopter arrived to take her and the body to the city.

She accompanied the body to the military hospital, where Lennox was officially declared dead from a single gunshot to the chest. Examination of the bullet extracted from the corpse established that he had been shot by one of his own men. It was an accident, an easy but fatal mistake to make in darkness among men wearing facial camouflage cream.

Still wearing the same clothes, Sara Jane had fought her way onto the ambulance taking the body to the mortuary. Medics had initially refused to take her until, screaming and flailing at anyone who came near her, she was allowed on board. Finally, friends arrived and took her home.

The story was pure horror. Stella raised her glass towards the bar and two more whiskies arrived. She read my thoughts with alarming precision.

'I know you don't want to get involved. I don't blame you. But she works for you. Help her. Talk to her. She has friends with her, but right now she wants to talk to you about the story. It will be catharsis for her.'

I didn't see how an article in a New York magazine could help this grieving lover, nor did I think Meredith would happily take an obituary article extolling the qualities of a heroic soldier in a rebel white regime. True, I had developed some sympathy for the white cause, but that did not extend to glorying their dead in the pages of my magazine, even if they agreed to publish it.

On the other hand, Sara Jane had been hired as freelance fixer for the magazine and therein lay an obligation. I would see her and offer what comfort I could.

•

The next morning I made my way to her apartment close to the city centre. I felt ashamed of myself. Here was a woman in her thirties losing the great love of her life, not in some gallant action against the enemy but as the result of a stupid accident.

Sara Jane had helped me in a small way. My immediate response to her personal tragedy had been to think of how to avoid any involvement. I kicked myself for such selfishness. Besides, this was by any yardstick a good story.

The apartment was in a two-storey block in a tree-lined side street. A notice had been pinned to the front door saying 'No callers'. I tapped lightly on the door and stepped back. A black cat sat on the windowsill with the curtains drawn behind it. After some minutes, the curtains were pulled back and a pale-faced woman looked out. She put a finger to her lips and pointed to the sign. I mouthed my name to her. She signalled for me to wait and drew the curtains again. A few minutes later the woman opened the door and handed me a folded piece of paper. I opened it and read, '*Meet me in an hour.*'

I did not have to ask where. She was sitting as usual at the corner table.

George was his normal unsmiling, inscrutable self. He looked at me and returned to his cocktail-shaker, fruit-squeezer and silver fork. I didn't want a cocktail any more than I had wanted a whisky the previous evening but felt I could not refuse. Hard liquor was a social requirement these days.

Sara Jane had a champagne glass in front of her. She was drinking a cocktail, not the fizzy stuff. She wore a black dress which made the little gold medallion stand out against her tanned skin. I was about to ask if she wanted another drink when she shook her head and gestured to the chair beside her. I sat down. George appeared with my drink. I put a hand out to her.

'I am so sorry.'

She took my hand, squeezed and let it go. She rocked back and forth on her chair for a few seconds and put her head in her hands, the fingers splayed so that I could see her eyes, red and blurry. After a minute, she straightened up and reached for her drink.

'Please don't feel sorry for me.'

'Is there anything I can do?'

'That's kind of you, but no. Everyone says the same thing. I don't blame them, but the only thing anyone can do is bring him back.'

'I'm glad you have friends with you.'

She took the small gold medallion and rubbed it gently and slowly between her fingers.

'Everything has been taken away from me,' she said. 'I feel as if all the clocks have stopped. That's right, isn't it? Grief is the thief of time, they say.'

She held out the medallion to me, pulling the gold chain tightly around her neck.

'Look at this.'

I saw the line of tiny engraved figures carved into the gold. I had seen them when we first met. They were clearer now: '17 S 31 E'.

'What is this?'

She shook her head, her eyes rimmed with tears.

'The geographic coordinates of this bar.'

'Really?'

It was all I could say.

'We met right here. I was sitting on a bar stool over there. Our very first date.'

She took a small handkerchief from her handbag, dabbed at her eyes, drank briefly and fingered the medallion.

'He gave this to me the first time he went back on duty after we met. We were sitting on the bar stools over there. He had it made because this was the most important place on earth for him. That's what he said.'

She pointed to the bar.

'George made us cocktails. Whisky sours, his favourite drink.'

'So you know George.'

'Everyone knows George.'

There were now several couples and a few men on their own in the bar. Sara Jane attracted the odd glance from people who recognised her from photographs in that day's papers. Lennox's death had been big news and led the TV bulletins.

We didn't say anything for what seemed a long time. She fiddled with the medallion, gulped back her drink and stared at the floor.

'He said if anything ever happened to him, I was to come here and drink a whisky sour. He said George would look after me.'

She suddenly raised her voice and said very loudly, so that the whole bar could hear, 'You'll look after me, won't you, George?'

George turned very slowly and looked at us. He raised the side hatch of the bar and walked over. He moved the way he made a cocktail, slowly and with deliberation. By now the whole bar was watching us. This was an unexpected bonus to accompany evening drinks. It was almost dark outside and in that darkness a war was being fought and people like Lennox were dying. But the usual routine of drinks in the Cancan Bar – cocktails with peanuts on the side and ashtrays that quickly filled – kept the dark night at bay. Isn't that what happened on the *Titanic*? People continued to play cards, dress for dinner, order drinks, make love perhaps, more frantically than usual, while the ship settled slowly into the Atlantic.

George lowered his head and said in a whisper, 'I will look after you, but you must look after yourself, Miss Shannon.'

With that, he returned to his position behind the bar. She was now drunk, as was I. I was glad. The whiskies and silver bullets were going to help both of us that night. We had yet to discuss her wish that I write a piece about Lennox. I was beginning to hope it had been forgotten when she said, with slurred, throaty words, 'I want you to write something for me.'

'Can we talk about it tomorrow? You're exhausted. It's not the right time.'

'You mean I'm drunk.'

'Yes, and so am I.'

'You saw Stella. She told you what I wanted?'

'Yes.'

'Right. Tomorrow,' she said.

She got slowly to her feet. I stood up. She placed a hand on my shoulder, leant forward and kissed me on the cheek loudly and for too long. The bar was rapt with attention. Over her shoulder the cancan girls danced on. She turned and walked unsteadily from the room. Everyone was watching. Her head was down and her shoulders hunched. She gave the same wave over her shoulder as before.

She went to the head of the staircase, swayed slightly and reached for the handrail. I wondered if I would see her again. The life had drained out of her as we talked. The woman I had met in the bar all those weeks ago had vanished. She needed help and I was not the person to give it to her. I walked quickly to the head of the staircase and followed her down.

The lobby was busy but there was no sign of her. I went to the main doors. The light of the illuminated fountains showed her walking across the square with a firm step, head held up and looking straight ahead. I felt relieved. She was a strong woman.

I wanted to get back to the room and make notes. Lennox's absurd death and Sara Jane's tragedy summed up the impenetrable stupidity of those who conducted the war. A perfect intro to a new piece, another 5,000 words.

The lobby was full of the kind of men war attracts: arms dealers, tobacco traders, salesmen of every type united in one aim – to break the sanctions that so far had had little effect that I could see on either the economy or the war effort.

Julia Milan emerged from the throng and skipped across the lobby with the coltish grace of the young. I noticed lascivious glances from the sanctions traders. She made to kiss me on the cheek. I pulled back slightly. She was wearing a cotton safari jacket over a tight T-shirt and slim-fit blue jeans. Her hair was tied back in a ponytail.

'Hello, stranger, want to buy me a drink?'

I told her I had to work. She put her face close to mine and sniffed.

'It looks like you've been working hard already. Who was the lucky girl?'

There was just a moment, a moth-flutter of lust, which told me that this sexually confident young woman dressed to attract would happily spend an hour or so in bed with me.

'I know what you are thinking,' she said.

'Do you?'

'Yes. Another time maybe.'

'I have to go,' I said.

'Lunch tomorrow at Sandro's. I have something to tell you,' she said and skipped away, carrying the eyes of the lobby with her.

•

I went back to my room, work forgotten, and slept until breakfast. Once again George was on duty. I had not seen Patience since the school play. I was sure she would have left a message for me. George just shook his head when I asked.

I ordered more coffee and carefully analysed the irritation, almost anger, that arose within me. We had promised to keep in touch, to mine nuggets of time out of every day to talk, meet and move gently towards that state of mind where two people can begin to share thoughts, jokes and long, soft kisses, mindless of who is looking. I was fooling myself. This was self-hypnosis, a hopelessly romantic view of a relationship that had hardly put one foot in front of the other.

Like most men who find themselves in love, or who tell themselves they are, I could relegate this inconvenient fact to join my collection of many other inconvenient facts. I was not sure that Patience felt the same as I did. She was not the kind of woman to admit to such emotion. Either way, why had she not sent a message through the most obvious and discreet channel?

I told myself to separate the personal from the professional, desire from duty. Patience was my sounding board, my way into nationalist thinking. Lennox's death would have been celebrated in the townships, or so I assumed. And what of the continuing raids in the neighbouring countries? The tempo of the war increased almost every day and with it the political temperature. I needed some insight into the minds of those in the majority of the population who could see that power was about to fall into their hands. That was why Patience was so important to me. On a personal level, I missed everything about her.

I could not hang around the school at night parked around the corner like a sneak thief. Neither could I go to the bar in the Victoria Hotel. It would be embarrassing. I called George over.

'Can you take a message?'

He nodded with a sigh. He was weary of running such errands.

I turned the menu over and wrote, *'Can we meet tonight? Your choice, Richard.'*

I folded it. He took it from me carefully and turned to the sound of someone snapping their fingers. A few tables away a man stopped snapping and beckoned.

George was a magisterial figure in the hotel where he had served since starting as a boot boy forty years earlier. Back then, the war was raging in Europe and the country was full of Royal Air Force crew sent to train in the sunny skies of Africa. The hotel was their social base and George had become their mascot, a plump urchin uniformed in the purple hotel colours. His photo was endlessly taken on the hotel steps posing with the aviators. He now stared out at old men in Britain from framed photos on their mantelpieces. Some still wrote occasional letters to him.

Patience had told me this. I thought of it as I watched George walk up to the finger-snapper and his wife. As he neared the table, the man held up the menu with a displeased face that demanded not just immediate attention but an apology for some crime committed by the kitchen. He was about to speak when George walked wordlessly past him. The look on that man's face would stay with me for a long time.

•

There were two telex messages waiting for me in my room. They had been slipped under the door in white envelopes stamped with the hotel crest. The first, from Meredith, congratulated me on my recent writing. She said I was getting to grips with majority nationalist thinking in a way few other correspondents had even attempted. My refreshing coverage had struck a much-needed balance in reporting from this stricken nation.

That was the word she used: 'stricken'. I looked out at the square, where everything was exactly as it had been before:

decorously dressed white women strolling past the fountains thinking of lunch; black women pushing prams or carrying shopping. Those sunlit figures moved in slow motion in my mind. The effect was hypnotic. I would not have been surprised if the ladies with parasols and little dogs had stepped from the boulevards of Paris in the Cancan Bar and joined the tableau in the square. It was exactly that: a painting that captured an eternal, unchanging scene, just as the founders of this country had planned it.

I opened the second telex, this time from the features editor. Meredith hated such intrusions on what she regarded as her territory. There was little I could do about office turf wars, but I felt for her. She got to her desk early, left late and ate alone in the commissary. She had no time for political games in the office, and as a result her colleagues had little time for her.

The features editor praised my work, but with such extravagance that there had to be a twist. '*We suggest you re-base to gain coverage of guerrilla operations and nationalist command thinking,*' it said. '*We would run a major feature to 5,000 words.*'

I smiled at this. Five thousand miles away, this intelligent man with a Harvard degree, a nice brownstone in Brooklyn and a mental map of every decent restaurant between midtown and Central Park could casually request, i.e. command, a correspondent to put himself in the line of fire. In this case, I was being asked to visit guerrilla camps in a neighbouring country under frequent attack from a professional army, air force and special forces units.

To what end? Snatched interviews with young men who would pump their AK-47 rifles in the air and shout the usual slogans? I already knew what would happen next. They would leave under cover of darkness to slide another knife into a wounded nation, picadors weakening an enraged bull with lances before the final assault.

And many of them would end up in a line of corpses in an army camp. Behind these young men stood the commanders, the politicians and the cheerleaders who knew that such slaughter was avoidable. At this stage of the war, negotiations, which one side would call a sell-out and the other surrender, were the only way forward.

I would learn nothing from visiting a guerrilla camp, even supposing I was allowed to do so. The irony was that I could learn, and indeed had already learnt, more about the currents of political thought flowing through the black community from visiting the Arcadia township. I knew where their ambition lay and what they were fighting for. I also knew, in the memorable words of Jeeze, that if there were a civil war after independence, it would be 'our civil war, not yours'. That summed up the deep well of bitterness and humiliation from which the African population, young and old, drew their water. I did not need to go to a guerrilla camp to learn that.

I sent a brief message back thanking the features editor for his warm words. I said I would look into the complex travel arrangements needed to move between two countries at war. I also asked him to check my insurance cover for work in a war zone. I thought that would give him pause and keep me where I needed to be.

I rested for an hour, planning a long piece for a magazine in France. My contract allowed me to write a certain number of pieces for other outlets. Then I spoke on the phone with my French editor, in a mixture of his bad English and my rather better French. His interest was very much in the French mercenaries who had arrived in considerable numbers and had already made quite an impact in the club.

This made me think of a wider piece on the mercenaries who roamed the world signing up for conflicts wherever the rate of pay was commensurate with the risk. My Paris editor was only interested in the French contingent because many of them were former members of the Foreign Legion. This outlier of the regular French forces had acquired a patina of romantic glory thanks to the softening filter of Hollywood and endless books. In fact, those I had met were uniformly psychopathic killers seeking to satiate bloodlust in another dirty war.

I was still on the phone when my eyes were caught by a folded slip of paper pushed under the door. It slid into the room with a slight rustle and lay there on the carpet demanding attention. This was becoming routine, but there was still something mysteriously seductive about the delivery of such a message.

I told Paris to call me back, hearing a swear word in return. The message was on the same menu I had handed to George at breakfast. It simply named a small roadhouse in an inner suburb and the time, 7 p.m. There was no signature, but I did not need one. My mood lightened. The day had taken a pleasing shape.

I was about to start work when there was a knock on the door. Without waiting for a reply, Marion entered to clean the room. I put aside my initial irritation at this further interruption. She offered to come back but I told her to work around me. I watched as she made the bed and dusted various bits of furniture. I told her to leave the hoovering until the next day. She frowned and said that the housekeeper personally checked all rooms later and would reprimand her.

'I will talk to her,' I said. 'Does she treat you well?'

'She is good to me.'

'In what way?'

'She helped get my children into school.'

'Where?'

'In the township.'

'So, you are happy here?'

'It is a good job.'

'What about the war out there, the boys, the fighting?'

'Let them fight. I just want my job and my home.'

This woman was an unlikely victim of vicious white racism. It was an initial and tempting viewpoint. After all, her lot would probably not improve in the inevitably chaotic years after independence. Inevitable because sharp minds like Jeeze recognised the internal war to come. The deep differences between people in the north and south made that certain. In his bitter words, the two nationalist sides would fight each other for their future, as had happened with the birth of most nations in the world.

And so I could argue to myself that Maid Marion, as she called herself in an unlikely nod to an English fairy tale, was better off under the paternalistic yoke of white rule than she might well be in the future. It was a lazily understandable view. But it was a trap; the *Gone with the Wind* trap.

Margaret Mitchell gave us happy blacks on a slave estate

in the Deep South ruled firmly but kindly by a family with the commanding figure of Scarlett O'Hara. But who was that long-forgotten African American actress, what was her name? The woman who had won an Oscar for the best supporting role? There she is, buried and forgotten in the footnotes of Hollywood history. Hattie McDaniel. Hollywood congratulated itself on what was at the time seen as a courageous liberal gesture. But Hattie was made to enter the ceremony itself by a side entrance and sat at a table far from the rest of the cast. She was even denied a seat at the premier in Atlanta. That was forty years ago.

•

Sandro's was the most popular restaurant in town but an odd choice, I thought. It was expensive and a place to see and be seen, rather than somewhere for a quiet conversation. I wanted the lunch with Julia to be over quickly. I had more writing to do and I needed to think about Patience. I was seeing her that night. I would buy a present for her. The only perfume in the shops was local. A leather handbag would be better.

Julia was dressed formally in a dark cotton dress. She had been at work and had to return after her lunch hour. She gave me a kiss on the cheek, sat down and picked up the menu.

'When are you going?' she asked.

'Going where?'

'To see Mum. You said you would.'

'Julia, I have talked all this through with her already. I'm rather busy right now.'

'Well, Mr busy-important-correspondent-who-has-forgotten-who-first-welcomed-him-to-this-country, she just said she really wants to see you.'

'What's the road like?'

'Safe in convoy. Please go. Just one more time. She wants to help you get the story straight.'

We are at war and we deserve our fate but it is not as bad for the Africans as everyone says. That was the story she wanted me to get straight. We ordered and ate quickly.

'What will you do after independence?' I asked.

'What a question! I haven't really thought about it.'

'Well, you'd better start thinking about it.'

'Who's in a bad mood today?'

'Sorry. I'm just very busy.'

'I'm going to stay if I can, but my boyfriend is going to leave.'

'You have a boyfriend?'

'I have always had a boyfriend, but not always the same one.'

She laughed at her little joke and looked at me for any reaction. I smiled. We were drinking water. She worked in a farmer's co-op selling dried food and clothing at discounted prices. She didn't seem worried about the future. She had known no other life than the farm and occasional visits to the city. She had the innocent confidence of the young that makes light of most problems.

The fact that going home at weekends meant driving in convoy on a road liable to be ambushed or mined did not seem to worry her. Her boyfriend left for long periods of call-up, but that did not worry her either. There were always others. She kissed me on the cheek and left. I watched her go and smiled as, without looking back, she gave a slight wiggle at the door.

•

That afternoon I bought a leather shoulder bag adorned with a thorn tree stitched in black on the side. It was beautifully done by local craftswomen. I thought it would please Patience. The hotel wrapped it for me in tissue paper.

She jumped up from the table and gave a little gasp of surprise when I gave it to her that night. She held it up, turned it round and stroked the smooth skin.

'Thank you. Thank you. Thank you,' she said. 'Where did you get it?'

I named a small shop in the part of town where Asian and Indian traders produced cotton fabrics and leather goods and where, with due discretion, one could change American dollars at black-market rates. We resumed our seats at a creaky wooden table in a restaurant lit only by candles and a few lamps hung from the ceiling.

'What have you been up to?' she said.

'Thinking of you.'

'That's not quite what I meant.'

'I've been writing, working and wondering why I'm drinking so much.'

'It's that awful bar.'

'Your uncle George wouldn't agree with that.'

I told her the story of George and the finger-snapping guest at breakfast that day. She laughed, shaking her head from side to side, so that her black hair wrapped around her face.

'I love that man,' she said.

'Let's go,' I said.

She put her hand on mine and bent across the table, forming her lips into a kiss.

'Let's eat first. I have something to tell you.'

We drank decent white wine and chewed sticks of biltong. I waited impatiently. I wanted to be out of there. I tried to think where we could go. I wanted her to come back to the hotel again. She would be wary. Maid Marion might surprise us in the morning.

She put a finger to her lips, looked around and then, with a needlessly theatrical gesture, looked under the tablecloth.

'They want to talk to you.'

'Who?'

'The people over the border. The commander, the big chief.' She named a name I had never heard before.

'How do you know this?'

'Does that matter?'

'Yes, it matters a lot.'

'I'm just a messenger. They know we see each other.'

'See each other?'

'They like your writing. They think you need to see their side of the story.'

So the features editor in New York and this terrorist leader, as he would be called by one side or freedom fighter by the other, both agreed. And Patience Matatu was the messenger.

'They must trust you,' I said. 'This is dangerous.'

'Only if you betray me.'

•

We lay in bed that night, breathing deeply and cooling off under the air conditioning, each in a private world of unshared secrets. She had said nothing when we drove to the hotel, but would not take the lift and hurried me up the staircase to my room on the second floor.

I was not surprised to find myself alone again the next morning. She had a school day ahead and the pupils arrived at nine o'clock sharp.

I sent Marion away when she knocked on the door. There was lipstick on the pillowcases and stale scent in the air. I put the pillowcases in the laundry bag and opened the windows onto the square. The same cast of characters were performing the same daily ritual. Time didn't stand still there; it went backwards. I left before Marion came back. George was not on breakfast duty.

They wanted me to interview a rebel leader in a neighbouring country, which was at war with the people around me eating their ham and eggs, porridge and fruit. They were at war with the mothers and nannies in the square outside and with everything those people stood for.

It would be a logistical nightmare. It would mean flying between several countries, each with their own visa demands. At the end of it all, I would get the same weary clichés I had to endure from government officials here. Worse still, I did not speak the language and thus would be unable to gauge the mood on the streets or even talk to women like Maid Marion. It only made sense if I fell into the trap of enjoying the inevitable high praise for a boring propaganda piece praising the nationalist cause.

I drank more coffee and thought about Patience. She was

much more than a messenger. She was part of the nationalist underground. The police knew all about her. She knew that. Yet she still promoted the cause. Every night she laid a sheet embroidered with the green and gold flag of liberty on her bed. All the young African men in the township wore those colours as T-shirts, just as young white men displayed the green and white colours of their national flag on clothing, posters and front lawns.

I wouldn't do it. My reputation as a fair-minded writer open to all opinions would be finished. That is how people still saw me, even if the truth lay elsewhere. I would explain that to the features editor. He would say he respected my decision. But in the bar later he and his colleagues would agree I had lost my nerve. I didn't mind that. I minded about Patience. She would not understand. She would be furious. I had to have a reason.

•

Bram had his arm in a sling when I saw him that night in Pinks. I had come for lack of anything else to do, and as usual at the end of the day I needed a drink. The familiar faces were there: Chris Raymond with the dreamy look of a drunk, Stella Knight surrounded by her acolytes. I wanted to join her group and listen to old-time stories of when the country was being hacked out of the bush and the main streets of town were laid wide enough to allow an ox wagon to turn full circle.

Bram, with a drink in one hand, raised an elbow and lifted his head to beckon me over. He was with a short, slim young woman wearing a dark trouser suit. Her hair was cropped, revealing a sharp-nosed face that seemed at one with her shiny patent-leather shoes.

'Meet a colleague of mine, Emma Lamb,' he said.

I shook hands with Emma.

'I'll get you a drink,' she said.

Bram gestured to the alcove table. We sat down.

'She works with me. Just started. I thought you would like to meet her.'

I was about to make a semi-humorous remark as to why I would want more than one secret policeman in my life when Ms Lamb returned, carrying three glasses of whisky on a tin tray, which bore the image of a stern-looking prime minister over the motto '*Fidelis ad Mortem*'.

We clinked our glasses. These two had the business-like air of those with an announcement to make. I had come to join Stella Knight's audience of admirers and now I was to be lectured on my reporting or given some prime source of intelligence. I should have stayed true to George and his silver bullets.

'What happened to your arm?' I asked.

'Flesh wound. Rock splinter,' he said.

'The bullet missed him by an inch,' said Ms Lamb.

'What happened?'

'Nothing to write home about,' said Bram. 'I understand that you have been invited to interview Felix Tongogara.'

I drank my whisky.

'Why would you think that?'

'Because your friend Patience Matatu has passed on that message to you. She was quite right. They do want you to go over there.'

'If what you are saying is true, it would be a good opportunity, wouldn't it? It would put me well ahead of this crowd.'

I nodded to the bar.

'Risky, though,' said Bram.

'How do you make that out?'

Emma Lamb, who had been staring intently at her shiny shoes, looked up and said, 'You would not be allowed back in this country.'

'Why not?'

'You would have given a propaganda platform to a Marxist terrorist who is trying to destroy us.'

'Don't be ridiculous. I would report fairly and in a balanced way, just as I do here.'

'What would Churchill have done if a British journalist had secured an interview with Hitler, Goering or Goebbels at the height of the Second World War?'

I looked at her again. The hostility was ill-concealed beneath a veneer of official politeness. Perhaps there was more to her than fake leather shoes. She leant forward, her face so close to mine I could smell the whisky on her breath.

'Ordinary young men, our people, are being turned into barbarians over there. They come back and steal and rob from their own. They cut the lips off any woman under the slightest suspicion of being a sell-out. They murder our farmers in hideous ways. They do this because Tongogara tells them this is the path to freedom.'

'And your troops behave like gentlemen, do they? They don't burn villages, kill civilians, throw the living wounded into burial pits and use methods of torture even the Nazis hadn't thought of? They don't –'

Bram banged the table with his glass.

'Enough,' he said.

He looked at Emma and nodded. She got up, shook my hand, swallowed the remnants of her drink and left.

'She's good, isn't she?' said Bram.

'If you say so. What's this all about?'

'She told you the truth: they will not let you back. You can see why.'

I drained the whisky. How had they known? Tapped Patience's phone, her house, her car? Obviously. The woman had no idea about her security.

'I am still going to go,' I said.

'I'll see you off at the airport,' he said. 'Just let me know when.'

•

Our meeting was over. More than ever, I wanted the peace that came with the sight of the shambling bulk of an elephant moving slowly to the river, sluicing the water over its back and ears and drinking deeply. The bushmen would have hunted these creatures with flint-tipped arrows and spears. Everyone through history here had hunted elephant, not so much for the meat, which was tougher than teak, but for the ivory. The bushmen had not survived but the elephant had. Until now.

I approached the group around Stella, who had taken up a position at the bar, one elbow resting on the counter next to the old sandwiches. Her cigarette was, as usual, in its tortoiseshell holder.

'Oh, you've had enough of the spookies, have you, darling?' she said. 'Join us for a drink.'

She introduced me to her courtiers, who included a former British hangman called Albert who was happy to tell you how many he had 'dropped' during his time with the rope – 'They all said the same thing at the end: "Make it quick."' There was also a sanctions-breaking tobacco salesman and Sam, a stripper at the Boheme nightclub who did interesting things with rifle barrels. Her weekend shows were a favourite with troops back from the bush.

Occasionally the group was joined by Stella's daughter Lisa, a sweet-looking young woman with long plaits who had spent some years working as a waitress in Florida. She was the only normal person in the place, I thought, until she told us that after she had been fired for an inappropriate relationship with the chef, to make some money she had appeared in a porn film. She told us with pride that she had played a cowgirl riding a horse through huge cactus plants that stripped off her clothing. It was an artistic porn film, she explained.

Finally, there was the ever-present Chris Raymond, whose appearance was even more dilapidated than when I had first met him; stooped and bearded, his face as pale as parchment, a fold of greasy hair curled over his collar at the back, he looked as if he had slept in his clothes for a week. If I had known how he was to change my life, I would have paid him more attention. As it was, I knew only what he told everyone, that he had been in trouble with the police back home in the UK and had fled to sanctuary in Africa. It seemed an unlikely story even then.

These people were the next best thing to elephants. Their company calmed me. They did not ask anything of anyone. They were prehistory, the remnants of a long-gone age, alcoholic eccentrics with a large library of memories they were eager to share. Stella presided over this group nightly, conducting the conversation. Everyone had their turn to speak, order drinks, tell a story or simply sink quietly into their drink. She would finish these conversations by recalling great days in her past.

They were simple people, content with their company, living on declining pensions in small suburban bungalows. With only an ill-paid servant to talk to at home, they sought solace here, refugees from the present as much as the past. You could find them on Saturday nights in any bar in the world.

I had drunk enough whisky and earned general disapproval by switching to water while answering questions about my time in the country. Had I marvelled at the mighty waterfalls that fed the great lake in the north? Did I know that this was once the best tourist destination in Africa?

No mention was made of the war because Stella did not approve of such talk. It spoilt the atmosphere, she said. My interrogation stopped when Quigley burst in, offering drinks to all. He was unusually sober and had just come back from a long trip to a mission station in the north.

He broke Stella's rule by describing the dangers of the journey and the risky lives of the missionaries. Stella did not seem to mind this departure from the normal run of the conversation.

'Tell us everything, darling,' she cried.

Quigley told us the most frightening moment came on a

dirt road when he was forced off the single strip of tarmac by a fast-moving farm truck. He was sure he would be blown up.

'They see you coming and force you off the tarmac just where the mines have been planted.'

'Who?' asked Alfred the hangman.

'Terrorists, missionaries – mate, I don't know, they're all the same.'

'Could just be an accident,' offered a whiskery major with a pink gin.

Quigley stuck to his story that he had been the victim of a terrorist murder attempt. It was an obvious lie, but it would play well on the wire agency he worked for.

•

Before I finally got to sleep that night, I considered a visit to a mission station. It was a difficult decision. I would have to sort out New York's request first. The proposed visit to a nationalist leader across the border would be dangerous. It would have to wait.

I needed to get deep into the rural areas with the least possible risk and talk to people who had dedicated their lives to the country and who understood the jeopardy of villagers in rural districts. Missionaries were a missing piece of the jigsaw. They were scattered around the country. Some had been there since the formation of the government in the 1920s. They were a mixture of Catholic, Protestant and sects such as the Seventh-Day Adventists. Patience had gained her early education at the hands of these people. She regarded them as saintly.

They may have been over-zealous with the leather strap, but she credited her general education and her deep knowledge of Shakespeare to their teaching. Missionaries of all faiths had also gained respect among the African people for the good works they did in remote parts of the country. For that reason the government and the security forces were deeply suspicious and correctly doubted their allegiance to the regime. I wanted to find out where the truth lay.

Usually when I arrive at such a decision, sleep follows. But I had a larger question to answer, which kept me awake until birdsong and dawn. My honeymoon with New York was over. That was clear. The irony was that as my writing became more popular with the readership, so the free hand I had been given to report as I liked was being withdrawn.

The pressure to go to a hostile neighbouring country and profile the guerrilla leader was one result. The editors who had left me alone for so long had suddenly become interested in the story. I felt possessive about this country and its warring people. I did not want anyone telling me how to describe the absurdities of two people fighting over what they both loved.

I had brought this nation out of the wilderness of the foreign news-in-brief columns and onto the inside pages and then the front page. My byline was now larger and the accompanying photo touched up to reveal a younger and more handsome man. The foreign desk told me fan-mail letters had begun to arrive, mostly from women's social groups asking me to address their gatherings and promising a small fee with supper and hotel accommodation.

No doubt, the obituary editor had been asked to expand the skimpy note about my life that all staff were required to submit. I had no intention of dying, but all the same I didn't want some unknown hack to write my life story and cast judgement on my successes or failures, to be filed away for the day of my death.

Death held no fears for me because, like most people, I could not imagine it happening. In occasional moments of self-indulgent melodrama, I even thought it might be a release from the lingering guilt about the Parisian affair and my growing attachment to a renegade cause.

It was time for courage, a quality I had notably lacked ever since joining the school gang lashing that poor French boy with stinging nettles. I would ignore what New York and Patience wanted. I would stay on to develop the story into which I had put so much effort.

It would look as if I was falling in with the wishes of Bram and his ghastly colleague. Patience would be angry. I would explain. I would tell her I felt written out, the hollow interior of my mind unable to translate the emotions of those waiting for victory and those fearing defeat. I needed to move forward and prove to Meredith Kaplan and her desk colleagues, maybe even to Patience, that the story lay here, somewhere between the Eastern Highlands, the northern lake and river frontier and the dusty cattle country in the south.

The choices swung like needles on a compass. North took me back to Green Creek Farm, where Layla Milan wanted to add to her story of settlement and war. In the city lay Patience, the township and the now forbidden Victoria bar. In every other direction lay those sidebar stories that add muscle to good writing: Sara Jane Shannon grieving over her lost lover, the mission stations dangerously beyond enemy lines and George, master of the Cancan and well armoured against insults in the breakfast room.

There were roles in Shakespeare for George. I wondered if Patience saw him in that light. Falstaff was the right image but the wrong character. Then there was Stella Knight, her hangman admirer, the charmingly inebriate Quigley, Bram and the lizard-tongued Emma Lamb with her shiny shoes. Somerset Maugham would have relished these characters. There were short stories or even a film to be written around these undistinguished denizens of Africa's dark night.

•

I came out of this reverie the next morning after a night of vivid dreams. The phone was ringing. The front desk said that a police officer was in the lobby with a message she had to deliver in person. Emma Lamb was waiting for me. We shook hands and she gestured to a sofa between two large palm plants.

'Shall we?'

We sat down as people passed to and from the main doors. The receptionist looked at us and then away as if he knew the reason for this odd meeting in a hotel lobby.

'I believe you knew Sara Jane Shannon.'

I knew then what was coming.

'Not well. She has helped me occasionally.'

'I am sorry to tell you she is dead.'

She had killed herself with the Beretta pocket pistol her lover André Lennox had given her. For her protection, that was why he had given it to her. To save her life, not to take it. She had shot herself in her apartment, sitting in a chair facing the window with a view of the plane trees on the street outside. A neighbour had heard the shot and called the police. There was a note scrawled in red biro on the floor beside the chair.: '*I'm sorry. I couldn't go on.*'

Emma Lamb told me this in a neutral tone of voice, looking at me for any reaction.

'Thank you,' I said, 'but why have you come to tell me this?'

'Bram thought you would like to know before everyone else does. You can see her if you want.'

●

There were two uniformed police officers in the room. They had laid her on her bed, still dressed in jeans and T-shirt, both now covered in dry blood. She had said her gun would stop a man at close range. The small calibre had not made as much of a mess as I imagined.

One side of her head had a small scorch-marked hole partially covered by leakage of brain matter. Her facial features were untouched. The gold chain with the small gold medallion was still around her neck. It was smeared with blood. I lifted the medallion slightly from her body and looked at one of the officers.

'For her family,' I said.

He nodded. I raised her head gently, unhooked the chain and took it off. I wiped it with a handkerchief. I looked at the officer again. He looked away. I put it in my pocket.

There was an almost empty bottle of vodka lying on the floor. Next to it was a small empty bottle labelled as sleeping pills. She had wanted to make sure. The officers were taking photographs. A mortuary assistant was waiting to take the body away. Sara Jane looked weary, sad and finally alone as she had been in life. Her beauty had gone. I looked around the room. The reek of blood and vodka clung to everything.

There were framed photos on her dressing table of Lennox in army uniform, Lennox with his arms around her, Lennox cooking over a campfire, face turned to the camera, laughing.

There were no family photos. I looked at the bookshelves. Collected poems of Keats, books on Middle Eastern history and Proust's *À la recherche du temps perdu* in translation. I opened the book, half expecting to find pristine pages of an unread text inside, but they were well thumbed and worn. *In Search of Lost Time.* I wish I had known. We could have talked about it.

There was only a police car outside to suggest anything undue had happened inside the small apartment. The trees were in leaf along a shaded suburban street, their branches meeting overhead to form a leafy arch; the small front lawns were carefully mown. The only sound was birdsong and distant traffic.

The calm outside denied the end to life in that small apartment. Sara Jane must have looked out at this scene in her final moments. She would have shaken a fist at the trees. Hers would have been a hurt beyond all telling.

•

I drove to the Frank Johnson School and left a note for Patience saying I would pick her up after school. There was only one place to go after that.

The Cancan was almost empty. George was polishing glasses. I sat down heavily on a bar stool. He began to reach for the cocktail ingredients when I ordered a beer, then changed my mind. Whisky sour was her cocktail. This is where Sara Jane went on the first date with the man she loved. I reached into my pocket and took out the gold medallion showing the coordinates of this bar. A gift of imagination from someone who must have cared for her deeply. I drank the cocktail and left.

I sketched out the story in my room that afternoon, the Remington clacking away like the cicadas outside. Sara Jane had shot herself because the man she loved, the man she was going to marry, had been killed. There was nothing else left in her life. The misfortune of war had taken everything away. In a final tribute to André Lennox she had killed herself with the gun he had given her, thus performing the old Hindu ritual of sati, although in this case the flames from a funeral pyre had become a bullet from a .22 Beretta pistol.

She had not even waited for his funeral. Now it was her turn. It was a good story for the magazine. I would weave into it the wave of anger and despair among the white population that had followed the downing of the second Viscount. On the opposite side of that coin lay the concealed joy among most, but not all, of the African population. Lennox was a much-publicised war hero for the regime.

Outside it had begun to rain. Nowhere in the world has rain like Africa. Night can fall in the middle of the day, bringing with it rivers from the dark heavens. It was getting dark and still raining when I realised that I had failed to pick Patience up. The gift of a lovely shoulder bag would not save me from the roiling anger that swirled within this remarkable woman.

Remarkable was the wrong word. It made her sound like a business executive. She lent passion to her opinions, had the courage to make the risky drives to the border and loved Shakespeare with an obsession driven not just by the language or the range of characters or the poetry, but also by the desire to challenge the white man in his cultural homeland. What if Shakespeare had been black? It would be a different world, was her answer. And she was right. She saw and explored the world in a very different way from me. That is why I had fallen in love.

Marion came in to turn down the bed and tidy the room for the night. She paused at the door, twisting her hands, looking embarrassed, glancing at me, then away. She had serviced my room for several weeks now.

I gave her a generous tip in US dollars, which would gain her much more on the black market. She gave a little bob and left. I wrote out a note of apology to Patience begging for forgiveness. I handed it to George.

•

Since Sara Jane had few friends and no living relatives that I knew of, and since she had worked for me, although with little effect, I made the funeral arrangements myself. There was a small brick-built Anglican church in town with a plaque outside giving the date 1921. The elderly vicar had read about Sara Jane's death and kept muttering to himself 'far too young, far too young' as we chose the hymns and readings. Not being a church man, although I like the liturgy and the music, I followed the vicar's suggestions. He recommended 'Guide me, O thy great Redeemer' as the first hymn and read the opening verse in a sonorous voice.

'Guide me, O thy great Redeemer,
Pilgrim through this barren land;
I am weak, but thou art mighty;
Hold me with thy powerful hand.'

We were standing by the altar in an empty church. The vicar was proud of his voice and spoke as if addressing his congregation. The words brought me to tears. Sara Jane had indeed been a pilgrim in a barren land.

I chose the reading, a familiar choice from the few funerals I had been to: Christina Rossetti's 'Remember'.

The vicar nodded his approval and disappeared into the vestry. He returned with a copy of the text.

'Very popular,' he said and asked me to read the opening lines.

'Remember me when I am gone away,
Gone far away into the silent land;
When you can no more hold me by the hand,
Nor I half turn to go yet turning stay.'

Sara Jane's death made three small paragraphs in the local press. All telling the same story: American photographer takes her own life. No mention was made of Lennox, whose death notices and obituaries had run over pages.

Funerals were held quickly. The mortuaries were small and

designed for a much smaller population. Black and white had separate cemeteries, a custom rather than legal requirement that suited both sides.

About fifteen of us gathered at the church on a warm and cloudy morning. A few of André Lennox's army friends were there, as well as Fiona Foxley, a photographer I had seen occasionally in the Cancan, always with a different man. Sara Jane's servant, who had cooked and cleaned for her, sat at the back, dabbing her eyes with a handkerchief.

Halfway through the service, the door creaked open. Several heads turned to see the latecomer. Patience was wearing a long, dark dress with the butterfly clasp in her hair. She went to a back pew, knelt in prayer and sat down. I felt ridiculously pleased. I decided not to attend the cremation as planned. I had no wish to see the casket slide through curtains into whatever lay beyond.

There was neither reproach nor even a hint of irritation when we drove back into town. She spoke quietly. Sara Jane's death seemed to have had a surprising effect on her. She understood why I had failed to meet her the previous night. She knew little about Sara Jane beyond what she had read in the papers. She knew I would be going to the funeral. It was a tragedy that only a woman could truly understand, she said. Lennox had betrayed her, that's why she killed herself. When I gently remarked that Lennox had hardly chosen to be killed, she replied that no man would understand what she meant.

We ate at Sandro's and continued talking. I could see that something beyond the funeral had upset her. She talked of George and how his work had won him promotion over the years, of the school, where another Shakespeare play was planned, then she looked out of the window and took a deep breath. Her face told me she was holding back the tears.

She drained her glass of white wine and asked for another. She told me that late the previous night the staff and their families at a mission in the Eastern Highlands had been massacred. Three couples, two single women, three children and a baby had been axed, bayoneted or battered to death.

I sat there for a moment without a word. Missionaries were supposed to be sacrosanct, allowed to run small schools, treat minor illnesses and do God's work, safe from the threats and predations of both sides. Most were known to be sympathetic to the nationalist cause. Several mission stations had gone further, actively helping the insurgents with food and medical treatment. But others had helped wounded troops while waiting for evacuation.

She told me she had been woken with the news in the early hours. I was too shocked to ask any of the obvious questions. These were the missionaries she had visited when she disappeared from the city. She knew them, if not well, then well enough to remember the names of the children. They were all from England and worked in the Pentecostal church.

'Men, women and children,' she whispered. 'Not just children: babies. Taken from the mission in the afternoon, lined up and murdered. They did not use guns for fear that nearby troops would hear the gunfire. I knew those people. They were good. They helped us, for God's sake!'

She folded her arms on the table and laid her head down. I put a hand on her head, stroking her hair with the yellow butterfly clasp. I could hear her sobbing. More heads turned. The waiter came over, asking if everything was all right. She raised her head and wiped away the tears. We had hardly eaten. I paid the bill.

I drove her back towards the township. We were halfway there when she told me to stop and turn around. She had to see George. For the rest of the journey, about twenty minutes, she talked without cease. She said that the massacre would be all over the TV news that night. The local and international press would be in full cry. This was a story that would break all round the world, followed by condemnation from every quarter.

The immediate question was the identity of the perpetrators. Both sides had shown themselves capable of barbarism, but I did not think government forces would kill missionaries.

I waited for her to defend what seemed indefensible. She didn't.

'We will blame your army, special forces, undercover agents and say they did it to blacken our name. But that will be a lie.'

'It's not my army.'

She looked across at me in the dark front seats of the car.

'Isn't it?'

'Stop it,' I said.

She shook her head and sat gazing at the headlights as they swept the road ahead.

'I know my people,' she said. 'This is what war does. You know why they did this? Revenge. Blood will have blood. Kill anybody white because that is what you have done to us. You know what happened in that last big raid? No, you don't, because you were too busy getting drunk and bedding that puppy girl. You killed hundreds, literally hundreds, of our people, men and women.'

'I accept and condemn that, but surely that doesn't justify this kind of atrocity?' I said.

'There were women in that camp, cleaners, cooks and medics. None were spared. So don't look at me like that. And don't give me your pseudo-Christian civilised values. Blood for blood – that's what this war is about.'

'I get that, Patience. I'm not arguing with you. And, by the way, I haven't been bedding that puppy girl, as you call her.'

She ignored the remark.

'I'm sorry, but this is what happens,' she said. 'This is what your people have done.'

Me and you, us and them, your people and my people. The same old story, and with what naivety could one expect it to be any different? I had forgotten the raids that were continuing almost every week. Many were unreported small actions by special forces intent on murder, whether insurgents or civilians. Pinks had been full of rumours for days about a major cross-border attack that would take every helicopter and plane in the air force. The raid had been a huge operation.

'Those raids target fighters,' I said gently. 'I accept civilians get killed, but they don't set out to kill missionaries and their children.'

For a moment, I thought she was going to jump out of the car. She gave me a look as if a fire had been lit behind her eyes.

She shook her head. 'Just take me to George.'

She went straight to the ladies' room at the hotel. Her face was tear-stained. Somehow the yellow butterfly clip had come loose. She held it in her hand.

I waited in the lobby, partially shielded from the comings and goings at the reception desk by the potted palms. The lobby hummed like a beehive. People were checking in, checking out, booking taxis, tipping staff, paying bills, asking for transport, questioning reception staff about the weather.

I heard a woman asking for the best restaurant in town. More than ever, I felt unmoored from normality. Even nations at war could hang on to a sense of the normal, judging from what my parents had told me about the London Blitz in the 1940s. As a doctor in central London, working long hours through the bombing, my father had seen his share of horrors. But the milkman still came most days, buses and trams moved along the streets, the pubs stayed open, serving weak beer.

There were no spirits except bathtub gin offered to friends on Sunday mornings before lunch. My job as a precocious ten-year-old was to serve the drinks. I swirled the Angostura around the base of the glass, poured in a large slug of gin and that was it. No ice, no slice of lemon, no mixer either. I watched them drink these lethal mixtures and always remembered the pleasure my parents and their friends took from such parties.

That was normal wartime life. People grumbled but got on with it. Humour and a belief that the past life would somehow return kept everyone sane. Here everything had become a kaleidoscope of make-believe, an old black-and-white film played slowly backwards. A small, outnumbered army and air force were fighting ill-trained forces bent on their country's destruction. There was courage and savagery on both sides.

Should I reveal my increasing confusion to readers in America and around the world and let them divine the truth behind a tormented nation? The magazine was proud of its overseas sales. It saw itself as an intellectual diplomat for decent liberal values. 'Fair to All' was the motto engraved in granite above the Fifth Avenue entrance.

How could I be fair to all when Patience was right? You can't stay neutral in this war. Choose your side, she said. The danger was that one side was choosing me. Patience emerged from the ladies' room, waved goodbye and climbed the circular staircase to the bar.

•

They laid on an ancient Dakota aircraft the next day to fly journalists and one or two devious-looking strangers to an airstrip close to the Holy Mount Mission. It was assumed that everyone who could loosely call himself or herself a writer or journalist would want to see at first hand the bodies of those slaughtered and hear the accounts of the African staff who had managed to glimpse the killings from their hiding places. I had received a message telling me to report to the airbase at 10 a.m.

Quigley turned up at the hotel to offer a lift. He looked sober. When I declined, he got out of the car and reached into a backpack and produced a flask.

'It's not going to be nice, but this will help.'

I told him I was not going. He looked incredulous.

'Why not?'

I shrugged and walked back into the hotel. The desk clerk handed me a telex. I didn't have to open it to know that Meredith wanted a full account from witnesses who had survived the massacre. I ignored it. The magazine paid good money, but I was not going to 'report fullest on massacre and aftermath'. I had no wish to add to the toll of dead I had already seen. I did not want the eyes of a dead missionary staring at me in accusation as Cephas Msika's had done.

What would I do there? Describe that collection of wooden huts gathered around a stone-built church, watch as the tarpaulins were drawn back to reveal bloody, broken bodies, their faces twisted in terror? That would only convince one side they were dealing with monsters while the other neatly reversed that view. Nationalists would churn out propaganda claiming that government special forces had committed the atrocity. It would make no difference. Everyone with a stake in this squalid war had already made up their minds as to who were the villains and who the heroes.

It was Freud, I think, who talked about hatred born of small differences. I carried that thought back to my room. I wondered whether Patience had found some consolation with George. She had always known this would happen. Her faith in the freedom fighters led her to believe that they were different from any other men under arms. Her sincerity was beguiling, but was it really honest? How many times had she told me she despised racial hatred?

Her struggle, as she saw it, was to right a historic wrong. She would teach pupils that hatred based on race, colour or class would end the world one day. She would make them reach for Shakespeare and read a tragedy by a man who knew the power of evil and the price that had to be paid. She wouldn't tell them that hatred and atrocity in wartime cut both ways.

I wanted to drive to the township that night, wrap my arms around her and tell her that young men with guns confronted with the slaughter of their colleagues would inevitably respond in kind. That did not excuse their barbarity.

I wondered whether I should have joined the press pack and gone like the good servant of a big media company to witness the victims of an atrocity in the mountains.

For security, the missionaries had built their settlement high up, with views of the country around. It had done nothing to deter the gang that had murdered them. There were no fences, dogs, searchlights or armed guards to protect them. Did they go to their deaths with faith unshaken, as did the Christian martyrs of old? Or did terrible doubt cloud their minds in the final moments?

•

I had promised myself an early sober night, an unlikely ambition in the circumstances. I walked across the square, hearing the music drifting from the hotel, just audible over the racket of the cicadas. The fountains were still.

The club was almost empty. I sat quietly in the corner with a beer. I knew very well what was coming. There is a scene in the film *The Way to the Stars* when a World War II bomber crew slowly enters the briefing room after a mission in which they have seen their much-loved commanding officer shot down. The men are silent, hunched up and hollowed out. They sit down, release their parachute harnesses, light cigarettes and stare at the floor or the ceiling. An officer begins the briefing in the usual clipped matter-of-fact manner, as if reporting a road accident. He is talking to a void.

This was the scene as the press corps came into the club.

Their clothes were covered in dust – kicked up by the aircraft propellers on a dirt strip, I guessed. No one spoke until drinks were in their hands. They muttered without looking at each other about the bumpy ride of the plane back, the terrible sandwiches laid on by the Information Ministry and the absence of any alcohol on the trip. No one paid any attention to me, for which I was grateful.

Fiona Foxley, the photographer, came and sat down beside me. Her dark hair, tied back in a ponytail, had turned grey with dust. Her bush jacket was stained with sweat. She was holding a glass of what looked like neat gin. Her hands were shaking.

'You should have come with us,' she said.

I nodded, trying to pretend I was giving the statement some thought.

'You should have seen what we saw.'

There was nothing to say. I raised my empty beer glass and caught the barman's eye. He came over with a whisky and a gin for Fiona. He knew what everyone was drinking.

'It was the babies. There were three of them.'

She drank deeply and attempted to brush the dust off her jacket. She lit another cigarette, blowing a plume to the nicotine-stained ceiling.

'You call yourself a reporter, don't you? Why weren't you there?'

I shook my head. Best to let the wind blow.

'My pix of those children will be on your editor's desk in an hour's time. They'll be seeing what we saw. Where's your fucking story? Don't you care?'

I put a hand out and rested it on her arm. She shook it off.

'That's the trouble with you hotshot magazine writers. You don't want to know what's happening. You don't want to see what we see. Know why? Because we get down and dirty, while you prefer to stay here where it's nice and safe and you can lunch on white tablecloths, drink fucking cocktails in that fucking Cancan fucking bar and write those long, fancy articles your bosses like so much in New York. "On the one hand, on the other" – isn't that your style?'

'No,' I said.

'No, what?'

'That's not true. I don't have to look at dead people to care as much as you do,' I said.

She jerked up, spilling some of her drink.

'You call those dead people lying there with their babies lies?'

She wasn't listening. This was a losing argument. I looked at the crowd at the bar. No one was paying any attention.

'Let's talk about it another time,' I said and started to get up.

She pulled me back and began to cry. She leant back in her chair, looking up at the ceiling, crying and smoking all at once, hot tears running down her cheeks. I felt like a voyeur. She looked at me through her tears. She finished the drink.

'I should never have gone. Fucking babies,' she said.

She was saying the same thing as Patience. You can't stay neutral in this war.

•

I walked across the square back to the hotel. I had hated being talked to like that. She was right. I should have gone to see dead babies. It was almost 6 p.m. I would take a taxi to the township and go to the Victoria. Too bad if they didn't like the sight of me. If she wasn't there, they would know where she was.

She might be rehearsing another play, Shakespeare no doubt. *Henry V* would work well with young minds; all that swordplay and 'once more unto the breach, dear friends'.

There was another possibility: she had gone off to one of her mysterious meetings. There was one night every week when she vanished. I'm just with friends, she would say. When I pressed her, she told me kindly enough to mind my own business.

'You cannot know all my secrets, just as I don't know all yours.'

Bram fell into step beside me near the fountains, as if it was quite normal to meet in this way. I knew I was being followed but did not expect such close attention.

'You should have gone,' he said.

I stopped.

'What do you want?'

'Hey, take it easy. I thought I might join you for a drink.'

'Another time.'

He nodded to the hotel.

'I'll be there later if you're around.'

He left, walking away under the trees, the darkness folding around him, leaving only a shadowy outline. I liked to think he was more than a shadow in a secret world, because I felt there was something decent in the man. But then that was the point of being a secret policeman, wasn't it? To project a comfortable image inviting trust and goodwill.

•

The taxi bumped its way into the township and stopped at the Victoria. The driver gave me the same dark look of disapproval as before and left, making his tyres squeal on the tarmac road.

The new barman who had taken the place of Cephas was on duty. Perhaps in tribute, he wore the same T-shirt with the red fist. The bar was much the same as before – the reggae music, card games and dealers swapping drugs for notes in a corner. I noticed a new addition to the wall posters: the standard image of Che Guevara with beret and gun. Everyone looked at me once, then away.

There was no sign of Patience, Charity or Rosie. I ordered a beer. The barman slid it in front of me, took the money and gave me the exact change, thus refusing the large tip I had included. He walked away to the other end of the bar. There was nowhere to sit. I drank at the counter and waited.

The barman had a brief word with a drinker. He came over to me. I braced to be told to leave or maybe, worse, to be taken outside and robbed, but he simply said, 'She's working late at school.'

This seemed strange after the terrible news that day. Then I reflected that this was exactly what Julia had done after the road ambush. She had gone to her swimming session as planned. Keeping to a routine and living life as normal was clearly a good antidote to shock.

The rehearsal was in full swing when I got there. She didn't see me. I sat at the back of the hall trying to work out which play her pupils were trying to perform. They were doing so with confidence and brio, shouting out the lines and moving around in striding steps, but playing what?

Macbeth, of course. Lady Macbeth was a statuesque teenager, probably sixteen or seventeen years old, who was urging her feckless husband to carry out the murder with real conviction. In a country at war, where so many young people were dying, it seemed an odd choice. But that was Patience.

She was standing beside the stage scribbling notes on a clipboard. She did not interrupt but let the play go on, even when the actors stumbled and forgot their lines. She waited while they collected themselves or took a quick look at the text. It was extraordinarily ambitious to ask these youngsters to learn so much dialogue by heart. For much of the rehearsal they read from the text, but many of the longer passages were delivered without assistance.

The action on stage stopped for a break for water. By some sixth sense, Patience turned and saw me. She smiled a warm smile. The anxiety I had felt about my intrusion faded. I walked to her. She allowed me to kiss her on the cheek. Her young players looked on curiously, then returned to their scripts.

I was about to ask gently about reaction in the township to the massacre but she sensed the question and shook her head.

'What do you think?'

'They were brilliant, but it's a bit bloodthirsty, isn't it?'

'You don't approve?'

'Don't be silly. Of course I approve. It's a wonderful thing to get these kids working like this after school. What do their parents say?'

'They can't wait to see it. If we do this well, the theatre in town will give us a short run.'

The main theatre was on my list to visit. I had not got

round to it because there did not seem much point. A few well-meaning white liberals had got together to run a playhouse on non-racial lines. A worthy cause, but African writers, artists and actors with any ambition had long since left the country. The theatre had fallen back on a steady diet of Oscar Wilde and Noël Coward, spiced up by the occasional Tennessee Williams. To stage a play there with a cast of African schoolchildren playing *Macbeth* was going to be a great adventure. I told Patience I would write about it.

She hugged me, warned me in a whisper not to go back to the Victoria and reminded me that she had said that before. Looking slightly embarrassed, she returned to her players. They had been observing our brief exchange with interest. We agreed to meet the next day.

•

I took a taxi back, feeling elated. Patience was extraordinary. A few weeks ago she had been helping smuggle young men and a few women, not much older than those on stage, across the border to fight and probably die. Here she was, only hours after hearing of a terrible massacre committed by her own people, opening those same young minds to the complex glories of Shakespeare's language and characters carefully crafted to please a Queen and draw laughter from the unwashed mass of groundlings.

Why *Macbeth*? I wondered. What message would these children take from a play that showed the bloody price of failed rebellion? I played with the thought that Patience was trying to stem the flood of recruits by showing just how high that price could be. When the play was performed, every seat would be taken. It would be one of the great events of the township year. And no one in the audience would miss the obvious lesson.

It was late when I got back to the hotel, almost eleven o'clock, but glancing up at the windows I saw the bar was still open. I took the circular staircase, remarking yet again on the one-sided story told by the white pioneers frozen in their silver frames, and went to my room.

There were two messages under my door. I showered, drank some water, lay down on the bed and left the messages unopened. They would only be more urgent but carefully phrased requests for coverage of the massacre.

Our readers needed to understand not just why the conflict was being fought to a bitter and obvious end, Meredith would say. She was always saying that. They also needed to be shown the reality behind the clash of entrenched cultures. What she really wanted was more front-line reporting. Violence, like sex, sells whether in print or on-screen. She didn't say that, but that's what she meant.

The public embraced the role of voyeur eagerly. Why not? It was natural. We humans have been fighting internecine wars since we crawled out of the swamp. War is a natural condition of mankind. 'Periods of peace and happiness are empty pages in the history of the world,' as some old philosopher said. If conflict was a constant, what was wrong with blood-and-guts reporting, or what the cynics in Pinks would call the 'screaming jets' approach to the war news?

Given the bloody finale that was approaching, that would be reasonable. It was certainly what every other journalist in town was doing. But I was not a journalist like them. I was not a war correspondent. I despised them.

•

I woke in the night feeling thirsty. The carafe by the bed was empty. I drank from the bathroom tap. It was 3.30 a.m. I opened the messages. The first was from a Mrs Honeymore Shannon in New York. It began: '*I am Sara Jane's mother. She told me about you.*' This was a shock, because Sara Jane had said she had not talked to her mother for years. She had certainly never mentioned a memorable name like Honeymore.

Mrs Shannon said how sorry she was that she had been unable to come to her daughter's funeral. They had been estranged for some years and she had heard the news from a neighbour who had seen it in the *New York Times*. Could she trespass on my time to tell her about Sara Jane's life in Africa, and why that life had ended so tragically?

I put the message aside. I wondered how she had come up with my name. Not that it mattered. I would write briefly saying I did not know Sara Jane well, but like most of her friends I knew she had fallen deeply in love with an army officer. But how to explain her suicide? From the message it was unclear whether Honeymore Shannon knew her daughter had killed herself. On reflection, she must have known. The paper would have made that clear, even in the coded way they report such things.

I would try to explain the nature of Sara's love, her total surrender to emotions that few of us experience. I paused. I was using clichés to express something I did not myself truly understand. Perhaps none of her friends did either. Sara Jane had been in love. That love had been brutally cut short, but why kill herself? That's what Mrs Shannon would want to know, as would we all. I began typing out a short note to her. They would be dead words, which would not help. I owed Sara Jane something more. I went back to the beginning.

She had been in her early thirties when she died. From one angle she was a lost soul seeking some meaning in a wayward life, very much the pilgrim in a barren land. Looked at in another way, she was a talented photographer who knew the power of her attraction to men and made her own choices in life.

According to her, and I still doubted this story, she had used that attraction to make a lot of money in a few months by selling herself to rich men in New York. 'You'd be surprised how many perfectly normal well-educated women do this,' she had told me. Well, I would be surprised, because frankly I did not believe her. It was part of the myth she had created for herself: the risk-taking photographer in Vietnam, the taboo-breaking call girl in New York. Two sides of a silver dollar.

That was the woman she wanted us to see. The image fitted her perfectly. I could see her using sexual charm to fly with the Marines into combat. That would be Sara Jane. The call-girl story was a clumsy attempt to wrap herself in the cloak of a social rebel, a young woman happy to upend the boring bourgeois moral code and expose the hypocrisy of rich men buying sex.

If she had really been a call girl, she would not have done so to expose hypocrisy. She would have done so to make money and to prove that a woman can choose to walk on the wild side just as much as a man. She always sided with the underdog. She liked the down-and-out loner facing long odds in life. I could see her at parties making a point of talking to the shy tongue-tied man in the corner.

In another life she would have made a fine radical politician. That is why she had been so sharp with me when we first met. I was everything she had grown to dislike and distrust: an entitled correspondent with the power of a major magazine company behind him, looking to gain some Pulitzer-winning glory in a dirty little war. She had changed when she saw me with Patience that night. Then she knew I was like her, an outsider happy to break unwritten rules.

This troubled me. Here was a woman from a broken home in New Jersey who had stolen a camera from a shop on 41st Street and learnt how to use it, and then years later had gone to repay the money with interest, only to find that it had become a porn shop. That's what she had told me. She would have found a brutal metaphor in that – if it was true.

Perhaps in revenge for her background, this woman had not hesitated to align herself with an outcast regime and throw herself into a relationship with its most famous, charismatic soldier. The rebel then found something deeper in herself. She had come to understand why this man was fighting. That had touched a nerve somewhere. His battle became hers. She sympathised with a society that was going to fight to the end. That was the way she saw the world. That was the way I was coming to see the world too.

I fell asleep thinking of Sara Jane and her gold medallion.

•

I awoke the next morning feeling like one of those wrecks salvaged from the deep that emerge with water streaming from a rusty superstructure. But in the depths of sleep I had found the words for Mrs Honeymore Shannon.

'*Those she loved will forgive her because we loved her too,*' I wrote. '*Yours sincerely.*'

That was true. Sara Jane was a pilgrim in a rebel country. I loved her for that.

I broke my breakfast rule and ate what the menu described as 'a champion way to start the day': eggs, sausage, bacon, tomatoes, mushroom and fried bread. There was no sign of George. I had put off opening the second envelope but did so over coffee. It consisted of several lines of poetry:

> *She's lost him completely. And now she tries to find*
> *His lips in the lips of each new lover.*
> *She tries in the embrace of each new lover*
> *To convince herself that it is to him*
> *That she gives herself, only to him.*
> *In Despair.*

I folded up the message, went to the front desk downstairs and asked for a packet of cigarettes. Any kind, I said. They were a rough, cheap local brand, a surprise in a country that grew tobacco. I didn't care.

I thought that Marie Claire and I had reached if not a settlement of some kind then at least a truce. The poem would have been a translation, probably from the French. It did not sound like Rimbaud, Baudelaire or Paul Valéry. Far too modern. Any poetry in translation can slip into modern usage.

I cursed her and lit a cigarette.

I went to my room, took the typewriter from its case and slid in a sheet of paper. I had no intention of replying with a line or two of Shakespeare on the disease of jealousy. Something mad from Dylan Thomas, perhaps, a mischievous magician who created rhythmic beauty from words that usually lacked any meaning beyond their place on the page. Marie Claire and I could duel back and forth, flinging bitter lines of poetry at each other. Perhaps one day she would leave me alone. Perhaps one day I would want her to.

•

There was a briefing at the ministry that morning. I would not normally have gone, but new regulations meant my press pass needed to be extended again. The rows of chairs in the conference room were almost all taken when I arrived. The press corps had grown to several scores of reporters, cameramen and hangers-on.

I sat at the back. Peter Fryer, the Director of Information, mounted a small rostrum and announced that there would be a facility trip in an hour's time to the scene of heavy fighting in the north-east operational area. Interviews would be arranged with troops who had been in combat and with captured terrorists.

'Guerrillas,' shouted somebody.

'Whatever,' said Fryer. 'But remember, these are the people who slaughtered the missionaries.'

Every hand went up when a count was taken. I slid down in my seat, feeling strangely guilty at not joining the general excitement.

Back in my room, I began to work on what I saw as the real story of the war. Here was a cast of characters, ordinary and extraordinary, who had been thrown together in this distant place like driftwood on a beach. The alcoholic Quigley, who cast a brilliant eye over a changing world through a veil of booze; George, serving cocktails to people he hated; the unknowable Jeeze; the British hangman who could recite the last words of every prisoner he dropped to their deaths; Marion, my room cleaner; Charity, the teacher who said she was too plump to swim.

The Greeks were wrong. Character is not fate. Fate is fate, a roll of the dice, a spin of the casino wheel. These people had found themselves here by chance. They could see what the soldiers and their commanders, the politicians and their agents could not see. As such, they were worth more than a few carefully coached words from a troopie who would no doubt describe the successful contact with the enemy as part of an overall winning strategy.

He would speak to the world's press with microphones pressed close to a face smeared with camouflage paint. A press officer would observe the scene with a tutorial eye. There would be footage of troops jumping into helicopters, of a gunner firing the .20-mm-calibre Browning at fleeing black figures. Why would I want to be party to such a propaganda circus?

The trouble was, my readers wanted the blood and guts of war, and who could blame them? Every film company, publishing house and newspaper editor knew that war stories, especially World War II stories, sold well. Audiences loved them. They tapped into something deep in our DNA: the fascination with, and need for, conflict.

War, with its heroism and horror, gave ordinary people the excitement denied them in their workaday existence, a view of a life as they wished to live it. Blood will have blood, as Patience had said. We like to watch it spill and flow from a safe cinematic distance.

I felt ashamed. I wasn't being paid to retreat into a sanctuary for pious minds. I wasn't here to cherish my high moral values. I wasn't here to pass on the views of a retired hangman. I wasn't here to describe the aching beauty of the mountains, rivers, lakes and plains that made this country one of the most beautiful in Africa. I might tell myself that I was a magazine writer who didn't need to get down and dirty with the rest of the hacks, as Fiona had said, and report the blood spilling out of this corpse of a country. But that would be my shadow self, talking to someone I had left behind long ago. Because that was exactly what I was here for.

•

I strapped myself into the hold of an old Dakota aircraft with the rest of the press corps. The pilot told us the plane had first flown at the battle of Arnhem in 1944 some thirty years earlier. No smoking was the rule. There were no windows. In semi-darkness we thumped and bumped our way through cloud until the aircraft steadied in clear air.

The pilot told us cheerfully that we were still in missile range. 'They've got no radar, but they can sure hear us coming,' he said.

I worked out that we would be two hours on the ground and then an hour's flight return. That would put me back in my room by early evening, in time to write up my notes. As so often, it didn't work out like that.

It was the second soldier who gave me the story I had been searching for, the story that would lift my readers from their morning commute to air-conditioned offices, a kiss on the cheek in the evening from a faithless husband to a faithful wife, a cocktail, steak supper in front of the television, summer camps for the children and winter sports on the slopes for the whole family. Those were my readers.

His uniform was stained with sweat. Dark patches on the sleeves looked like blood. He was sitting on sandbags with the sun behind him, so that his face was half shaded. In spite of the camouflage paint, I could see he was exhausted. There are things you see that you can never unsee, that remain with you in dreams or nightmares. That soldier's shaded face smeared with sweat, dust and camouflage remains with me.

His eyes were not the vacant eyes of those poor bastards in Vietnam looking sightless and shocked after combat. They stood out from the mask of his face lit by some inner fire, the adrenalin rush after close-quarter combat. His hands shook slightly as he lit one cigarette after another. A press officer stood nearby with a tape recorder. No photographs were allowed.

His description of the fighting was brief. His unit had set an ambush outside a village known to be feeding terrorists. Claymore mines had been placed across the dirt track leading from the village into the bush. The villagers always took another track down to the river. An unusually large number of fighters had been seen making their way towards the village just after daybreak. He said 'fighters', not 'terrorists'.

The mines had been detonated by remote control when the group entered the kill zone. A few terrorists – here he changed the name – had been killed immediately, but the rest, including the wounded, fought back, using grenade-launchers and rifle fire. The contact was close, both sides no more than 30 metres apart, firing through a thin screen of bush across the track. In a few minutes it was all over.

He lit another cigarette and looked at us, his eyes moving from face to face as if making sure he could remember everyone listening to his story. Someone asked how many had been killed.

'We counted ten bodies, but more will have died. Most died on the track from the claymores, others crawled away into the bush and began firing back. They were brave bastards,' he said, and got off the sandbags, ready to leave.

'Your casualties?' someone asked.

There was a long pause here. He looked up at the sky, then down at us, and lit another cigarette.

'We lost one, with two wounded.'

'What about their wounded?'

'There weren't any.'

'Tell us what it feels like to be in close combat. I mean . . . erm . . . were you scared?'

Everyone groaned and turned to look at the questioner, a young woman with several cameras slung around her neck. It was a perfectly fair question. He smiled at her.

'We were all scared, them and us, but when you start firing you're in a different world. Training takes over.'

'Why were there no terrorists wounded?'

'There were.'

'What happened to them?'

'We shot them,' he said, and walked away.

The promised interviews with captured terrorists would not take place.

•

That wasn't the whole story. I could have built a book around that soldier when I found out later what had really happened. He had stood over the wounded with others in the unit. They were too badly wounded for interrogation. One bullet each in the head. That way they saved ammunition and made it easier to search the bodies for documents.

As he had raised his pistol to the last of the wounded, the dying man had looked up at him with cloudy eyes and whispered '*esche*', the local-language word for 'chief'.

He looked more closely at the man bleeding heavily from the chest and stomach. Age and agony had changed the face, but he recognised the cook who had worked for his family for years. Godwin had risen from gardener to kitchen boy and then to a full cook. He had grown up with Godwin, eaten the food he prepared, kicked a football around with him (much to his parents' disapproval), smoked forbidden cigarettes with him behind the compound huts. At Christmas he would smuggle the remains of the turkey and cake down to the servants' quarters where Godwin lived with his family. One day, Godwin had vanished, leaving his wife and children behind.

'*Esche*' – the word struggling from a mouth bubbling with bloody froth.

He had looked at Godwin for a moment. Their eyes met. Then he shot him.

I learnt all this later. It was then I knew I had a story that would make my readers pause at the water cooler and repeat it in the bar after work. It would win me praise, sacksful of readers' letters and maybe even a bigger by-line.

The cook who became a rebel fighter and his friend, his master's son, who became a soldier. They had met in the bush with their guns, one with a true belief in the righteousness of killing, the other trapped in the coils of a war he knew to be lost but happy to kill all the same.

It was only when I talked to that soldier later that I knew I was getting closer to the real story of the war.

Chapter Twelve

'Tell me about your girlfriend, the French one.'

Patience was sitting on the sofa in my hotel room dressed in a slim black dress that fell from neck to knees, black disc earrings and giraffe-print shoes. The same butterfly clasp was slid into her hair. She had heard I had been on a facility trip to the operational area. I never knew how, but I had given up worrying about such things. I had long learnt that in this town everyone spied on everyone else. Even the switchboard girls in the hotel could be bribed to reveal guests' conversations.

She had told me she was coming to dinner in the hotel that evening. She didn't ask, she just told me. She brushed aside my mild objections and said that a township girl was as entitled to dine at Franklins as anyone else, which, while true, did not exactly conform to the unwritten rules of the hotel. Nor did it make much sense of her previous refusal to eat at a white man's table, as she put it. I decided not to mention that.

Patience knew about Marie Claire because she had heard me

cry out her name one night, not during our lovemaking, which would have been embarrassing, but during a nightmare. I had woken with a strangled shout and called out her name. At the time, she had pressed me no further when I explained that I had once had a girlfriend in Paris and that our relationship had ended sadly for both of us.

'What happened?' she said now.

'I told you, it was a brief affair, which ended badly.'

'Tell me more. I am curious.'

'Why? I don't ask you about your ex-lovers.'

'Oh, I have had lots of lovers, have I?'

'I didn't say lots. Of course, you've had boyfriends. Look at you, you're gorgeous.'

With that she got up, walked across the room to a full-length cheval mirror, posed this way and that and finally turned, looking back over her shoulder.

'Lovers, not boyfriends,' she said. 'Boyfriends are for little girls. Buy me a drink.'

It was early in the week and the Cancan was not full. The management had recently put the prices up, blaming sanctions and a shortage of wine and spirits. The real reason was to discourage what they called 'unwanted customers', a euphemism for the shabbily dressed journalists and their hangers-on who inhabited Pinks and who occasionally wandered across the square seeking peace and a quiet drink.

George, imperturbable as ever, served the usual silver bullets and handed us dinner menus. Our table had been booked in half an hour's time, he said. I looked at Patience. She smiled and nodded.

She raised a glass and clinked mine.

'What's it to be, your French lover or another famous victory in the white man's war?'

I told her about my Paris affair. It was a relief. For the first time I could try to make someone understand the collision of feelings from which I seemed unable to free myself, the bubbling mix of guilt and desire, the longing to turn back time and lie with her in the sun while barges chugged past the floating piscine on the Seine and the boys watched the girls with their tops off, just as I knew they were watching Marie Claire. She was fair-skinned and came from Brittany, where she said there was as much rain as sun in the summer.

My Paris memories were of water spilling down the gutters in the morning, bald old men playing boules on sandy strips beside the boulevards, the hunt for rare books in the stalls along the Seine and the pleasure in finding a water-stained edition of Baudelaire's letters to his mother, half the pages missing but still a painful record of a man at the mercy of his own mad genius. Marie Claire was always there.

And so I went on, twisting and turning, letting George give me another bullet, easing the flow of further confessions.

Patience looked at me throughout, sipping her drink, her face slipping from slight smile to frown while listening to this confessional incantation. I knew the questions were coming. She was like her name, but she wanted her say. There was silence and a long pause when I stopped.

'You're a bloody fool,' she said finally.

I shook my head.

'Why are men so stupid? You're still in love with her.'

It was then that I wanted her above all else, to possess her, to hold her. Somehow, I had to anchor her to my life, never let her go. Marie Claire was a memory I had enshrined in some remote part of my psyche, a memory to be recalled with the masochism that attaches to guilt. I wasn't in love with two women. I was in love with Patience Matatu.

•

She was sitting on the bed the next morning, the sheets kicked back, quite naked, when there was a knock on the door. I was fresh out of the shower with a towel around my waist. Before I could say anything, the door opened and Marion came in.

She looked at Patience, then me, then back to Patience. She frowned, squinting her eyes as if doubting what she was seeing. She had probably walked in on many a couple in various states of undress or even tumbling around in bed. But I doubt she had seen an African woman in a white man's bed. For a few seconds, no one said anything.

'I'm sorry,' Marion said, backing out and beginning to close the door.

'Stay,' said Patience. 'Don't mind me.'

With that, she swung her legs onto the floor, wound the top sheet around herself and walked into the bathroom, trailing the sheet behind her. Marion watched her as if witnessing a visitation. She stepped back into the corridor, closing the door.

'I'm sorry,' I said to the door.

The door opened a crack. Marion's head appeared.

'I'll come back later, sir,' she said.

•

I looked closely in the bathroom mirror that morning. I was not the same man who had crossed the border so long ago, or so it seemed. I certainly wasn't the same man I had been in Paris a few months before that. I tried to calibrate the events that had reshaped my life.

First, an assignment to the most beautiful city in Europe as the base for writing about European affairs.

'Skip the politics,' Meredith Kaplan had said. 'Give readers what they really want: the people big and small, the food, the wine, the smell of the place. Paint them a picture of somewhere they will never visit except in their imagination. Give them the paint box, allow them to imagine they might one day travel to these foreign places you visit.'

She was always saying things like that, advice born of a wish that she too had been a correspondent in the field, where in her own mind she would have done a much better job than me.

A military coup had then taken me to Lisbon and on to Africa, where the old colonies were crumbling. Sitting on a hotel balcony one evening in one such colony, looking at the Indian Ocean lapping at a long beach, I wondered how much time I could spend there and whether I could get a boat out to the islands. A waiter arrived with a cold beer and a telex message: '*Exforeign probrady. Cross the border immediate.*' They were asking me to go to a country whose name meant very little to me. What I did know I didn't like. They could have sent anyone.

The face staring back from the mirror now was older, more worn, stamped with the look of a man who needed a slug of gin before lunch. There were dark crescents beneath hooded eyes. I felt a moment of unmanly self-pity while running a razor over the rough bristle of a four-day beard.

Chapter Thirteen

I met Emerson in a smart bungalow in the Indian quarter of town. I was given no other name for him. Patience had arranged the meeting after much discussion. She listened to my reservations carefully and did not argue. She told me Emerson was the internal leader of the nationalist forces, a man hunted by Special Branch and certain to be tortured if caught, and then probably killed.

I had wanted nothing to do with an interview, since it placed in jeopardy my whole assignment. Talking to such a wanted man would inevitably lead to discovery. The secret police had informers everywhere. I would be declared a prohibited immigrant and expelled. And for what? More one-sided propaganda, more banal statements about liberation and freedom, more evasion of simple truths about the slaughterhouse of war and the sacrifice of a generation to satisfy the vanity of men who wished to be seen as warriors? Such men were greedy for war. Victory was a prize there for the plucking; there was no need to prolong the conflict.

Inevitable negotiations would lead to independence.

Patience was not angry with me. She understood my reservations. But she said Emerson was essential to understanding the future. His vision was shared with the very people I had declined to meet, the leadership in exile. This was an arrangement that suited everyone, she said.

I cannot pretend that I was honest about this meeting. The more I heard about it, the less I wanted to meet the man. But Patience was as seductive as the sirens of old Greece. And so after dark, and with two changes of vehicles, I was driven to a smart bungalow. I was asked to look at the floor of the car throughout the journey. Patience said nothing except a few clipped words to the driver.

I was taken through a large, well-furnished living room to a terrace at the back. There was a swimming pool and, at the far end of a long garden, cricket nets. This must have been the house of a wealthy businessman. He had probably left the country for the duration.

The man I met was bearded, wearing a black beret and blue overalls. Wrap-around dark glasses concealed the upper half of his face. He looked like a cartoon gangster. The hair at his temples was grey. I placed him in his sixties. Behind him, sitting silently, was another man in a mask.

I was beckoned to sit down and took an uncomfortable wooden kitchen chair. A servant poured tea and placed the pot on a small table beside me. There was a brief exchange between Patience and the man I was to interview. Then she turned to me with a smile.

'He bids you welcome and says he appreciates the risk you are taking. The interview is off the record. The aim is to help you understand our struggle more clearly. You may make notes.'

'Will he be talking in your language, with you translating?'

'No,' Emerson said, 'we'll speak in English.' The voice was low and measured.

I saw the man in the mask shift in his chair and lean forward into the light. He held a small tape recorder in his hand.

'We will be recording,' he said. His voice was husky and faintly familiar. He had a barely visible crescent scar just below the hairline.

I drank the tea. It was very strong. Without asking, the servant poured me a second mug.

We talked for about an hour. For much of it Emerson told me how, like Patience, he had been taught by missionaries and how he had joined what he called 'our great cause' as a schoolboy, running messages and buying food for those hiding from the police. Towards the end of this long speech, I looked at Patience and briefly raised my eyebrows. This was a waste of time, as I had thought it would be.

As if sensing my disappointment, Emerson said suddenly, 'I don't hate white people.'

'I didn't suggest you did,' I said. 'What do you feel about them?'

'Contempt.'

'What about the ordinary people, whites born here with ancestry going back generations: do they have any rights?'

'The post-war settlers came out here for an easy life with servants and sunshine. The original pioneers were different. They carved this country out of unbroken bush.'

'You salute that achievement?'

'Of course not.'

'But it was an achievement?'

'Without our labour they would have got nowhere.'

Here he raised an arm and slapped his muscled forearm.

'Without this, the country would still be bush.'

He looked around and nodded at the immaculate lawn.

'They had no right to plant the Union Jack on our land. But you Europeans wanted your empires, didn't you? It was a game you all played, you were like children with new toys. But history turns and now it's our turn.'

I was irritated. I had heard so much talk of these people joining the cause as schoolchildren, doing errands for those on the run, leaving home without a word and travelling for combat training in foreign lands, finally returning to fight in a war. But the prize for which so many were dying lay within reach now. They couldn't or wouldn't see it.

'Why are you all being so blind?' I asked.

Both men stiffened in their chairs and stared at me.

'What do you mean?' asked Emerson.

'You don't have to chop the tree down to pluck the apple,' I said. It was Sara Jane who had told me the quote, saying it was an old Arab proverb. I think she had made it up, like most of her life. I sometimes wondered if she had ever been to the Middle East.

'What is that supposed to mean?'

I said nothing for a few moments and pretended to write in my notebook. It's a good tactic when you are on top in an interview like this.

'The war is unnecessary. You are only fighting to redeem your shame.'

'Shame?' The two men spoke almost as one.

'Shame that it took you so long to take this country back from the colonisers. You don't have to do all this killing – it's vanity. The country is yours. Six million against 250,000. If your people don't get up in the morning, the economy stops. Farming, industry, tourism, the railways, hotels, bars and restaurants – they all stop. How long do you think the government would last? You're fighting for majority rule when you already have it. You don't need an AK-47 to prove that. You need organisation. Think about it.'

The man with the faintly familiar voice jumped up and muttered something, probably curses.

'The interview is over,' he said.

The big man stared at me. Patience got up and smoothed her skirt in a gesture I knew well. She glared at me and began to walk to the door.

'We should go,' she said.

'No, stay,' said Emerson. 'Maybe he's right.'

•

She said nothing in the car on the way back, but linked arms with mine and leant against my shoulder. I could feel the yellow butterfly pressing into my hair. When we got to the hotel, the driver parked in a side street around the corner.

'You took a chance tonight,' she said.

'I hardly think he was going to shoot me for stating the obvious.'

As I got out, she kissed me once very quickly, trying not to let the driver see, but he caught us in the mirror. I watched the car drive quickly away. I hadn't noticed it before. It was a mud-spattered Audi. I wanted her to stay. I almost ran after the car to try to stop it. I wanted her to have a coffee, a drink with me, anything but driving off into the darkness.

I had agreed to everything she had asked that night. I would not reveal the meeting to anyone. I had listened to a supposedly senior guerrilla commander hidden away in the civilian black community. I would treat our talk purely as background. Much of what he had said was tired old rhetoric, but he had given me an insight into why so much of the African population continued to work for the white minority.

I climbed the stairs past the bearded pioneers and wondered what they had really wanted from this country when they planted their flag here and started building a fort. The column had trekked up on horses from the south, to do what? Extend the British Empire, search for gold? Or was it just the old law that nature abhors a vacuum. Except it wasn't a vacuum. There had been people here.

John Milan's grandfather had bought his acres with a blanket and a bottle of brandy from an old chief. 'Good brandy from France,' he had said, as if that had made a difference.

A travesty of justice, or the beginning of a farming economy that would employ labour and help build a thriving nation? Whichever way you looked at it, it didn't matter now. It was over. My readers would hardly be interested in the long-ago doings of a few white men in this country.

I passed the Cancan, not sliding so much as a glance at the bar. I could hear it was full. George would be there, a rock around which a river flowed. Perhaps his grandfather had also swapped land for brandy.

There were no messages under the door.

I lay on my bed in the dark watching the light patterns on the ceiling. I had drunk too much tea. It would keep me awake for hours. The man had been interesting. He oversaw the smuggling of boys across the border and held the brighter ones back, so some could stay and join the police or army – a smart move. He said they needed teachers so their kids could learn the real history of their country. I did not ask what story this new history would tell, but I guessed it would not include white rule, except in most condemnatory terms.

'The whites took everything from us, but not the memory of our lost land,' he had said.

I made a note of that.

He had also told me the government was covering up the occasional missile attempt on civilian airliners, but I had guessed that.

I refused to go down to the bar. I had written about it in my last piece, describing it as a bubble of trapped time in which the wealthy could travel to the past, drink overpriced cocktails and indulge their nostalgia. Here one could 'ride a cock horse to Banbury Cross', as the old nursery rhyme had it, and for a few silver bullets drinkers would no doubt see rings on her fingers and bells on her toes. Whoever she was.

I had thought this was quite clever, but for my pains I received readers' letters saying I should not spend so much time in smart bars patronised by the white elite. I should spend more time with local people. If only they knew.

I looked at my watch. The luminous numbers had faded over the years, but I could just make out the time: 11.30 p.m. There had been no message from Marie Claire since she had sent me the poem. I had finally tracked it down. A translation from the Greek poet Cavafy, better known and admired in France than elsewhere. I wondered if she had found a new boyfriend. Almost certainly. I would send her a brief note, using her office telex. She got in early, long before the bosses, and so it was safe. Just a little something to say I still cared for her. That would be sensible and kind. I wondered who the boyfriend was. Not English; this time, she would choose some smart French executive, maybe a married man in her company. I hoped not. She was worth more than that. She was worth more than me.

I had a shower, turned up the air conditioning and picked up an old standby for sleepless nights, a much-thumbed paperback of Chandler's *The Long Goodbye*. Reading the opening pages was like singing a hymn in church: the words known by heart, every note and chord in place, the intense pleasure of what had been remembered from childhood. Familiarity does not breed contempt; it beckons people like me to safety.

I read for several pages but sleep would not come. It was 1 a.m. The city was quiet. I looked out of the window. The night was cool but not cold. Temperatures in the high country stayed well between the extremes. There was no one to be seen. The occasional car passed, driving too fast. The fountains in the central square had been turned off.

I dressed and walked down to the lobby. A night porter slept at the desk. He would not be disturbed until the early risers came down to jog around the streets. Everyone would be asleep in their bedrooms, some never to wake. The hotel refused to comment about the suicide of their guests, but I heard they were regular. People driven by loneliness or despair would have a decent meal, a bottle of fine wine, a last cigar and then the pills or pistol. Sara Jane had chosen both, to make sure.

I walked into the street, across the square, past the Diplomat Hotel, now closed and quiet. Pinks had finally flushed the last of the late-night reprobates into the street. Paula the receptionist would have gone home. She had told me once that the hotel served twelve different kinds of marmalade for breakfast, the sort of trivia one remembers. Most had been imported from abroad. I made a mental note to include that in my next piece; local colour that showed the oddball nature of this place.

Black, white and brown drank, argued and flirted in that hotel. Many wound up in bed together after a convivial evening of drinking. Paula was always booking late-night, last-minute rooms. Nobody minded. The tradition of racial segregation was ignored in the Diplomat. In the morning, those lovers would descend to a darkened dining room lit with twinkly lights on fake branches nailed to the walls. Whatever the time of day, the Bird and Bottle was shrouded in deep shadow, with only glimmering lights by which to read the menus.

It was just another touch of madness. In the Diplomat Hotel, the festive lights in the dining room, the twelve different kinds of marmalade for breakfast and the alcoholic insanity of Pinks were signs of the normal.

I walked on, thinking briefly of Paula, another refugee washed up on a foreign shore. Her Scottish accent was the first thing one noticed, a soft back-of-the-throat purr like the sound of the sea curling onto the shore at low tide. She dressed smartly in black skirt and blouse and presented every guest with a beguiling smile.

One evening she had asked me for a drink in a house in the suburbs. We drove there in separate cars.

'Everyone sleeps with everyone in this town,' she said. 'Because everyone is frightened. It is just a way of blotting out the world. Better to feel guilty about sex with a stranger than have to worry about the war.'

There was no rejoinder to this remark, but it was a good quote.

She had given me a quick hug. 'It's getting very close,' she whispered. Then we had gone our separate ways.

Now, on this restless night, I turned back towards the hotel, reflecting on others who had washed up in this place – empire-building pioneers or ruthless land-grabbing colonisers, gold-prospectors, missionaries, immigrants seeking sunshine and servants, mercenaries seeking cash for killing – and now, like flies to a corpse, the journalists had arrived. And I was one of them.

There was a long telex from New York waiting in my room. It had been laid on my bed – too thick to be pushed under the door. Much of it was a reprint of a feature article in an Italian magazine, which had been translated and carried by a news agency.

A note from the foreign editor said, '*For your interest. Suggest you do not do likewise.*'

That meant of course that I should indeed do likewise. I could guess what had prompted the message. The Italian TV crew I had flown with to the forward airfield had finally persuaded the army to allow them to fly into combat on Fire Force missions. A cameraman and reporter had been given a ride on an Alouette 'K-car', the command aircraft which circled the fighting below using cannon fire to support the ground troops. The Italians with pilot, gunner and two troops made six in all on the helicopter, which was well over the load for which it had been designed. However, that was the way the war was being fought: every rule broken, every border crossed.

The copy was graphic, as I had surmised earlier: a golden arc of spent shell casing curling out of the helicopter, the earth below erupting in fast-moving dust puffs as bullets tracked fleeing fighters across open ground towards the shelter of the bush, ravine or even an anthill – shelter few of them reached. The endless noise of firing, with the loud whoosh of grenades rising above the staccato rattle of automatic-rifle fire. Finally, the moment when the pilot spotted a grenade-launcher aimed at him and flung the chopper sideways, dropping height. The missile went past with a loud hiss. It was a well-written piece, which came across vividly, even in translation. It might as well have been the script for a western. This was war glamorised and packaged for a television audience. I had no intention of flying around watching men being killed below me.

The Italian footage must have been very dramatic. Careful editing would have brought the story of a war-winning use of airpower and brave ground troops to TV screens around the world. Those images would have been on a network news channels the previous night. That's why I had got the package from New York. I could see what had happened. One of the company's many vice-presidents must have been at home, supper eaten, children in bed, watching the scene on CNN News. 'Hey, honey, come and look at this.' His wife would have come in from the kitchen and watched briefly, before saying over her shoulder as she returned to the dishwasher, 'Don't you have a man over there?'

Chapter Fourteen

I joined the convoy the next morning. We lined up, a few cars and motorcycles. At the front and back, machine-gun-mounted trucks guarded the convoy. The trucks had been fitted with light armour plating, which gave some protection to the men manning the guns. They looked impossibly young, almost schoolboys. The call-up age was eighteen, but these gunners looked younger.

I was going back to where I had begun my story. Although deep in the operational area, there was at least cold beer, quiet company and some gossip to be picked up at the Shamva Country Club. The Milan family would be at home, shielded by the bells on the wire, buried grenades and the belief that it would not happen to them. My visit would be a surprise. I hoped they would be pleased to see me.

There was also the embarrassing excitement of being under military escort on a much-ambushed road. Such attacks had never happened before lunchtime, I was told. I was not reassured. I planned to write a piece about the journey under convoy partly to satisfy New York that I was prepared to take reasonable risks, but also because on the road to Shamva the recent history of the country unfolded with the changing landscape: fat cattle on white-owned pastures rolling into the dusty reservations where the livelihoods of men and livestock had to be scratched from thin soil.

On this stretch there was plenty of cover in thick bush that lined the road. If I am honest, I half hoped for an ambush from which I would emerge unscathed and able to report my bravery under fire, as the Italians had done.

Layla Milan welcomed me after the disappointment of an uneventful journey. She hugged me as if I had been expected and told me Julia was inside, and here she leant forward confidentially and lowered her voice: 'With her new young man.'

She fussed off to warn the cook of another visitor for lunch. I settled into a comfortable wicker chair on the veranda. The view was calming. From the pool and the compound my eyes lifted to the blue hills and granite outcrops that gleamed in the sun.

I must have fallen asleep.

'Hey, wake up, you!'

Julia wrapped her arms around me from behind, almost tumbling me out of the chair. She was dressed in a short cotton frock. Her hair looked different, a shorter cut giving her the schoolgirl-urchin look. The come-hither eyes, touched up with too much mascara, stood out on her pale, freckled face. It was impossible not to feel the physical pull of this young woman. My mind briefly flicked back to the hours we had spent . . .

'Come in and meet Raphe,' she said, taking me by the hand. 'We're just about to have lunch.'

It took me a few seconds to adjust to the gloom of the dining room. Everything was as before: the animal trophies, the framed photographs and the gleaming silver pheasants. Raphe was sitting at the table, half turned away from me.

'Raphe, darling, meet the writer I told you about. He's doing a story on us.'

Raphe stood up. He was in army fatigues, with lieutenant's flashes on his shoulder. He nodded. I stared at him for a second. He was the soldier who had given the interview sitting on the sandbags with the misty-eyed look, the troopie who had been in combat hours earlier. He looked at me without recognition.

'We've met before,' I said.

He looked at me again and shook his head.

'I don't think so.'

We ate cold chicken and drank beer. Raphe slid me questioning glances. I decided to let him work it out.

After lunch we sat on the terrace with coffee and small brandies. Julia kept looking from Raphe to me, as if to separate the present from the past. Our brief hotel liaison was to be forgotten.

Raphe suddenly looked hard at me.

'Of course. That press briefing the bastards made me do. You sat in the front. There was that woman photographer from . . .?'

He looked at me to supply the answer.

'She was a freelance.'

'Yeah. It was a good question.'

He stopped and lit another cigarette. In the distance I could see helicopters flying low over the bush like distant dragonflies. There were four of them. No one else seemed to notice.

For the next half an hour Raphe told the full story of his brief contact, much as I detailed earlier. Watching Julia as he described hearing the whispered word '*esche*' and putting a bullet into his old cook, I saw a moment, a shadow, on her face.

She asked him to repeat the story, wanting every detail of that brief exchange of fire and the killing that followed. She watched him closely.

'Did you feel anything?' she asked.

'When?'

'When you shot him.'

'No. He had tried to kill me.'

'You were very brave,' she said, and pulled her chair next to his, leaning across to give him a quick kiss on the lips. It was as if I wasn't there. She ruffled his hair. He pulled his head away.

'It was just training. Shooting a man dying on the ground in front of you is not brave.'

She looked down at the servants' compound some several hundred yards away.

'"*Esche*",' she said. 'It makes you wonder, doesn't it? We think we know our house staff, but . . .'

There was a pause.

'I wonder why he said that,' she said.

'It doesn't matter,' Raphe said, and pulled her onto his chair, wrapping his arms around her.

She looked at me, smiled quickly, then kissed him again with a long, lingering kiss. She had liked hearing how the renegade cook had been killed. It had excited her.

I got up and walked into the house to say goodbye to Layla Milan.

'They seem very happy,' I said.

'Huh, they're young,' she said. 'Anyway, how long has he got?'

I thought about that remark the next day. It stayed with me on the drive back. It was safe to go so late in the day. There had been a big military operation in the area. The dragonflies I had seen were the helicopters carrying troops into action.

Chapter Fifteen

A hotel room is a lonely place. I began to hate mine. Bed, bathroom and desk; sleep, washing and work. The ordered calm of the square, the trees and the fountains seemed an obscene contradiction to the fighting that was getting closer to the city.

In my room I could faintly hear noise from the Cancan below, a temptation made more inviting by the knowledge that two large late-night whiskies was the only way I could get to sleep. I have never drunk alone in a hotel room. The bar was the only place for such solace.

I resented staring at the keys of my Remington, hoping for the words to come. The typewriter was like an old dog waiting for its bone. I was stuck reporting a cycle of news, much as a doctor might record the last days of a cancer patient. The end was inevitable, the descent towards death variable, but the outcome always the same.

Turning such stories into another feature for a magazine was becoming impossible. I had surely said all that could be said about this small, land-locked corner of Africa: the coming independence, the tribal rivalries between white and African and, above all, the sheer absurdity of this war.

I amused myself by coming up with an obviously fabricated story to see if anyone would notice. I tapped out a report stating that government forces in an area of high rebel activity had sent helium-filled balloons across the bush carrying local-language surrender offers. Suspected of containing explosives or some deadly poison, the balloons had been shot down, alerting troops to rebel positions.

This was fanciful nonsense, but I knew every news outlet would demand follow-up stories from their correspondents. The Information Ministry would refuse to comment but would not deny the story. They would see some advantage in it. My colleagues in the club – and by now I had been forced to accept that I was one of them – would know there was no truth in the story but would repeat it with various exaggerations.

I added suitable flourishes. Some of the balloons carried miniature recorders playing Mick Jagger singing 'It's All Over Now'; a nice touch, I thought. I read it through. It was brilliant. It would fool everyone

I tore it up and threw it in the bin. Patience would find out and be livid. I would be fired when the truth came out. A childish waste of time; proof, if I needed it, that I was losing touch with reality.

A message pushed its way under the room door. Hidden hands slipped messages into my room almost every night. I liked that. My ghostly postman kept me in touch with New York, Paris and occasionally an elderly aunt in the suburb of Dulwich in London. This message was local. One small and spidery line of handwriting slanted across a plain page of paper.

'*We need to talk. J,*' it said.

•

Unusually, the street outside Pinks was dark. Both nearby street lamps had stopped working; this was not odd, given the shortage of spare parts in a sanctioned economy. The entrance itself was well lit. A swarm of dazzled grasshoppers circled in the pool of light. I went in.

'Hi, stranger,' said Paula. 'They're all up there, the usual crowd.'

'Jeeze?'

'Yes, he's with Bram.'

That was Jeeze's problem. He was always with people he shouldn't be with: Bram, big TV networks, Red Top taxi girls, local journalists. He treated them all as his confidants, the only people he would trust with his information.

Jeeze was in the information game. Buying and selling hot snippets of news. He was good at it. More often than not, his tips about strategy disagreement in government or new arms acquired by the nationalists would turn out to be true.

When he told an American TV reporter that the Russians had shipped old T-34 tanks to the guerrillas to help defend their bases, he was laughed at. It was true. He would draw his contacts aside in the most theatrical manner and whisper the time and place for a rendezvous. He made sure everyone saw the important company he kept.

He came flying down the stairs two at a time and jumped the last four steps, landing with a thump. He looked at Paula and me.

'In a hurry,' he said, 'can't stop.'

'Hey, what about your note?' I asked.

'Oh, yeah, sorry. I've got something for you. I'll be back later. Stick around.'

Then it came to me, the husky-voiced whispering man behind the internal commander I had interviewed. Jeeze. I had not seen the small scar on his head but there was no doubt. It was him.

He bounded out of the door into the street. I went to the entrance to see him running up the road. A car door swung open. He got in. It was hard to see in the dark, but it looked like a beaten-up old Audi.

I went up to the club and straight to the bar. I ordered a Scotch and took a quick look round. Stella was at the bar talking to a shambolic Raymond, who had somehow secured a job at the Information Ministry. Quigley was holding a bottle of beer in each hand, rocking back on his feet and laughing. He was alone. There were others I did not know. Bram was lounging against one wall.

'If only your readers could see you now,' he said.

'I'm not in the mood,' I said.

'Drinking smuggled Scotch with these relics,' he said, waving his glass at the bar crowd.

'Your point?'

He levered himself off the wall. He was smiling.

'I want to offer you congratulations, my friend.'

'I'm not your friend.'

He nodded to the alcove.

I sat down. It was better to get this over with now. I decided to say nothing. Bram was probably going to tell me that a 'prohibited immigrant' order awaited me at the Information Ministry in the morning. That would be a relief.

He joined me. A few curious faces from the bar followed him and then turned back to their drinks. For a minute or so Bram said nothing. He looked at me, at the ceiling, back at me and then at the bar. Clearly a Special Branch technique.

He said, 'You have done us a favour.'

I said nothing.

'You met a wanted terrorist leader the other night.'

I said nothing.

'We know exactly what was said, who was there and where you met.'

I shrugged. There were only four of us at that meeting. Patience, myself, the leader and a man I now thought to be Jeeze. There was also the servant with the tea. It must have been him.

'We picked Emerson up after you left.'

I said nothing.

'He's talking.'

I felt sick. The meeting had been set up by the Special Branch to tape the big man talking to me. I had been used as bait. Sara Jane was right. Don't even trust your mother in this town.

'I had every right to meet him. Their side of the story is important; you said so yourself.'

'I agree. We knew where Emerson was. We could have picked him up anytime. But we wanted to hear him talk to someone he trusted to see what he really knew. You can never trust info you get under torture. As I said, you did us a favour.'

Again that sick feeling. I had been set up.

'What do I get – a prize?'

He leant forward so his face was close to mine.

'I think you are beginning to see that there is something worth fighting for here.'

'You told me that the war was lost.'

'It is, but this way we are going to get a peace deal we can live with.'

'Which way is that?'

'Fighting on.'

'Is this what you have sat me down here to say?'

He shook his head.

'I think your friend Patience may be in danger.'

'You said that before.'

'Not from us.'

Quigley was weaving his way across from the bar clutching three bottles of beer. He banged the bottles on the table in front of me and said loudly, 'No more Scotch, my little lovebirds.'

'Fuck off,' said Bram.

Quigley saluted, stepped back and began to lose balance, his feet just keeping him upright as he tottered backwards across the room until he collided with the bar.

Emma Lamb appeared in the doorway and beckoned. Bram got up and left without a further word.

I looked at the empty crisp packets on the counter, the last of the stale sandwiches, the crush around Stella, the once-grey carpet black and sticky with spilled drink, the clouds of tobacco smoke laying a fresh coat of nicotine on the stained ceiling. It was hard to imagine a more sordid venue for the trade of rumours, lies, propaganda and maybe occasional truths that drew journalists here from around the world.

Pinks wasn't a private club. It was just a room with a bar. In theory, anyone could walk in for a drink. Nobody dared, apart from those buying and selling news: stories of secret negotiations, back-door diplomacy by superpowers, peace talks, the latest civilian atrocities committed by every side, further devastating cross-border raids in which only the camp dogs were left alive.

It was easy for me to sit there and pretend I wasn't part of this grisly market place. I could win readers and please my editors with phoney phrase-making and moral ambivalence. I could reassure them that I was a mere spectator wrapped in the warmth of civilised values while this country turned into a wilderness around me. But I was not an onlooker. The night I had walked into the Cancan I had become part of this shadow world. I had been given a small part in this tragedy. Bram was right. I did care.

A small, nagging doubt crept like a mouse into my mind. That's what drink does to you: it feeds the imagination, seeding doubts, replacing the best with the worst. I didn't think Patience was in any danger from her own people. The idea that she had become an informant was absurd. She had led me to a big story, the last interview with a nationalist leader before his arrest and detention.

What had he actually said? Platitudes, patently disingenuous gestures to the white community. Shared power was a nonsense and he knew it. 'You cannot share a cake, but you can give a decent slice of it to people you wish to work with,' he had said. Nice words. But the cake was there to be eaten by the victors; that was the reality, as cold as the occasional frost that gripped these African highlands.

Quigley was weaving towards me again, clutching another bottle of beer. I wondered if he ever left the bar. I brushed past him and, hearing a sharp curse, turned to see him descend slowly to the floor as if helped by an unseen hand.

•

I began to write the story of my interview with Comrade Emerson. The journey in the old Audi, being told to look at the floor of the car, trying to flick a quick look out of the windows, hearing the grunted rebuke of the driver – it all made a good intro.

The fact that Emerson had been detained hours after I met him was an embarrassment. Was Bram right that they could have arrested him anytime but wanted to hear what he said to a trusted journalist? That was me, a trusted journalist. They knew I would be asked to keep certain things off the record – shipments of arms into the country and so forth. In fact, he had told me nothing of the sort.

My trusty Remington failed me again. The words died on the page. The snap of the carriage return no longer drove me on. I didn't know how to tell the story. I wondered if I had a story at all.

Welcome distraction arrived with the soft sound of my mysterious postman pushing an envelope under the door.

The unsigned telex read:

In the silver mirrors of my mind,
I see the girl I left behind.
If only I could take her hand,
Try and make her understand
Why the promises that he made
Were promises that he betrayed.
I didn't mean to end like this,
Selling love for a vampire's kiss.

So now I was a vampire. I had no idea where these lines were from. Definitely not Cavafy. Perhaps she had written them herself. I crunched the telex into a ball and threw it into the wastebasket. No doubt Marion would retrieve it in the morning and read it. I wondered if she was paid to pass on such findings.

•

The school holidays made it easy to find Patience the next day. She was at home and frowned when she answered the door.

'I told you not to come here.'

'Emerson has been arrested.'

'I know.'

She had been crying. For a moment, I saw in her face what I had never seen before: fear. She could express her feelings so well. Anger, love, lust, laughter, the satisfaction of matching a Shakespeare quote to the occasion – that was the face I knew, a face I had held in my hands, whose lips I had kissed. Now it looked worried, almost frightened.

'Something bad has happened,' she said.

She was twisting her earrings as she had before. They were new, deep-blue amethysts.

'I know.'

'No, you don't. Go back to the hotel.'

She half closed the door.

'You can't expect me to leave like this.'

'I am not expecting anything. I'm telling you to leave.'

I asked her for coffee, almost pleading. She shook her head and closed the door.

•

A strong black-sugared coffee in the rooftop café at Sandersons department store did not help make sense of what had happened. The thought that Patience really was in danger had twisted around like a snake in my head as I took the escalator to the top floor.

There was a woman in front of me with two blue canaries perched uncomfortably inside a small birdcage. It reminded me of the story of Winston Churchill returning on a rainy morning through bombed-out London in the war. He had seen a long queue outside a shop and ordered his car to stop. He sent his detective to find out more. It was a pet shop. The queue was for birdseed. The prime minister sat back, cigar aglow, and told the story that night at dinner. Victory was certain. Hitler would never break such people, he said.

Seeing the woman with her canaries brought me to a different conclusion. The white community, especially the women left behind, would sustain normal lives for as long as they could, not in the belief that victory was possible, but that life would become unbearable if defeat was finally recognised.

The view from the top floor again rebuked the notion of war. The city was spread out under the sun as if nothing had changed. The high-rise offices and shopping malls gave way to suburbs, which in turn rolled into the fields and bush seen dimly through heat haze. The grid of clean-swept streets, the occasional sunlight off fountains, a splash of green for municipal gardens – it all promoted the belief that an ordered existence was possible here in the heart of southern Africa.

Wondering about the blue canaries, I turned to the local paper and drank coffee. Always start with the small ads, the births, marriages and deaths. That had been an early lesson in my craft.

There were guns for sale, cars, lawnmowers, spare tyres and all the bits and pieces of everyday existence; ads for houseboys, garden boys and kitchen staff. Death notices had occasional references to those who had died on 'operational duties'. Otherwise, the notices were mostly of seventy- and eighty-year-olds, almost always men. There were no Africans mentioned in these columns. They had their own township papers to record such events.

The news was the same as ever. More military successes, increased airline flights out of the country and a surprising story about the growing number of whites leaving; surprising because these pages were censored by the government.

News-in-brief items told of a burst dam in the west, three couples getting married at the same time in the same church, a body found three kilometres out of town on the road north, and the news that Jimmy Edwards, a big-name comedian from England, was flying out to entertain the troops.

I wished I had not thrown Marie Claire's poem away. It was good, a burnt offering from a wounded heart. I wondered again if Marion had read it. Perhaps she went through the rest of my belongings, turned out the pockets of my only smart jacket, examined the bed sheets. Was she Bram's bedroom spy? She probably had no choice if she wished to keep her job. I had checked for cameras and microphones hidden in the room, pulling up the carpet, running hands over wallpaper and feeling slight bumps. Nothing.

I walked the stairs to the ground floor, keeping an eye out for caged canaries. Perhaps the woman had taken them shopping with her as company. Maybe there was a pet department in this huge store.

The sun was strong, reflected from glass-fronted buildings onto hot streets full of vendors selling ice cream, sandwiches, grilled corn cobs and cheap trinkets. One had a stall full of pictures of a stern-looking prime minister on tea towels, place mats and mugs.

I decided to lunch at the Diplomat, where the Bird and Bottle was said to have received a consignment of large prawns from the coast. The gloom of that ill-lit restaurant would be soothing. The other advantage was the absence of any colleagues from the press. They had all been banned after a drunken lunch and arguments over the bill.

Paula was on the reception. A thin smile, then she frowned and beckoned me over.

'Heard what has happened?' she whispered.

'Tell me.'

She was about to reply when four guests impatient to pay their bill appeared. Their car was hooting outside. She put a finger to her lips and mouthed the word 'later'.

The prawns were excellent, shelled and grilled with just the right amount of lemon juice and hot sauce. They were served with a side dish of rice. There was no wine worth the name, but cold lager was a better choice.

I dismissed Paula's words. Quigley had probably punched a troopie and ended up in hospital or jail. Perhaps Stella Knight had been discovered in a lesbian embrace in the ladies' loo – the domestic dramas in this small town were endless.

I leant back, ordered a pack of cigarettes and a local brandy. The thought that had been gathering slowly in the back of my mind, a cloud on the rim of the horizon, had now begun to take shape. I would leave this country – and take Patience with me.

Someone else could chronicle the final days here. Patience would come with me. She loved me as I loved her. I ordered a second brandy. She knew that independence would bring civil war. She would be a prophet without honour in her own country.

In any case, the end might yet be years away and in that time the Special Branch would surely pick her up and try to turn her. It wasn't difficult to do in most cases. Captured guerrillas were the easiest. Their families were effectively used as hostages. Far from bending to the imperative of peace talks, the regime was proving ruthless in pursuit of its survival.

The daydream bubble burst with the second brandy. Patience wouldn't come with me. And I wouldn't leave. If Meredith Kaplan decided I had been here too long – and she would have been right – I would if necessary stay as a freelance. Daydreams born of cold beer and warm brandy are deceitfully seductive.

•

I spent the afternoon with my Remington to make up for a misspent lunch. This time the words came easily. I was going to write a major personal article, allowing the reader to see the painful compromises forced upon correspondents like myself. I set out the title at the top of the page in capitals: 'HOW I LOST MY HEART IN AFRICA'.

This would be the story of a love affair with a people at war. I would write it as an opera in which heroes, heroines and dark-cloaked villains were swept away by divine furies, a romantic tragedy ending in the sweet agony of defeat and death.

In this confessional I would admit that I had become part of the story. I was biased because I had become involved. I cared passionately about the black nationalist cause. I saw their righteous struggle as redemption for a brutal past.

Equally, and here came the surprise that would make them sit up in New York, I sympathised with the white community and understood their pride in what they had created.

The way they clung to the hope that the western world would recognise their achievement and ride to the rescue was pitiful. I found affection in that pity. I saw them as sailors of old clambering to the highest yard on the mast, firing muskets as the wreck of a mighty war ship sank beneath them. An overblown image most certainly, but there was a truth in there.

Patience would no doubt have the requisite quotations for my opera from Macbeth's dying days, Lear in his madness or perhaps something from *Richard III*.

Even my faithful Remington seemed to rebuke me at this point. I was casting the cloak of romantic grandeur over the last stand of a racist white regime. Writers like me are supposed to hold themselves to the highest standards of impartiality, allowing their readers to decide on moral censure or otherwise.

How many times had I damned, both in print and to anyone who cared to listen, the so-called 'committed' journalists bending the truth in the service of their own political prejudice? I was one of them now, and it was too late to go back. The day was done, the night had come. That sounded like Shakespeare. I would try it on Patience.

The thought of Patience made me pause at the typewriter. She would be horrified by any such revelation. It would be ruinous for both of us.

I went to the window and looked out. I have no idea what prompted me to do so. Intuition, sixth sense – I don't know. But I do know I had no choice. I let my eyes wander over the street scene, the central square and fountains, the ever-blue cloudless sky, as if hoping she might magically appear. After some minutes, a muddy blue Audi drew up at the hotel entrance. No one got out.

I ran down the stairs to the lobby, taking two steps at a time, brushing past startled staff. She was in a corner partly screened by the potted plants, talking to George. She was whispering to him while he listened and nodded. I could not see her face properly. George looked his usual sombre self.

I stepped closer. She turned and looked at me with a pained frown. She said something to George, who immediately left by a side door. Patience nodded to the front door and walked rapidly into the street.

I thought for a minute she was going to get into the blue Audi. Instead, she walked across the road into the square. I followed, almost getting knocked down by a passing motorcycle. I joined her on a bench shaded by trees.

'I was going to call you,' she said.

'Good. I want to talk to you.'

'Let me talk first,' she said.

She lit a cigarette, drew deeply and exhaled the smoke. She gave a long sigh, shook her head, stared at the ground for a moment and then straightened up.

'Jeeze is dead,' she said.

'What? How?' It was all I could say.

'His body was found dumped on the road north outside town.'

Of course. The news-in-brief item: a badly beaten body found at the three-kilometre post on the Shamva road. That was why Paula had been so anxious to talk to me.

He had been tortured, Patience said in a flat monotone, as if this was an everyday occurrence in the life of a local journalist. She pre-empted my who-why-where-when questions.

'They killed him.'

'Who?'

She threw the half-smoked cigarette away and lit another in a swift movement of her hands.

'Our people. My people.'

'*Your* people. Why on earth?'

She lit another cigarette.

'I had nothing to do with it,' she said.

'But why, for God's sake!'

'He was a traitor. An informer.'

'How do you know?'

'Who do you think told Special Branch about the meeting with Comrade Emerson? Who told them I was helping boys across the border? Who told them we were having an affair?'

'Were we? Are we?'

The morning had been so surreal, the news of Jeeze's murder such a shock, that what followed seemed quite natural. We spent the afternoon in bed at the hotel, smoking, looking at the ceiling. She didn't say a word. There was no point asking questions. She just smoked one cigarette after another. I got up and found beer and a half-bottle of gin in the fridge.

'Put it back, it's probably cane spirit,' she said.

I had to laugh. She sat up in bed and asked what was so funny. I told her that was what Sara Jane Shannon had said when we first met.

I didn't care if it was witches' brew. I filled a plastic tumbler with ice, doused it in cane spirit and knocked it back in one. Patience drank beer from the bottle. She fell asleep in my arms. I felt her move gently with every breath and felt the stirring of the uncontrollable pulse of pleasure that came with our lovemaking; I wanted to wake her, taste the sweet kiss of flesh and skin leaving love in its slipstream and lifting us both as if in flight. Some birds make love on the wing, they say, joining as one while gliding together for a few seconds as seed and egg fuse before breaking away, never to meet again. A one-flight stand.

Moving gently to look at my watch, I saw it was six o'clock. The hours had slipped past by like a cat in the dark.

She woke when I was in the shower and joined me. The stall was too small to allow any movement for two, so we just stood there under the hot water, my hands on her breasts, her back against my chest.

I wanted to hear much more about the killing of Jeeze, but this was not the time. She got dressed quickly, wrapped a scarf around her wet hair, then kissed me; a long, slow kiss that half made me think she wanted to stay the night.

'Let's go somewhere,' I said.

She shook her head, ran a finger down my nose, across my lips and onto my chin.

'I'll see myself out,' she said, and blew me a kiss from the door as she left. There was no point asking her where she was going, home presumably, or when I would see her again. This was a one-way affair, if 'affair' could reasonably describe our relationship.

•

Jeeze's death had become front-page news in both the white-owned and African press. The latter, although governed by censorship regulations, was allowed to function with greater freedom than their counterparts for reasons that were never clear to me.

News coverage and editorials in the *Daily Herald* kept carefully clear of any mention of the war, even when military operations featured African units, but were remarkably critical on matters such as housing and educational provision for the majority population.

Without actually pointing the finger at government agents, the *Herald* insinuated that Jeeze had been murdered because of his pro-nationalist opinions, expressed with vehemence both in the press and to the western media. The interviews he had given American network stars such as Peter Jennings of ABC had incensed the government.

This made Jeeze a hero, and he was duly celebrated as such in township demonstrations. Banners were paraded around the streets carrying crude images of his face and a lavish funeral was attended by thousands. There was no body; that had vanished into a morgue.

The white-run press hinted darkly that he had been killed because of his open praise for the role of African members of infantry and special-forces units. It was perfectly true that Jeeze saluted those troops on the spurious grounds that they were acquiring skills useful in the creation of a post-independence army.

I didn't think this had anything to do with his murder. News reports that confirmed he had been tortured. There were burn marks on his hands and feet, probably inflicted by a lighter. Someone had suspected Jeeze of being an informer. He had been at my meeting with Comrade Emerson and had probably recorded our conversation for his Special Branch handlers.

I went back to the hotel. Marion was wearing her ironed and starched uniform. She had opened the windows. She gave me a deferential nod. I looked around the room to see if there was any evidence of my afternoon with Patience. Marion probably knew anyway. I decided to take the Remington into the square and write on a bench. Marion looked embarrassed and said, 'Please, sir.'

She pulled a carefully folded piece of what had been crumpled paper from her pocket and handed it to me. Marie

Claire's poem. 'In the silver mirrors of my mind.' I looked at her. She smiled shyly and went back to making the bed.

•

Trying to write in a public square, sitting on a hard, slatted bench with passers-by stopping briefly to stare, dogs sniffing at your shoes and children playing games nearby, was impossible.

I wanted to write a big feature around the life and death of Jeeze. I am immodest enough to admit that I saw this as a prize-winning piece that would take my readers into the dark heart and bright future of this nation.

It was difficult because it needed context. The only lesson I could offer was one in which everybody in this brutal war was betraying everything and everyone they believed in. That was a gothic horror story that would not appeal to my readers.

What they wanted was hope. They did not expect a happy ending born of this chaos, but they hoped for at least the prospect of a better future. I was writing for decent middle-class liberal Americans anointed at birth with the belief that hard work, faith and love of country would help build a better future for them and a better world for all. That optimism had survived the catastrophe of the Vietnam War and the two unimpressive presidents that followed. Hope shaped the way my readers saw the world. I felt bound to try to match their expectations.

My colleagues delighted in disaster, plundering their thesaurus of doom-laden adjectives to describe the horrors of the present and the nightmares to come. I too had occasionally been guilty of this, because the more one exaggerates present dangers and future disasters in any situation, the more space editors give such stories.

I take nothing away from war correspondents who describe every shot and shell from the front line, but I sometimes wonder what they are there for. In this case, there was no danger to any of us except for the mad Italians flying on Fire Force missions. I learnt later that the cameraman had been killed driving through the darkened streets of Beirut. His taxi had hit an oncoming truck loaded with crates of Coca-Cola. There was a lesson for us all there somewhere.

The story of Jeeze was going to be unusually dark for my readers. The first question was simple. If, as seemed likely, Jeeze had betrayed his own cause, why? The answer came to me more easily than I had thought. The character of the man was his undoing. Jeeze loved the intrigue of buying and selling information and the importance it gave him. He would use contacts in the police or his own nationalist colleagues to pass on snippets of privileged information to the big players from the American networks. They bought him drinks and meals and paid well for his information. That gave him the power to be treated with respect in Pinks and in the Victoria in the township.

Jeeze loved the idea that people came to him for information. We all saw him whispering with Bram in the alcove of the club bar; he was no doubt doing the same with senior nationalists in the townships. He was engaging, with his buck teeth and gurgling laughter. He was everybody's friend, the man we all needed if we wanted to check out a story or find a new line into government thinking.

Jeeze had appeared in newspapers around the world, named as either a government or a nationalist source, depending on the story. He was quoted anonymously in TV programmes from Washington to Tokyo as a senior government official.

So how had Jeeze crossed the line and why had he taken the risk? Patience had said her people had killed him. I had no doubt that was true. There was only one reason. They had found out that Jeeze had become a government informer, one of Bram's secret sources. He would have been very well paid in American dollars, lodged in a foreign account. But why, when it was so obvious that Bram and his colleagues were working on the wrong side of history?

Bram would have flattered him and promised him that his role would never be revealed. Jeeze would have been told that in a power-sharing government he, Jesus Amari, would hold a senior position in the Information Ministry. He might even become minister. That would have been enough. That would have swung it. That would have sent Jeeze on the road to his death at the three-kilometre mark. The torture inflicted on him was not just a meaningless act of savagery, but a warning to others.

There was irony in this story, because the more I investigated Jeeze's past – and here Stella Knight was surprisingly helpful – the more I understood him. He was one of five children from a family of ambitious African traders; he had been sent to a private white secondary school, which offered a limited quota of places to African pupils. After school, he had won a scholarship to a university in the big country to the south. This was a rare achievement. Not surprisingly, this gave Jeeze the sense of superiority and self-importance that marked his career as a columnist and media fixer.

His carefully curated image was that of the man in the know, with contacts in high places. Given his apparent allegiance to both sides in the conflict, that was true. So far, so good. Then the temptation of money and the prospect of real political power had dislodged common sense.

The story was titled 'The Man Who Knew Too Much'. It was given the same prominent display as before, but this time the two-page spread occupied the centre pages, with a large, graphically enhanced image of Jeeze. My own photo by-line had also been enlarged and boxed off. I had done very well out of Jeeze. The feature closed my account with him.

•

I had spent wearisome hours tapping away on the Remington in that hotel room. I needed a change. I decided to move hotels. That may not sound much, but it would be a big move and somehow it might give me fresh ideas. Patience would approve, because I intended to move to the Diplomat.

This would mean saying farewell to George, the Cancan Bar and Marion, my secret-agent room cleaner. I saw George that night for a farewell drink, half hoping that Patience might be there. It was the sort of surprise she enjoyed. There had not been a word or message from her for five days.

The bar was full with what looked like arms salesmen. George had the silver bullet in front of me almost before I had slid onto the bar stool. The cocktail was as good and as lethally refreshing as usual. I beckoned George and suggested we might meet outside the hotel the following day. Just for a quiet word, I said. I wanted to explain my departure, thank him for his help and perhaps tempt him to the Diplomat on his evening off. George shook his head and said it was against staff orders.

I moved to the Diplomat the next day. I knew there would be a price. Pinks was full of drunks at the end of the evening and the only other bar was on street level and was patronised by a lower class of local whites. It was rightly called the Riff Raff Bar. My hotel room was smaller and the walls were thinner, but at least I would be spared the bearded pioneers staring sternly from framed photographs on the staircase, the fake Parisian glamour of the Cancan, the starched tablecloths and folded napkins in the La Fontaine restaurant.

I would miss George and Marion, but I told myself that once I had left the hotel, I could never go back. This was nonsense, but I liked to persuade myself that I had made a clean break with the past few weeks in this city. I had moved one step closer to leaving. This was irrational because, although I had become too involved to be a fair-minded observer, I had no real intention of leaving.

I would stay and follow the story to the end. I would stay because when I finally left, I wanted Patience to leave with me. I was sure George would tell her I had left Franklins. She would happily meet me at the Diplomat, and we would make love again – it had been at least ten days now – in that thin-walled room.

The school holidays had ended. She would be back in her classroom now, working on another play, a reprise of *A Midsummer Night's Dream*, which had been a favourite with pupils and staff. She had laughed when she told me how difficult it was to explain to her pupils why Bottom was called Bottom and why he wore a donkey's head in the play.

'What did you tell them?'

'I said that Shakespeare had a great sense of humour and knew that laughter was the best medicine for Londoners in the plague years.'

I wondered whether she had been involved in Jeeze's death. I wondered too whether the Special Branch was still watching her and whether Bram had been right. If she really was in danger from her own people, he surely would have told me.

I knew so little about her. She never discussed her family beyond saying that she was not married, had been schooled by missionaries and had no children. I had tried to find Charity at the school, but she was always away, or so I was told. It was as if a door had been shut in my face. Jeeze had warned me that I was not welcome anywhere in the township, although that may have been just another lie.

I went to Pinks most nights. It would be typical of her to turn up without warning. And so it turned out, on a Friday night some two weeks after I had last seen her. I was at once pleased and angry. She had not told me she was coming. She was talking to Quigley and Stella. She looked over, saw me, smiled and beckoned me to come over. A kiss on the cheek, a glass of watered whisky with ice, and I found myself listening to Stella describing the coming peace talks in Geneva. I didn't want to hear this, although she was better informed than most of the press. I steered Patience to the alcove table.

'Where have you been, for God's sake?' I said.

She placed a hand on my arm.

'I'm sorry.'

'Sorry? Is that all you can say? I've missed you. I was worried.'

'It's just that . . .'

'Just that what?' I said.

'I've been very busy and I wanted to . . .'

She twisted her hands, looking nervous.

'I wanted to put you out of my mind.'

'What are you talking about?'

'This is hopeless, Richard. How can we be together like this?'

I had no idea what she was trying to say.

'What are you talking about?'

There were tears in her eyes. She smiled, not the thin-lipped smile from when we first met, but a big, open smile.

'Richard, this is for you as much as me.'

'What is?'

'That we stop. I have thought deeply about this.'

'Stop? Just like that? I'm not a bus. I can't just stop. I love you, don't you understand?'

'And I love you too, but think about it. This is my home. I will never leave. You will have to leave. You have a job, a career, and there's nothing we can do about it.'

This was such a shock and the casual nature of her remarks were so utterly out of place in such squalid surrounds that I did not know what to say.

I was angry. I told her I would quit my job. I would find work in the new nation that emerged from the fires of the old. She liked those words but insisted that I was not being rational. I was a well-known magazine writer. I was a candidate for a Pulitzer Prize. How could I possibly stay here?

We talked back and forth for what seemed like hours. Quigley acted as barman, ferrying drinks and crisps to us.

He was sober, thoughtful and asked for no payment. 'Have it on me, sport,' he said. In the end she sat there crying. People ignored us, although I saw Stella take some interest. Finally, Patience looked up.

'Why did you move from your hotel?'

'Because it was ghastly, like a museum.'

'Even your favourite bar.'

'Especially my favourite bar – not George, though.'

'And your lovely big room overlooking the square?'

'That too.'

'And that cleaner who spied on me?'

'Marion. I tipped her well.'

Silence settled on us. She drank the gin, tilting the glass back until the ice cubes slid onto her nose. She put the glass down, wiped her nose.

'What's your room like here?'

'You can just about squeeze two people in.'

'Show me,' she said.

We were both rather drunk by this stage, but that didn't make any difference. I wanted to cancel out the conversation. She gave in to weariness and perhaps desire. Afterwards she lit a cigarette from a rare pack of Benson & Hedges. We talked about Jeeze.

She said his death had been like losing one's religion. You worship your god, faith becomes your shield, then your god suddenly vanishes. The years of worship had been wasted.

'That's what it felt like when we found out about Jeeze. We had trusted him. He was a hero in the townships. He gave us good information, or so we thought.'

'Like what?'

'They smuggled in big new Bell helicopters – God knows how with the sanctions. Shipments of new night-sights for the FN rifles. That sort of thing.'

'How did you find out he betrayed you?'

'We worked it out. Simple maths. Two plus two equals four. He confessed to everything.'

'Under torture?'

'Yes, a lesson to others.'

'How was he killed?'

'You don't need to know.'

'But you know?'

She shook her head in irritation rather than denial.

'Were you involved? I mean, I would understand. It wouldn't matter, it . . .'

She sat up in bed, pulling the sheets up to her neck.

'For God's sake, Richard, you have just made love to me – and now you're asking whether I was involved in murder!'

'I'm sorry, I'm sorry, I'm . . .'

She stopped me with a kiss.

'It's a fair question, you idiot. You hardly want to be lying in the arms of a woman who put a bullet in the head of your old friend Jeeze. If it makes you happy, I had nothing to do with his death.'

After a while she said, 'I know they're going to recall you. Fresh voice, fresh eyes – that's what they'll want.'

'I'm not leaving.'

She rolled over, sat up and straddled me, her hair falling over her face.

'Be honest with me, Richard. Let's just face the facts.'

'Why? Do you want me to go?'

'I don't. I'm just being realistic.'

'I'm not leaving. Believe me. Whatever happens here, we will stay together.'

She looked at me. There was a sparkle in her eyes, maybe more tears, maybe the gin. She kissed me gently, so that her hair fell over my face.

'Beautiful,' she whispered.

She finished dressing and slid the yellow butterfly clasp into her hair.

'When will I see you again?' I said. 'And no Shakespeare quotes, please.'

'Parting is such sweet sorrow,' she said, and stuck her tongue out at me. She closed the door behind her.

I got out of bed. The door opened again.

Patience put her head round and said, 'George is not happy. He says if you go to the bar at seven you might get a free bullet.' Then she was gone.

•

After my departure from Franklins – which saved the company a lot of money, by the way; the Diplomat was half the price – life speeded up. It was as if I had been paddling in the shallows and now found myself in deep water.

The bush war which had flickered furiously far from the comforts of urban life got closer. Rockets were fired at oil installations in the suburbs. A dentist in a wealthy white area had casually watched his gardener stripping and cleaning the lawnmower while having a beer on his terrace. The gardener was laying the parts carefully in order. He oiled each one with care using an old rag. The precision with which this was done struck the dentist as odd. It only came to him later. The man was stripping the lawnmower as if it were a weapon. The police found grenades, AK-47 rifles and ammunition in his lodgings. He told the police he was waiting for the call.

The war both in the bush and across the country's border intensified. Each side was seeking territorial advantage to improve their bargaining power at the long-heralded peace talks. The talks had been regarded as a fantasy ever since I had been in the country. Now it looked as if they might actually happen.

Stella Knight made the remarkable observation that the talks were like Omar Sharif's entry in the film *Lawrence of Arabia*: a figure dimly seen through shimmering heat waves in the desert, gradually taking shape and form as he emerged from the haze.

'One of David Lean's greatest cinematic tricks,' she said. I must have looked surprised because she said sharply, 'We're not all peasants here, you know, Richard. We do have a cinema club.'

'We're going to need more than a few director's tricks to get the talks going,' I said.

'"*We*"? Richard, I do believe you have begun to care for us,' she said.

Indeed, I did care. The independence talks, as they were called, would end the war, allowing elections to take place, leading to a new nationalist government. That was the plan widely forecast in the press. The colonial power would mastermind this miracle with a sleight of hand, allowing its diplomats a swift retreat to receive accolades in their London clubs.

No one mentioned the blood sacrifice that would follow this seismic power shift. I was less worried about the white minority, who would be useful for any new government for a few years at least. I did fear for the many Africans, mostly young men, who had signed up for service either in the army, police or their support organisations. I had never believed that these young men had joined the white cause to acquire expertise useful to a nationalist government. They had done so for money or sheer excitement, or maybe even believing they were on the winning side.

•

One morning Paula handed me an envelope containing a neatly handwritten invitation to the wedding of Miss Julia Milan of Green Creek Farm in Shamva and Lieutenant Raphe Loxton of 39 Steppes Road, Highlands. The wedding was to take place in the Anglican chapel in Shamva, with the reception at the Milan farm.

I wondered how long she had known this young soldier and what Layla Milan thought of the rush to get married. Lieutenant Raphe Loxton had been fresh from battle when he sat before us with that glazed look of shock. He had been in another world then, and I doubted he had come back. A wartime wedding in a hurry. Maybe she was pregnant.

At least the wedding was something positive to think about. Despite the prospect of peace talks, I preferred Jeeze's prediction: a fight to the finish. The columns of death notices in the daily papers were lengthening. Women with black armbands were carrying bunches of flowers in the streets. Black-market rates for the local currency were soaring.

Families were breaking up as wives took their children on holiday abroad, never to return. Their men were left behind facing long periods of call-up. The army was now inducting all males up to the age of sixty-five. Women volunteers were deployed to man back-room operations. Posters appeared on billboards showing uniformed women holding sub-machine guns over the slogan 'Your women are fighting for you'. There was a positive response to this call.

'For sale' signs on the cheaper houses in white-designated areas sprouted like mushrooms. The dentist's garden boy with hand grenades under his bed was not the only one waiting for the call. Master and servant eyed each other with suspicion. Government assurances that a negotiated peace would not bring the white nightmare of majority rule became laughable. Even the controlled press cast doubts on such statements.

The distant bush war had truly come to town. I wove these little stories into one of my best articles for the magazine, or so I immodestly thought. I knew I was repeating myself, but equally I knew that my readers wanted the answer to the central question. 'War is a world, not an event', as someone said, so why had a small, friendless and outnumbered community chosen such a fateful path into that world?

There was a much deeper loyalty to the country than I had imagined. Layla Milan had expressed this to me on my last visit in an illogical but emotional way that I found moving. I had made a note of those remarks, but had forgotten them until I went through my notebook.

Layla and I had been sitting in the dining room while Julia and Raphe Loxton sat hand in hand, smoking and sipping drinks, on the canopied double swing seat outside.

'If there is one single thing I want you to tell your readers, it is this,' she said. 'We love this country and we love its people. Does that sound strange?'

'Frankly, yes,' I replied. 'These people are your servants. It's easy to say you love them.'

'And just as easy for you to accuse me of condescending racism. But it happens to be true.' There was not much I could say to that.

'My family go back over eighty years in this country,' she said. 'We were simple folk. We knew how to carve farms out of the bush, dam the rivers, build roads and railways, but we did this with the Africans we found here. They worked alongside us. It was a partnership, but we never saw it that way. We didn't know how to share it. That was the mistake.'

These words so closely mirrored my own thoughts at the top of the Sandersons store that day that I thought she must have read my piece in the magazine.

'That's an unusual attitude,' I said. 'So what was the point of the war?'

'Search me,' she said. 'Ask those toy soldiers in town.'

These thoughts made very good copy, which I placed prominently in the article. They gave it the headline 'The Bush War Comes to Town', with a picture of a white woman laying flowers on a headstone.

•

I sent the piece off at about four in the afternoon, mid-morning in New York. It was timed for that week's Saturday publication. I was in my room feeling pleased with myself and preparing to go to Pinks below when the phone rang. It was Meredith Kaplan. This was highly unusual. Meredith never liked phoning correspondents around the world, on the grounds of expense.

'Thanks for the piece, very good. We plan a big show for it.'

'Foreign-page lead?'

'There are other big stories in the world, Richard.'

We exchanged the usual small talk about the weather, American politics. Reagan was campaigning to become president, which didn't sit well with Meredith and her colleagues. We talked about the latest sales figures and how our competitors were doing. None of this was the point.

'You have done a great job, Richard,' she said finally.

Staff correspondents hearing those words from their editor know that bad news is coming.

'Thank you, Meredith.'

'You have had a good run there. How do you feel about a change of scene?'

'I would like to see it through to the end. Makes sense.'

'The end never seems to come, though, does it? Maybe fresh eyes and ears?'

'Meredith, if you think I have done such a good job, why not let me stay?'

'OK, but are there any personal reasons for this? Professionally speaking, we would like you to move on, but we always respect family reasons.'

So they know about Patience, I thought. So what? It was

my life. But how had word got back to New York? I cast my mind back. Sara Jane was dead. Of course: Jeeze, the man with a mouth like a torn pocket. He had gossiped to one of the network stars, probably Jennings.

'My private life has nothing to do with anyone,' I said.

'All right, Richard. Let's step back and think this through. But one word of warning. Don't get too close to the story.'

'Meaning what?'

'Meaning some people think you have become too involved.'

'Who is "some people"?'

'Richard, I am really busy. Bear in mind what I have said. Once again, congratulations.'

Stepping back meant I probably had another month. There would have been a lot of politicking in New York about me. The six-o'clock-cocktail crowd from the home desk who thought fondly of Marx would have decided I was too soft on the old regime. They would have preferred a tumbrils-to-the-guillotine approach. They would have hated the subliminal sympathy for the regime in my writing. Perhaps I hated it myself. Perhaps I found moral complexity in a conflict that presented the outside world with a simple choice. Either judge the white regime as crypto-fascist, bent on suppression of the majority, or accept that the country had been created in an unequal partnership in which the majority had, to some extent at least, benefited from the minority. It was easy to understand why so many young Africans were crossing the border to take up arms. But why were so many also joining the regime's security forces?

Patience would have torn me apart for such heretical views – indeed, she had done so – but at least she had, warily and uneasily, acknowledged that sometimes, just sometimes, jeopardy lay in lazy thinking.

Chapter Sixteen

The rainy season was coming early this year. Grey castles of cloud piling up in the sky again. I had woven the weather into my writing because, as Sara Jane had said, the war was to a great extent weather-dependent. The weather meant a lot to my readers too, especially in the Midwest.

I was surprised when Paula handed me a cable clearly sent from Paris. It had been brought over from Franklins. I had not told them where I had moved. I do not know whether I had forgotten Marie Claire or deliberately put her out of my mind. I was sure she had not forgiven me.

I was hopeful that the cable might tell me of an ending, that she had found a new love and wished to meet again sometime as old friends. Experience told me this was never going to happen. I knew she followed my writing, because *Le Figaro*, her favourite reading material, had published most of my work in its weekend magazine, suitably translated.

The message was brief: '*Please call me this evening after six.*'

We had not spoken on the phone since shortly after I had

arrived. I did not relish the thought. She was pushing on an old bruise and knew it. I put the cable away. Paula smiled at me more with pity than with pleasure: another reminder that everyone knew everyone else's business in this town.

I climbed the stairs to the bar, comforting myself with the thought that many great writers (Hemingway, Faulkner, SSteinbeck), and some great actors (Richard Burton, Trevor Howard, Richard Harris), had been alcoholics.

They were all there, an unchanging tableau rather like the painting of the Last Supper: Stella, Quigley, the hangman, Sam the stripper, the sanctions-busting salesman, the old major, Fiona, Chris Raymond and Bram lounging against the wall with a glass in hand. Who was the Judas? Maybe we all were.

Nothing had changed. Stella was dressed as if she had stepped out of one of those period country-house soap operas so beloved of British audiences. Bram was wearing a jacket and tie. He was never off duty. I went straight to the bar.

'Fancy a snifter, old man?' said Raymond.

I ignored him, ordered a whisky and joined Bram.

'I hear you may be leaving us,' he said.

'Do you listen in to *everyone's* phone calls?'

'Only those that might be important.'

'And my talk with my editor ranks as important?'

'I said "might".'

I leant against the wall beside him and took a sip of the whisky.

'Enjoy your drink. The barman says that's the last of it.'

'What?'

'Local stuff only now, unless you go back to your old hotel.'

'Tell me about Jeeze,' I said.

'It's been in the papers. Nothing to add.'

'Come on, Bram, he was your man, that's why they killed him.'

I said this just loud enough for the bar crowd to hear. They turned to look at us. Stella pointed her cigarette-holder at Bram.

'Is that true?'

Bram steered me to the alcove.

'What are you trying to do?'

'Hadn't you noticed? Journalists ask questions.'

'Not in full view of that crowd.' He jerked his thumb towards the bar.

'Fair enough, so what's the answer?'

'You cannot play with both sides in the same game.'

'How was he betrayed?'

'Ask your girlfriend.'

'She doesn't know.'

'Maybe she knows more than you think.'

'You blackmailed him, didn't you?'

He shook his head.

'How long have you been here?' he said. 'A year, months, is it? And you've learnt nothing. The only reason you're still here is because you work for an American magazine. Remember that.'

Chapter Seventeen

The call came through in time. The line was good, the voice from Paris strong.

'Richard?'

'Yes.'

'I hate you. *Tu es un salopard minable, infidèle et égoïste.*'

'My French isn't that good.'

'You're a shallow, selfish, cheating bastard.'

'This call is being taped.'

'Good. I hope the whole country is listening.'

'What's the point of calling?'

'I just want you to know that nothing has changed.'

'OK, I get it, so . . .?'

There was a long pause. I could hear the sound of a cigarette pack being torn open.

'I want a favour for a friend.'

Virginie Ducroix was a freelance photographer. Her work had occasionally appeared in *Paris Match*. Freelance photographers were arriving in numbers, hoping for that one picture that would lift them from obscurity. Although they were a burden to an overworked press office, they brought in valuable foreign exchange.

'She's coming out. I want you to help her.'

'How exactly?'

'Stop playing games, Richard. Just give her some advice, introduce her around.'

'When is she coming?'

'Soon. I will send you details.'

'I may not be here much longer.'

'Oh?'

'It's complicated.'

'OK. By the way . . .'

'Yes?'

'I miss you.'

The line went dead.

•

Days passed without a word from New York or a sign of Virginie Ducroix. I doubted the government would have denied her a visa, since the French were known to be breaking sanctions by supplying spare parts for the Alouette helicopters.

I say 'known' because while we knew that to be true, no one reported it. We told ourselves that the war had entered a final phase and that sanctions were no longer an issue. I had never tried to get to the truth of just how international sanctions were being broken by traders in arms, raw materials and medicines. That was a red line for the Information Ministry people and to cross it meant expulsion. In my early days, I might not have accepted that trade-off. Now it didn't seem to matter.

There were still a few French mercenaries to be seen in the Riff Raff Bar, noticeable by their hair cut to the scalp and arms heavily tattooed with the double-barred Cross of Lorraine and love hearts dedicated to girlfriends. They had been a disaster on operations, partly because of language problems, but also because they were unable to distinguish African villagers from rebels. Several small-scale massacres had been hastily covered up, or so we heard. These rumours were probably true, but that's what they remained, rumours.

Time had lost its meaning. The days had faded into weeks and the weeks into months. I felt as if I had spent my life here. I was exhausted, propped up by alcohol and the Remington. However tired, however drunk, I could always slide paper into the machine and write.

Patience was also exhausted. On our nights together she fell into my arms and went to sleep. 'Don't fool yourself', she would say. 'This is sex, not love.' She was working long hours, taking classes by day and rehearsing plays in the evening. Her disappearance one evening every week remained the same maddening mystery. Where she went and with whom I knew not. It was better not to ask. It usually happened on Thursday nights. I would phone the school those evenings to be told she had left early. No, they did not know where she was.

The sense of an ending hung heavily on all of us. The prospect of Julia's wedding provided some slight relief. I had seen little of her since lunch at the farm that day. She was sharing an apartment somewhere in the suburbs, working in a clothing factory. The swimming pool was closed. She occasionally appeared in the club, where she badgered me to introduce her to Patience. When I did one lunchtime in the club, she flung her arms round her, until Patience gently pushed her away.

'You will come to my wedding, won't you?'

Patience gave me a look and said, 'Well, let's see.'

'No, let's not see. Just say yes. It's just family, really. Richard is almost family, aren't you, Richard?'

'Of course I can't go,' Patience said to me later. 'Their farm was bought for a blanket and a bottle of brandy. The groom is a killer in the infantry. I can't celebrate the wedding of a settler farm girl and a murderer.'

We were talking in the alcove. She was speaking too loudly.

'Quite right,' shouted Quigley from the bar. Stella had turned her back.

The next day she changed her mind.

'I will come with you,' she said quietly. 'I would like to see a white farm behind wire with all those bells on it.'

'Why?'

'It tells me we've won.'

'You won the war a long time ago,' I said.

We were talking in a township café at the end of a long school day. The date and place for peace talks would be announced the next morning. I had the news from Chris Raymond, who passed it on as 'Exclusive just for you. Can't stand these Yanks. Fancy a snifter, old man?' I had decided by now that there was more to Raymond than a moth-eaten old drunk. He was acting.

I filed the story to New York. The peace talks were to be in London in one month's time. Despite the rains and low cloud, the fighting had intensified. Several thousand young guerrillas were in camps across the border, better trained, better armed and with high morale now that victory was in sight. It was hardly a secret that the regime was planning ever more large-scale operations against this threat. A savage finale to the war was coming before both sides sat down behind polished tables with carafes of water, notepads and a shared conviction that nothing would be achieved by such a farce.

Music drifted into the café as a band marched past. Drums, flutes and horns created a stirring sound that was rather too martial for the occasion. The Salvation Army, uniformed in dark-blue trousers and jackets, were parading with banners saying 'Christ is Peace and Joy'.

'I hope that's true,' said Patience.

'It will soon be over,' I said, and leant across the table, taking both her hands.

'I'll believe that when it happens.'

In our endless discussions, we had talked about the here and now of the war, the white flight, the long-buried enmities that were surfacing in nationalist ranks, the death toll and terror inflicted on the civilian population, the crowded hospitals, the acts of gallantry on both sides, the weariness that had settled on everyone like chalk dust in a classroom after the end of the school day. Every time I had raised the subject of the future, our future, Patience just shook her head.

'We may all be dead by then. Why make plans and tempt fate?'

'There's Shakespeare in there somewhere,' I said.

'It boots not to resist both wind and tide,' she said, looking at me with the smoky grey eyes I had first seen when we met in the Victoria. There was doubt in those eyes, then as now. 'You think we have a future here?'

'Here or wherever,' I said. 'I want to marry you.'

I don't know who was more surprised. I spoke those words quite casually and without any forethought. In fact, I had imagined doing so on bended knee in the Cancan with George serving champagne in fluted glasses. The words had slipped out. A proposal made but not accepted, a promissory note of a future neither of us had even talked about.

She sat back, breaking my handhold, and laughed, not in mockery but in embarrassment, I think.

'*What* did you say?'

'I said I want to marry you.'

'Richard, you cannot propose in this shabby little café. What if I say yes? Where's the champagne? Admit it. You just made that up. You don't mean it.'

I got down on one knee, picked up the silver salt cellar, held it out to her and said, 'Patience Matatu, will you marry me?'

She took the salt cellar from me.

'Don't be ridiculous. Get up. Everyone's looking.'

At tables nearby people had turned to watch this spectacle. I sat down. She took my hands again. There was no doubt now in her eyes. They were bright and shiny.

'You flatter me, you stupid fool, but it's … too soon. We don't know what's going to happen.'

And that is where we left it. I tried to argue because, having made a fool of myself, I felt there was nothing to lose. What was the point of waiting, and waiting for what? We were in love, I told her, but she said that was not the point. Then she irritated me by quoting Shakespeare again. I quoted back the one about love being an 'ever-fixed mark', but I couldn't remember the rest.

We both laughed, which was the best way out for both of us. The café owner waived the bill, wishing us good luck. Patience insisted on paying him and left for her school. She turned on the pavement and blew me a kiss.

•

Paula beckoned me when I got back to the Diplomat.

'You have a visitor upstairs,' she said.

Virginie Ducroix was short, bespectacled, with a bulging shoulder bag and brown hair tied tightly back into a pigtail. She was drinking beer from a bottle and talking to Quigley in heavily accented English.

I introduced myself and drew her aside. Quigley followed us to the alcove table, resisting my attempts to shake him off. I bade her welcome, asked about her flight and the reception at the airport. She said she was surprised to find everything apparently normal, without any sign of a country at war. I asked about Marie Claire. Beyond acknowledging that they were close friends, she would not be drawn.

'She asked me to give you this,' she said, pulling a small package from her shoulder bag: *Les Fleurs du mal*, the poems of Charles Baudelaire with an English translation that I had left behind in her flat. We used to read it to each other, she in the French version, me in the awkward English translation.

To my relief, Fiona Foxley appeared in the bar and I was able to introduce them. As photographers, they had a great deal in common and fell into animated conversation.

•

I thought stupidly that the wedding reception at the Milan farm might prompt Patience to look kindly on my proposal, but she said nothing throughout the strange journey there, from the moment we set off in the morning convoy.

We were now being protected by armoured cars rather than machine-gun-mounted trucks. There were some twenty cars waiting to take the road north. At the halfway mark, where the tribal reservation began, the lead armoured car began firing into the bush. We could see nothing and heard only the noise of the heavy machine guns.

We never learnt what had caused the shooting.

Julia and Raphe had been married that morning in a local chapel with just their families present. She was flushed with excitement and looking very much the beautiful bride when she greeted us at the poolside.

There were some thirty people gathered around the pool, mostly women wearing dresses that were too dressy and the hats that only come out on such occasions. The staff were serving drinks from a bar under a marquee.

Everyone turned as Julia ran to greet us. She hugged us both, Patience with excited extravagance, then turned to the other guests and said, 'Richard and Patience, everyone, just up from town.'

With that we were ushered into the marquee and given glasses of white wine mixed with soda water. 'The best we could do,' said Julia. 'Come and meet some people.'

The guests had been well briefed. The presence of an African woman at a white farmer's wedding was unusual, to put it mildly. The ripple of interest among the guests had been evident when we arrived. I left Patience in a bubble of women and walked over the lumpy turf to Layla Milan.

'I hope you've turned these things off,' I said, pointing to the small mounds.

She laughed. 'Moles make a mess, don't they?'

I had to laugh with her. It was a good joke on me. I should have put it into the first story I had filed.

'Doesn't she look beautiful?' said Layla.

Julia was wearing a long beaded white dress, her hair pinned up and crowned with a wreath of flowers. The dolphin tattoo had been covered in white gloves.

'Stunning,' I said.

'I just wish he could take her away from here, start a new life somewhere, Europe maybe.'

'Can he do that?'

'No, he can't, and anyway he won't. They will be here for the duration. She will live with us while he is on call-up.'

'That's not ideal.'

'That's the way it is. Anyway, small mercies, they seem very keen on each other. One can't ask for more.'

I looked over at Patience. She was being introduced by Julia to one group after another. There were very few male guests. The plated food was served and a small group of musicians began to play versions of songs from great musicals. 'Some Enchanted Evening' received several encores. Patience was now talking to the staff, listening carefully with bowed head. Layla Milan was watching this with interest. I looked at my watch. It was getting close to time for the return convoy. They would gather three miles down the road.

We said our goodbyes, kissed the bride and shook hands with the groom. On the way back Patience asked me what we had given them as a wedding present.

'Dinner for two at Franklins,' I said. 'George will look after them.'

She nodded. We were in convoy now, travelling at speed.

'That was a surprise,' she said suddenly,

I waited, keeping my eyes on the road. We were driving through the reservation.

'We have images of people, don't we?' she said. 'We stick a label on them. These people didn't fit any label. I expected them to be racists, blind to the world around them. But they were different.'

'In what way?'

'There were a couple of frosty bitches who pretty much turned their backs, but the others were curious. They asked a lot of sensible questions and tried to make me feel at ease. They weren't patronising. If anything, they seemed fearful about what was going to happen. I appreciated that.'

She spoke without looking at me, staring ahead. The women had wanted to hear her views and seemed to accept that peace and independence would not be on their terms. Repeatedly, they wanted to hear what the nationalists were going to do. They used that word 'nationalist'. They didn't say 'terrorist'. They asked what was going to happen to the farms, and would they be forced to leave?

'I said I was just a teacher, but they seemed to know better. They had obviously been told all about me,' Patience said, taking her eyes off the road and looking at me.

'Not guilty.'

We drove on. I could see that all the passengers ahead, mostly women, had their rifles pointing out of the car windows, presumably with safety catches off. Since there were sharp bends in the road, this made me nervous.

Shortly after we left the reservation, Patience began to laugh. I looked at her quickly. She went on laughing, then stopped, dabbing her eyes.

'I'm sorry, I just can't help it.'

The convoy had speeded up. We were in the outskirts of the city.

'Just can't help what?'

'That salt cellar. You weren't serious, were you?' she said, and broke into giggles again.

Drunk I may have been, I said, but I had meant my proposal and knew we had a future together. The rattle and whine of the old Peugeot going flat out to keep up with the convoy stifled my words. The conversation ended on that note. She went to sleep on my shoulder. We continued in silence for the rest of the drive.

I tried to persuade her to come back to the hotel with me, but she said she was tired. I offered to drive her home to the township, but she said she would take a Red Top taxi instead. She kissed me goodbye on the cheek and suggested we meet by the fountains the following evening.

•

My memory of what happened next is clouded by anger at my stupidity. Perhaps no man could have grasped what was really going through her mind that afternoon at the wedding.

I should never have taken her there.

She was late for our meeting. I had been sitting by the fountains watching the sparrows fly in and out of the spray for twenty minutes before she arrived. We talked briefly about her school day. She was planning another Shakespeare production, this time a real challenge for the school, *As You Like It*, a comedy that would surely defeat her pupils. I had been baffled and bored by the only production I ever saw.

Then she spoke almost without pause for ten minutes. She talked in a low voice without looking at me. She must have prepared what she said carefully. I watched the sparrows as the words flew at me.

'I cannot go on like this, Richard. *We* cannot go on. I have long known we come from different worlds, but that would not matter if I thought we could find a new world together. Yesterday at the wedding I realised how far apart we really are.

'It would have been better if those people had been the racist bullies of my imagination, but they weren't. It would have been better if the groom had not been a man who had killed my people and would kill again. It would have been better if somehow I could have found a bridge there, a feeling that we could all share the same future, that we could all rebuild this country after independence. But we can't.

'We have different destinies. I didn't like those women very much, but they were decent in their way. I understood them, and that only made it worse, do you understand that?'

I shook my head. There was nothing to say.

'We can pretend we have a future together, but do we really?' she said. 'I am going to stay here. My people have fought for the future of this country. We will build it up again and, frankly, we don't want your help.

'Your people built this place with our sweated labour; you gave us nothing in return. You took away who we were, made us believe in our own inferiority. That was the cruellest punishment of all. That was our shame. We have redeemed it now. We've won. We don't want to go on with you. You didn't share this country with us, so why should we share it with you?'

She fell silent and looked away. I looked at the fountains. The sparrows had flown away. It was well past six. The lights round the square had come on, casting shadows in the gloaming. I hoped to break the moody silence and take her away from this place, the square, the fountains.

She began to speak again in the same low tone, again with lowered eyes.

'I am sorry, but it is the same for us. We may say we love each other, but that's not real. The women I met yesterday were nice to me, kind even, and said they had heard all about my Shakespeare plays. They said they wanted to share the future with us, turn time back and start over. But it's too late. Everything is too late.'

'But what has this got to do with *us*?'

'Everything! Be practical, for a start. I have said this before, but you never listen. You are a well-known writer for a famous magazine. Are you going to give that up? Where would we live? Your favourite city, with that girlfriend breathing down our necks? Of course not. And in any case, you threw her over, didn't you? You betrayed her. That was brutal, you said so yourself. You have been wallowing in self-pity ever since. Why wouldn't you do the same to me?'

'Because I love you.'

'I love you too,' she said, and hugged me, holding me tight. 'I really do, but it's too late.'

It was dark now and cold. She got up and walked away without a kiss. I could not find the words to say anything, not even goodbye. I watched her disappear into the ink of the night. I sat there without moving for a while. I needed a cigarette and a drink. Silver bullets were made for moments like this. I walked to Franklins.

•

I had written nothing for the magazine in ten days, which was unusual. The desk had not complained or even contacted me. Their attention was on the Middle East, where events in Israel, Syria and Lebanon were building to another regional war.

I envied the correspondents there, men and women I knew. They had a big breaking story that was moving to a climax, which would dominate the world's media for weeks. I was stuck in a small country with a small war and small-scale peace talks, which nobody really cared about.

Kissinger had briefly cast his shadow over us and had moved on. It was time for me to do likewise. I could choose my next assignment, although it would not be the Middle East, which is where I really wanted to go. I hated the repetitive nature of war reporting, but I did envy the glamour, the headlines and the huge audiences that radio, print and TV gained in that part of the world. That was power.

In any case, there was no reason to stay. Patience's bitter words milled around in my head, impervious to reason. She didn't really mean what she had said. It was a reaction to the wedding party that would pass. She would not regret her words, because many of them were true, but she would have the sense to see that I could hardly be blamed for the past in this country. I cursed myself for taking her to the wedding.

As for us, how could I deny what she had said? Was I really going to give up my career with a prestigious magazine and become an African-based freelance reporting a circular story of decline and fall? Colleagues would be winning prizes, gaining acclaim and becoming media celebrities while I was here, and for what? For love. And I did love her. I wanted her now as never before. I was desperate to keep her in my life. But maybe she was right. It was too late.

The next morning a short story in the local paper caught my attention. Pentecostal missionaries had returned to the mission station in the eastern mountains where the massacre had taken place months earlier. Patience had visited the mission, where she had helped stage a play for the local children. The lead missionary, Michael Munnion, was reported as saying that three families would start their work again as an act of faith.

'We believe in our God, just as we believe in the essential goodness of all humanity. What happened here was an act of evil. To fight evil we must forgive. "Father, forgive them, for they know not what they do," said Christ on the cross. That is why we have come back here. To forgive, but never to forget.'

Those words were my story. God against the gun.

The drive down a thin strip of tarmac on a dirt road in the middle of what the military called a 'high-intensity operational area' was an act of madness.

I thought it might make Patience see the risks I was prepared to take to bring the world's attention to people she cared about deeply. This would be my last story in this blighted country, a story of Christian courage and compassion in the face of danger. God against the gun, as I said. A compelling headline on a story that would make her see how much we had to lose.

I wasn't religious, but I had always admired the faith of those who were. I wish I had had the spiritual comfort of faith. The worship of God would have made sense of my life. Instead of which, I was driving down a dangerous road feeling sorry for myself.

There was no sign of life when I arrived. The sun gave warmth and colour to two long bungalows beside a small stone chapel. On the grass in front a silver plaque had been bolted onto a craggy rock bearing the names and ages of those who had been murdered.

I had grown up in a suburb of London where many German rockets had fallen during the war. The simple memorial plaques were exactly the same there as here: a few brief words with the date of the attack and names and ages. What tugged at the heart then as now were the ages of the children who had died.

I was looking at the plaque when a voice called out.

'Can I help you?'

Michael Munnion was a short, wiry man in blue jeans and a bush jacket. He watched me warily from a distance. He relaxed when I told him why I was there.

'We don't get many visitors,' he said. 'Come in and have some tea.'

We drank from china cups on a veranda that ran the length

of the house. I told him of the brief paragraph in the paper that had made me curious. I was thinking of writing an article centred on an obvious question: why had he come back with his wife and two other married colleagues after what had happened? The question loomed larger after he told me the story in precise detail and without emotion.

I don't think he was trying to impress me with his courage. If anything, the brutal facts of the massacre made his return and that of his colleagues look like supreme folly. Patience had already told me some of the details, but she had suppressed, or had not known, the true horror.

I fetched a bottle of whisky from the car. We both needed a drink. It was getting cold, so we went inside to a sitting room furnished with comfortable armchairs and a sofa. Michael circled my single repeated question with various lengthy expositions on how faith in God was the quintessence of Christianity and how faith was central to any religion.

'If you do not have faith in the existence of God, what is the point of our existence on earth?' he said.

'How can faith protect you from another such atrocity?' I asked.

'Because if we don't have faith, we don't have God, and God commands us to forgive.'

I was beginning to enjoy this theological debate and thought it might make a piece. Journalists are such self-centred bastards.

'I accept that,' I said, 'but does God really want you all to come back and put your lives at risk after what happened?'

'Did God really want Jesus to die an agonising death on the cross?'

'That's a lawyer's answer, Michael. I am not a religious man, which may be why what you have said hasn't made any sense at all. You have not given any reason for you to be here, except for a bizarre desire to honour your slaughtered colleagues by repeating their tragic mistake.'

'Now you are talking like a lawyer. Religion is not rational; that is the whole point.'

To change the subject, I asked about the pastoral work of the mission. Michael gave me details of the religious teaching given to African villagers in the area and the clinics, which provided basic medical advice and treatment.

I resisted the strong temptation to say that since the dawn of time the local population had worshipped their own gods, so why should we try to convert them to ours? As for medicine, there was no doubting the effectiveness of penicillin, aspirin and other modern drugs, but to evangelise about such medical wonders without taking into account long-developed local remedies, many based on herbs, seemed arrogant.

The whisky began talking. I made the mistake of suggesting to Michael that the murdered missionaries had sacrificed themselves and their children out of vanity: they thought their good works somehow raised them above the bloody war around them. They may have looked up at the hills at night and prayed to Jesus, but in those hills were men looking down on this unguarded settlement with bloodlust. Was that so hard to understand?

We had both drunk enough whisky to lose our tempers. Finally, he got up and left, pausing at the door to point me to the sofa.

•

I was certain that my sacrilegious remarks would bring a bolt from above in the shape of a landmine on the drive back the next day. The heat shimmering off the tarmac and a thudding headache made driving difficult. The unctuous piety of these people continued to irritate me. I gave up the attempt to stay on the tarmac strip. What was the point? They could lay a mine anywhere on the track.

I took a circular road around the city to drive through the township on the way to the city centre. I drove to the school and parked the car a short distance from the entrance. It was 2 p.m. on a Friday. She would have finished lunch in the staff canteen. Her pupils would be at their desks with their sandwiches wearily waiting for another afternoon of Shakespeare.

Patience was a creature of habit. I knew what she would do next. She came out, paused, cupped her hands to light a cigarette and walked across the street. She stood by the lamp post, exhaling smoke, looking up at the grey-white sky.

I cautiously got out of the car. If she had turned in my direction, she would have seen me. Instead, she threw the cigarette away and returned to the school. I could so easily have gone up to her, but I knew that she would have given me that same sad smile and told me to go back to the hotel. There was no point. She surely could not have meant what she had said by the fountains, but this wasn't the time or place.

I made plans to leave that night. I would take a plane to a country in the north with a palm-fringed Indian Ocean shoreline. The peace talks were due in three weeks. Nothing would happen in the meantime except the daily treadmill of news: the body count, ambushes, landmine blasts on major roads. It would be somewhere to shake off the dust and forget an invisible war with its pious missionaries, the drunken crowd in Pinks, spies, informers, traitors and a compliant workforce waiting for the wheel of history to turn.

I telexed New York to say I was taking a break. The reply was swift and brisk. 'Understood and approved.' There was no congratulation on my work or interest in why I had chosen this moment to leave a strong story.

In the club that night, I asked Quigley to step in and cover for me. He looked puzzled, then gave me a beery hug and ordered us both a beer. 'Try and stay sober,' I said.

Stella was not happy. She spoke with the imperious tones of a queen to her courtiers. 'We are within sight of peace talks and you're leaving to lie on a beach? That makes no sense, Richard. We are all tired of this bloody war. But we're sticking it out. Why are you so special? What has happened to you?'

Her courtiers turned briefly from the bar to hear these unkind words, frowned at me in agreement and turned back to their usual discussion about the black-market rate.

In the alcove, Virginie Ducroix had been watching this scene with Emma Lamb. She waved to me to come over. This was the point of the club. Everyone was always there.

'Will you do me a big favour, please?'

'Maybe.'

'I'd love some perfume. I'll pay you of course.'

'I know nothing about perfume, what sort do you want?'

'Chanel No. 5 if you can get it. It's expensive but . . .'

'. . . you'll pay me. I know.'

I sighed, sat down, looked at her and nodded.

'You are coming back, aren't you?' she said.

'Of course he is,' said Emma Lamb.

'I am supposed to be keeping an eye on you,' I said. 'What are you doing with a secret policeman?'

She laughed. Emma did not look amused and Quigley came and placed a further bottle of beer in front of me. I left, giving Virginie details of my hotel on the coast in case she needed me. I felt responsible for her. They had been talking about mine-proof vehicles. Virginie was going to use one on a trip into the bush.

As I left, Emma put a hand on my arm and said, 'We will keep an eye on her for you.'

She saw me look at Virginie.

'No, not her.'

Back in my room, as I packed quickly, I wondered why the Special Branch were helping an inexperienced French photographer to go dangerously deep into hostile country on dirt roads. An easy way to get information without the risk, perhaps?

George made me a farewell cocktail that night, insisting that I try a new version of the Manhattan, which he had learnt from an American businessman: a bourbon whisky base, sweet vermouth, with a slice of lemon instead of bitters. I took one sip and switched back to my usual. I told George of my travel plans. He asked when I was coming back. I don't know, I said.

Chapter Eighteen

I t was a mistake. I had a room in a pleasant beachfront hotel with a large balcony overlooking the Indian Ocean. Much as advertised in the brochure, the palm trees whispered at night outside my window and the sea curled small waves onto a well-swept sandy beach only a few metres away.

Grilled fresh fish from the ocean and exotic fruit cocktails were served under the palms on pewter platters. There were deep-sea fishing trips, nightly music, dancing and local markets to explore. The other guests were an interesting mix of a honeymoon couple who argued loudly about their room, middle-aged women hopeful of romance, and elderly men who would slip into the palm groves at night with young Africans who looked more like boys than men.

I limited myself to beer and tried to read the few books I had brought with me. Even a rereading of Chandler did not prove a distraction. Closer inspection of the romantic notion that my departure might remind Patience of what we had found in each other revealed a wishful fantasy.

She was not going to repent her decision. I remembered every word she had said by the fountains. They played in my head in endless reprise. She had every right to refuse a future as an exile from a country she had fought for. I had proposed marriage to her like a circus clown. She had rightly laughed. I would return and do so properly; for better or for worse, I would remain at her side.

The BBC World Service brought me news of the war I had left behind. The nightly broadcasts told of manoeuvring by both sides, the division within the white regime between those who wished to fight on and those who saw the futility of doing so. The prospect of power was sharpening old rivalries among the nationalists.

The progress of the war, a contradiction in terms if ever there was one, was going as expected. Rebel deployment of Soviet ground-to-air missiles and restricted government airpower was the major story. Quigley would be busy.

•

My plane landed shortly after sunset. A taxi took me straight to Franklins. I'd had enough of the Diplomat. The city was darker. Fewer street lights were working. Power lines from the big lake had been sabotaged, I learnt later. I checked in and went to the bar. George had shaken and poured my drink before I had sat down.

I had been away for only a week, but he seemed to have aged. He looked tired. The lines on his face were deeper. The moustache more grey than black. I handed him the note I had carefully written on the coast. I had used hotel paper with a graphic of palm trees on the beach across the top. He put it behind the bar without a word.

I wanted to tell him that it was urgent, that Patience should read it as soon as possible, that in the note I had dared to hope that we might find the love we had lost, that I would wait forever for a reply, that I would . . . And so it went on, love and hope imprinted in ink on cheap hotel paper.

I walked to the Information Ministry the next morning. Returning correspondents had to report to a press officer. Peter Fryer was busy but someone else wanted to see me. A bearded man smelling strongly of whisky and looking as if he had just been run over by a car greeted me in his office. It took me a minute to recognise Chris Raymond. A nameplate on his desk said 'Acting Chief Press Officer'. He flipped through a file in front of him too rapidly to read anything. He paused at one page, looked up and waved the file at me.

'Says here you like a drink.'

I shrugged. He looked at his watch.

'Care for a snifter, old man?'

I looked at my watch. It was 10.30 a.m.

'A little early for me.'

'Just a quick one?'

Without waiting for a reply, he produced a bottle from a drawer – decent Scotch, I noticed – placed two shot glasses on the table, filled them almost to the brim and carefully slid one across the desk to me.

He raised his glass, and drank.

'You certainly upset our missionary friends.'

I sipped my drink.

'They've made a formal complaint, saying that you had no

permit to be in the operational area and had no right to visit them without notice. They said you were "unmannerly" and "insulting to their Christian faith".'

'What's this got to do with the ministry?'

'Absolutely nothing. They're a bloody nuisance. They try to buy off the terrs with food.'

'In which case, why did you want to see me?'

'Lighten up, old boy,' he said, pouring another glass and raising the bottle to me enquiringly. I shook my head.

'You need a new permit extension and I just wanted to meet someone labelled here' – and he peered at the file – 'a "curate's egg".'

'What does that mean?'

He looked again at the file.

'Says you're a curiosity, neither one thing or another. Sort of an in-between man. Are you an in-between man?'

'You tell me.'

'God knows who writes these things,' he said, pushing the file away so abruptly that it slid off the desk onto the floor.

He held up the bottle again. I shook my head.

'Are you sure?'

I had been called many things, but never a curate's egg. I thought of other insults that had come my way, most less literate than this one. The curate's-egg crack would be useful in a personal farewell piece summing up my assignment here. As for Raymond's early-morning appetite for whisky, who could blame him?

•

I was looking for coffee afterwards to wipe away the whisky taste in my mouth when a voice hailed me from across the street. Layla Milan hurried between the traffic. She wore a black armband on the sleeve of her dress.

Catching my glance, she said, 'You haven't heard?'

I shook my head.

'It's Raphe.'

'Oh no.'

'The military police have taken him.'

'What?'

She took my arm as we walked down the street.

'Julia is in pieces but is being very good about it.'

'I don't understand.'

'I'll let her tell you. She's been waiting for you to get back.'

We parted on a street corner. She gave me a quick kiss on the cheek. I was to meet Julia in a bar next to Franklins that evening at eight. The place was a known haunt of off-duty troops, an odd choice.

She was sitting in a corner sipping a drink through a straw. The bar counter was lined with uniformed troops. At the far end a soldier was standing, sleeves rolled up, with a catheter in his arm leading to a bottle of fluid held head-high by a fellow soldier. Both men were drinking beer. The soldiers were all talking, but not loudly.

Julia looked up and smiled. She was very pale and her freckles seemed to have melted into her skin. She had lost weight.

'I'm so sorry,' I said. 'What are you drinking?'

'Lemonade. I am trying to stay sober. But it's hard. I'll have vodka or gin, it doesn't matter now.'

She raised her glass to me. I could see the dolphin on her underarm.

The soldiers parted to let me buy the drinks and went back to their beer.

'I was stupid. I should never have done it,' she said. 'I just thought that . . .'

I waited.

'I just thought that if we got married, it would somehow protect him and keep him safe. I thought God would not let a just-married man do that.'

'What happened?'

She drained her glass in one. 'I'd like another of these.'

I was about to get up when a soldier appeared with two drinks and a small bucket of ice.

'I'm sorry,' he said.

She almost cried then, but smiled, thanked him and wiped away a few tears. She looked down at the floor, resting her head on her hands.

'It was so stupid. Raphe was with his call sign on tracks close to the border. Usually they can tell how close they are: footprints, body odour, torn leaves – that stuff. This time the terrs were good. They knew they were being tracked. So they backtracked and set an ambush. Two of Raphe's team got killed. Raphe was hit in the thigh, but it was only a flesh wound. The terrs took a lot of wounded and fled. There was a nearby village. Raphe went in. They tried to stop him.'

She paused. I went to the bar. The trooper with the saline drip was waving his beer bottle at the barman. I returned with two vodkas. The gin had run out. We sat in silence for a while.

'They were all trying to hide in their huts. He went in and shot them all, women and children mostly, some old men. He reloaded, kept on firing. They caught up with him when he ran out of ammunition. He is in the stockade now. They won't try him; you can't in this war. They'll hush it up. He will see a psychiatrist. They'll say he had a mental breakdown and leave it at that.'

'God, that's awful.'

'That's the man I married.'

I thought back to the soldier we had interviewed at the airbase. The hazy look, the eyes clouded by smoke. The man who had shot his dying cook. That last word, '*esche*'. At the farm he had been just a normal soldier happy to be on leave with a beautiful girlfriend. The same man had celebrated marriage to this young woman by a swimming pool with staff serving cold drinks from a marquee.

'I'm so sorry.' There was nothing else to say.

'I've been to see him. He didn't recognise me. Divorce, I suppose. I'm not playing nursemaid to a madman for the rest of my life.'

'What about his family?'

'I don't want to talk about this any more. Do you mind? Let's just say there are no happy endings here.'

She looked up and turned to me.

'What about you?'

'What do you mean?'

'Are you going to marry that nice girl?'

'If you mean Patience, I wish I could.'

'Why don't you?'

'We've broken it off.'

'Shame. She was lovely. The servants have not stopped talking about her.'

This was not what I wanted to hear. I had received no reply to my note. I did not wish to be reminded of what I had foolishly lost. My Indian Ocean reverie about winning Patience back was just that, a dream. She had made herself clear, not once but twice.

'What are you going to do?' I said.

'I can't stay here. Leave, find a job down south?'

'And the farm – your mum?'

'You'd better talk to Mum about that.'

The eyes of the bar followed us to the door. I said again how sorry I was. We were standing on the pavement. She looked at me, a suggestion unspoken but alive in her eyes. She shook her head and walked to the taxi rank. She had been a girl when I first met her. Since then she had survived a road ambush, been married and was now about to divorce. She had grown into a woman. She had made mistakes but she was right about one thing: this was no country for happy endings. I never saw her again.

•

The talks in London surprised everyone. The intransigence of the nationalists crumbled under the pressure from neighbouring states anxious to end a futile conflict on their borders. The regime faced equal pressure from a world weary of a small faraway war. In the context of rivalry between the great powers, the war I had grown used to, a conflict that had changed my life, didn't matter to anyone else.

The final days before the ceasefire produced memorable cameos. The hotel staff at Franklins, both black and white, went on strike, parading outside the hotel with banners demanding big pay rises. The sight of both races linking arms sent a shock wave through the city. George was not among the protesters.

One Friday evening, the busiest night in Pinks, the door burst open to reveal a young woman with a bandage around her head and an arm in a sling, walking on crutches. Virginie Ducroix hobbled into the room to a round of applause. She had survived a mine blast on a tarmac road.

She accepted a drink and flung her arms around me. She had been travelling with others in a well-proofed vehicle with metal plates under the chassis and sandbags on the floor when they hit a supercharged mine.

'Where?' someone asked loudly.

'Mount Darwin road, not far from Shamva.'

They had been the lead vehicle and the main target for the small-arms fire that followed. She had been thrown onto the roadside. She lost consciousness briefly and came round to find bullets hissing overhead.

A rebel fighter was sprawled beside her, clipping a new magazine into his rifle. His stench mingled with the reek of cordite was a smell she would take to her grave. The fire fight was going on across the road. She was on the wrong side.

The club fell silent. A real story had walked through the door. People were writing furiously in notebooks. A camera flashed.

Virginie paused and held out her glass, which was swiftly refilled. A chair was offered and she sat down.

'Go on!' said a voice.

She thought she was going to be either killed or abducted. The shock had given way to terrible pain. The man beside her was firing on automatic, his face buried into the ground, not looking at any target.

She described the noise as like the loud crackling of wood thrown on a fire. There was no other sound. She tried to roll away. She heard a groan and saw blood seeping through the camouflaged clothing of the fighter beside her. She could remember nothing else until she woke up in the back of a truck.

The club emptied. This was a good human-interest story. TV crews went to get their cameras and the print hacks to file. Virginie began to cry and was comforted by Fiona.

Bram had slipped in, hearing only the end of this story. He beckoned me and nodded to the door. I had hoped that Patience might turn up. There had still been no reply to the note. I didn't want to pursue her at the school. We had to meet on equal terms somewhere. She would have hated that story. More futile deaths as the old regime clung to the shreds of a tattered flag. She would have said something like that.

Outside, the night was chilly. We stepped into the darkness, away from the pool of light outside the hotel.

'It's too late,' Bram said. 'It's over.'

He sounded bitter.

'What are you talking about?'

'We surrender to the colonial power – your country, Richard – they hold elections and a new African nation is born.'

'Is this what you have brought me out here to tell me?'

'There's something else.'

'About Jeeze?' I said.

Bram rarely smoked but he lit one, handed it to me and lit another.

'No. He was stupid. A bad boy in a bad boys' war.'

He walked away without another word, but paused just within earshot.

'St Peter's church tomorrow morning.'

Chapter Nineteen

The church was on the borders of the township. It was known for its choir and was well attended by township residents and the liberal-minded from the minority white community.

I heard the deep-throated rumble of the organ as I approached. The music was familiar, but I could not immediately place it. It sounded like an anthem from the American Deep South. Then the choir came in, riding on the crest of the organ with a tune familiar from schooldays that I could not place.

The church was a solid brick building constructed in the 1930s with funds from evangelical groups in America. It was larger and grander than any other church serving the African community and looked as if it had been shipped in brick by brick from some prosperous town in the Bible Belt.

The ornate door opened with a push. The pews and pulpit were partially lit from sunlight filtering through stained-glass windows. The body of the church was mostly in darkness. A polished brass handrail gleamed around the top of the pulpit. At the end of the nave, two choir stalls faced each other in a halo of light from lamps strung from ceiling rafters.

The altar was covered in an embroidered white cloth on which lay silver ornaments. Above, a large cross rose towards the roof bearing the crucified figure of Christ. The crown of thorns had been painted gold. The interior was larger than the outside had suggested. I was surprised. The size and rich ornamentation of the interior were unexpected.

I mention these details because like many people I find the subdued splendour of a church pleasing. There is comfort in the peace one finds in church even if, like me, you have no regard for religion of any kind.

A thin, reedy character was conducting with a baton. I took my seat at the back and listened to the music. There were six African choristers, men and women, in each of the facing stalls. They were wearing everyday clothes. It was a mystery as to why Bram had sent me here, unless he had become a devotee of choral music. Or perhaps it was his idea of a joke.

I concentrated on the singers. In the middle of one row, half hidden by those on either side, I caught a flash of yellow. I looked more closely. A large yellow butterfly hair clasp. I moved seats the better to see, glad of my place in the dark.

This was her secret. This was the door into another world she had talked about, her escape from school, from Shakespeare and the struggle. This was the balm for her soul she had mentioned. This was the secret of the weekly disappearances she had been so anxious to conceal from me.

But why? I could only admire her pursuit of inner calm in this way. Perhaps she thought that singing in a Christian church was alien to the traditions of her people and alien, above all, to the violence of the struggle.

Perhaps in this church she sought redemption for the atrocities committed in the name of liberation. Lightning does not choose where it strikes, she had said, but lightning brings us the storm and the rain. That's what we need to wash away the shame of colonial rule.

'Washing away with blood?' I had asked. She said Christianity had been born in blood. Blood will have blood. It was one of her favourite sayings.

I scanned the rest of the choir carefully. Patience would not be alone in the pursuit of balm for the soul.

Charity was sitting beside Patience, wearing jeans and a black clenched-fist T-shirt. A familiar figure, not easily recognised in an unfamiliar surrounding, sat on the opposite choir stall. He was the only one wearing a cassock, which partially concealed his bulk. George, master of the silver bullet, was singing an unlikely mix of religious and pop music.

There were flyers on the seats, which told me there was to be a choral concert that night to raise funds for two township schools.

The choir moved on to sing what the programme said was Mozart's *Gloria* in B flat. Then 'Hear My Prayer' by Mendelssohn. Pieces by Fauré and Beethoven followed, with diversions into popular mainstream music. 'Some Enchanted Evening' seemed to be everyone's favourite. It reminded me of Julia's wedding.

I closed my eyes and went to our last conversation. She had been clear. She had been firm. But she was wrong. The music lulled me into a light sleep. My reverie was broken by a voice and a light tap on the shoulder.

'What are you doing here?'

She was standing looking down at me. Beside her Charity stared at me as if she had seen a mouse.

'I came to hear your choir.'

'No, you didn't. What are you doing here?'

'Does that matter? The choir was beautiful.'

Charity turned and walked away. Patience sat down beside me.

'Richard, you cannot follow me around like this. I have a private life and that is what it should be – private.'

'I see no harm in listening to your choir.'

'You're being childish. Who told you we were rehearsing here?'

I picked up the flyer.

'It's hardly secret, is it? You have a public performance tonight. It stands to reason that you would be rehearsing this morning. I happen to like choral music.'

'Don't take me for a fool, Richard. I know why you are here. But I have made my decision. It's best for both of us.'

'Does it occur to you that you might be wrong? That we could find happiness here. We loved each other; you said so yourself. Why throw that away? Don't we at least owe it to each other to try to find a way to make this work?'

'Make this work? We're not talking about a broken clock, Richard.'

I could see George drifting past in the background. He glanced at us with a look of disapproval and walked on.

'OK, at least let's talk. Surely we owe each other that?'

'Do we, Richard?'

'Do you love me, Patience?'

'That's not the point.'

I picked up a prayer book and slammed it as hard as I could against the pew.

'It's the whole bloody point. You love me and you know it. That's the bloody point. What do you think I'm doing here?'

'Stop shouting, and stop being so dramatic. Did you put that poor girl in Paris through all this?'

'That's not fair.'

'It's not fair to track me down like this. Our affair is over.'

It was the second time she had used that word 'affair'. 'A passing physical passion' I think is the dictionary definition.

I got up. Everything I felt for this woman, any hope I had of sharing those feelings with her, was crumbing away in the pews of a darkened township church.

I looked at her properly for the first time in this exchange.

'I'm sorry. I shouldn't have come.'

'Don't look at me like that,' she said.

'Like what?'

'That little boy let's-have-one-last-drink look.'

•

I couldn't persuade her to come to Franklins. I thought the presence of George might have helped. She refused. We went to Sandro's. The waiter brought two glasses of red wine. She sat facing me. The look on her face was that of a weary teacher with an unruly class.

'We're just hurting each other, Richard. We can't go on doing this.'

She had not lifted her glass from the table. I clinked it gently with mine. She reached for it. We touched glasses and drank.

'I understand,' I said. 'But tell me about the choir. The singing was beautiful.'

She sighed in exasperation and told me she had been singing since her mission-school days. She had a good soprano voice and had been encouraged to practise by Mrs Haworth, the same woman who had introduced her to Shakespeare.

'You mean you got Shakespeare by day and singing lessons by night?'

'I was lucky. They were good people.'

'Tell me more about the choir.'

'No, Richard. I am only here to make it less painful for both of us. Don't try to pretend this is a normal conversation.'

She took my hand across the table.

'Tell me you understand. This is over.'

'I don't really understand, but I'm not living in hope, Patience. I'm just interested in your singing, the choir. Why didn't you tell me, why the big secret?'

'Because it is part of me I don't want to share; not with you, not with anyone. It's private. When you sing in a choir, you lose yourself. It's like stepping out of your body. You leave everything behind.'

A waiter came for the order.

'Another glass of wine and then I must go,' she said.

I nodded and asked for the same. We sat looking away from each other for a few moments.

'Just tell me why. Make me understand, because I don't.'

'Look at me,' she said. Her eyes locked onto mine. 'When I talked to those women at the wedding reception, it took me back to the mission and made me think of Mrs Haworth. That dear woman gave me everything; those wives and their husbands took it away. Their whole life was based on denying me what Mrs Haworth had given me. They were born into a world they did not understand. I have told you this already, but you don't listen. Your people didn't just take our land, they took away who we were. Do you get that?'

'Of course I get it. I've written about it.'

'No, you haven't. You're like those women. They were not stupid. Some were well educated. They're not evil. They were not racists by choice. They were racists by birth. They could never have stood up for us, because they were born to believe we were all servants. That is when I knew we were separated by too much – that life together was impossible.'

'That didn't stop you coming back to my bed.'

'Lust makes a fool of us all, Richard.'

She got up. Her wine was untouched.

'I am not going on with this, Richard. I came here to try to make things less painful. I am not going to be drawn into an argument.'

'You know I love you.'

She bent down, kissed me on the cheek and whispered, 'Men's vows are women's traitors.'

I had been talking to a different woman, a stranger. People don't really understand one another, they survive on fantasies about each other in which truth hardly finds a lodging. I don't know who said that, it was just one of those sayings that drift around in my head like autumn leaves in the park. I stood up. She gave me a brief hug and gently pulled away.

She began walking to the door.

'What are you going to do?' I said

She turned. 'I'm going to speak for the dead.'

I held her long after she had walked out into the street.

•

My time here had been a trap. I had stayed because love in a time of war made good copy. The love of the land by two peoples divided by history. Perversely I saw romance and agony in that story. That is why I had stayed, bitter though the end might be.

After the years of war, the reality of independence was an anti-climax. The transfer of power was peaceful. A nationalist government took office. Flags were lowered and raised. Some of the old regime took new roles in the government. In the Cancan nothing much had changed. George dispensed the same cocktails. The same faces were there most nights.

In the La Fontaine restaurant waiters in black suits, white shirts and bow ties were still guiding diners to tables carefully laid with silver cutlery on white tablecloths. I supposed that Marion was still cleaning bedrooms and sifting through wastepaper baskets.

I didn't ask anyone about Patience. She would be teaching English to a classroom of teenagers by day and persuading them to perform Shakespeare at night. She would drink beer with Charity and Rosie at the Victoria Hotel. She would swim in the pool below the small waterfall wearing the same long, clinging swimsuit. She would go with George for weekly choir practice. She was right. There was no point in us seeing each other again.

For a few days I held onto the idea that there was still work to be done. There would be a bloody settling of accounts by all sides. A signed peace treaty cannot end years of killing overnight. Blood will have blood. I decided to stay and write an end piece for a story that had devoured my time and attention for years. That's what it felt like: years.

There are moments when the truth is too painful to face, when a lie subdues the qualms of conscience and offers the easy way out. The lie I told myself ended with a brisk call from Meredith Kaplan.

There was to be no more prevarication. I was a popular writer with a loyal readership, but the time had come for a new assignment. I was to take a staff position in the Middle East bureau based in Beirut.

Meredith made it clear that I could not refuse the posting. And why should I? The position with a base in Beirut was all I could hope for. A chance to test myself against the formidable opposition of celebrated top American and European correspondents.

It was a tantalising prospect. Prestige and prizes represent success in a profession such as mine. There would be a price, though. There was always a price. The shameful compromises, half-truths and above all betrayal of both friends and principles. There is no reporter who has not cut a story to suit the required version of the truth – a truth conveniently shared by his editor and readers.

The job would mortgage me to a career and the shallow fame that came with it. I had kept hidden my unpleasant inner self from the woman I loved, the beautiful Patience Matatu. Perhaps she had seen that in me. 'Men's vows are women's traitors.'

•

I went to Pinks that night to say farewell. Patience and I had already said our goodbyes. George would no doubt hear of my new posting and pass it on. There were new and old faces at the bar. The old faces briefly wished me well and returned to the topics of the day: the power shortages, which had cut off air conditioning across the city and the fast-rising black market. Chris Raymond detached himself from the bar.

'I hear you got a new job. Care for a snifter, old man?'

I thanked him and declined. I didn't bother to ask how he knew.

The new faces were gathered around Virginie Ducroix. She had a pronounced limp and a long curving scar down her left cheek. The battle-hardened look of a war veteran in pigtails gave her an aura of sexual promise. She had taken full advantage of her attraction, I gathered.

'Hi, Richard, I have news. Marie Claire is getting married.'

She saw my surprise. And followed me to the alcove table.

'Are you sure about this?' I asked.

'She called last night and insisted I go back for the wedding.'

'Who is she marrying?'

'A man who runs bakery shops. Nice chap. I've met him.'

The man with the bakery on the corner where she bought her croissants. He was a young entrepreneur planning a string of shops across the capital.

'When is the wedding?'

'A month's time.'

•

She would be back from work now. Soon he would be climbing the narrow stairs of 150 Rue de Rome, all 114 steps to that single room under the eaves, the door open at the top, the glass of red wine waiting. She had regarded me as deceiving and dishonest. An unflattering portrait I was forced to acknowledge. I wondered how long her affair with the baker had been going on.

It was 6.30 p.m. I was leaving in the morning. I had crossed one frontier on arriving and now I was to cross another.

Patience and I had parted for one reason only. Strip away the emotional whirligig of our relationship and the passionate protestations of enduring love and one salient truth emerges. Ambition had trumped love.

As for my sexual duplicity, I could not really be blamed. My brief afternoon hour in bed with Julia – or was it two? – was an act of compassion for a young woman traumatised by a road ambush that had almost killed her.

That is what I told myself.

Chapter Twenty

My flight left for Geneva early the next morning. A connecting flight took me to Beirut late that night. I reached the apartment around midnight. It had been rented by the company in a smart area of the city. The view from one window was of a string of lights along a broad seafront boulevard. In the other direction, a dark ridge of mountains was speckled with lights.

After the alcoholic haze of my year in Africa I was determined to make a new start. I had a small whisky and went to sleep.

I wrote two letters the next morning. The first, to Marie Claire, congratulated her on her forthcoming wedding. I hoped she would find the happiness that we had lost. She would not like that. It laid the blame for the end of our relationship equally between us. That was neither true nor fair, but I was weary of sackcloth and ashes.

I made a little joke about the baker's shop, saying I now knew why she had taken so long to get the breakfast croissants. She would not find that amusing. She always said the English sense of humour was inexplicable to foreigners, especially the French.

The second letter was to Patience. I wrote a breezy account of my flight and first impressions of Lebanon. I said it wasn't really a nation state, more a collection of tribes with flags and guns. That wasn't original. I had lifted it from the title of a book. The pretence of the letter was that we were still lovers, although separated by circumstance and distance.

•

I had been warned to avoid the Commodore Hotel, which provided room, food and drink for visiting journalists. It was described to me by the desk as a suitable setting for the opening scene of *Macbeth*, a witches' kitchen wherein was a frothy brew of rumours, lies, debauchery and drunkenness.

If ever there was a commanding invitation, that was it. The entrance of the Commodore led to an echoing hallway with a bank of lifts on one side and on the other a long semi-circular bar in which there were two solitary drinkers. Beyond was an almost empty restaurant. A bank of wire-agency machines lined the far end of the hall, clattering reams of paper into wire baskets.

A sharp-suited manager appeared, guided me to the bar and offered a complimentary drink. He didn't have to be told I was another visiting journalist. The barman had never heard of a silver bullet. He made me a pink gin; two drops of Angostura in a wine glass whizzed around with ice followed by large measure of gin.

He told me with a shrug that the press corps had decamped to a valley over the mountains where a hostile power had deployed surface-to-air missiles. Another saga in the permanent conflict between tribes with guns was about to be written into the history of the region. It had been going on since biblical times.

There comes a moment of clarity in life when everything changes. It is like watching a thick crust of snow sliding from a roof in spring: the glistening slates of a house long hidden by winter suddenly and silently emerge in the soft sunlight. You cannot choose where lightning strikes, as Patience said, but for a flickering moment you can see the road ahead.

My career as a magazine writer ended under the light of a fireworks party, a suitable celebration of a new life ahead and a mark of mourning for the life I had left behind. The phone call from Meredith had been brief and brutal. Fears of a recession had led to a drop in advertising. Subscriptions were down. Senior management had decided to cut staff. That meant me. I was to leave the company. There would be a severance package and the grateful thanks of the editor-in-chief.

This wasn't the real reason. Only a week before, I had been given a new assignment and praised as a popular writer with a loyal following among readers.

'This is bullshit,' I told Meredith. 'This has nothing to do with staff cuts. I am better than anyone you have abroad. You know that. So the truth, please. Why me? What have I done wrong?'

There was a long pause at the end of the line. She wasn't chewing gum this time.

'You got too close to the story,' she said finally. 'I tried to warn you.'

'What the hell does that mean?'

'Don't do this, Richard. You know what it means.'

'I don't know what it means.'

There was a long silence on the line.

'Is this your decision?' I asked.

'No. I have been a great admirer of your work. But I couldn't fight for you. There are big staff changes. I'm leaving too.'

This angered me more than my own dismissal. A great desk editor and servant of the company had been fired, or 'let go' in the current parlance, for reasons deep in the personal politics of the newsroom.

I told her how sorry I was and we left it there. There was nothing else either of us could say.

I ate supper in a small fish restaurant on the Corniche. A fireworks party in a nearby house celebrated a birthday or a wedding. I raised a glass to the distant figures dancing on a terrace. The sparkling colours cascading from the sky seemed a good omen for the future. I would cable acceptance of my dismissal to New York in the morning. There was no point fighting it.

There would be a brisk and increasingly irate exchange of messages over the terms of severance. In a bar near the office, over evening drinks, once-admiring colleagues would find good reasons to explain my departure: a nervous breakdown, an affair with an African woman, obvious sympathy for a rebel regime. A curt demand to bring my expenses up to date would end my employment.

Once my anger had subsided, helped by a bottle of wine, I decided to send a message to George at Franklins. He would pass on the news. Patience would be surprised, maybe even pleased, for me. I raised another glass of wine to the cascade of fireworks and said her name loudly. People at nearby tables turned to look at me. The wine was a strong red from vines grown in the valley over the mountain. Red wine and rockets. A good title for a feature, but I would not be the one to write it.

•

I awoke the following morning without regret or anger. I sent off the various messages and scanned the morning newspaper for a new apartment, somewhere up on the hill so I could see both sea and mountain.

I had never planned for this moment, because I was stupidly arrogant enough to believe that the magazine couldn't do without me. I had been a star writer. Again and again, I turned over various reasons behind my sacking – for that, put brutally, was what it was. The truth, I decided, was more prosaic than Machiavellian. Meredith Kaplan had fallen foul of office politics and I, as one of her favourites, had been chosen to be dismissed with her.

I swept away such dark musings with the cheerful thought that I could finally write a long-planned book: *The Mad Genius of Baudelaire* would rescue the greatest of French poets from the world of academia. Marie Claire and I had spent hours reciting his poetry and debating his place in the history of literature. She saw him as a major figure in the French canon. I placed him on the world stage, an innovator who influenced Joyce, Eliot, Auden and a host of American writers.

My departure from the magazine played out exactly as I had

thought: a series of emails about money and a refusal to pay any onward airfares. From George and Patience I received no reply. I told myself I didn't mind.

I found my apartment. Two bedrooms with a large living room and a terrace halfway up the hillside. I engaged a maid and bought a car, a second-hand Citroën that made a sound like the roaring lion that opens many Hollywood films.

I settled into my new life. The days turned into weeks. I took Baudelaire from infancy to the trauma of his father's death when he was just six years old. My life became a comforting routine. I worked in the mornings and lunched with a glass or two of wine. The maid cooked well, usually grilled fish and a range of local specialities: tabbouleh, hummus, kibbeh. I slept and read in the afternoon. An evening swim in the open-air pool by the seafront and then back to revise. Whisky on the terrace and bed long after dark.

I was enjoying my monkish isolation. I told myself that I didn't miss my job on the magazine. I did, of course. Wounded pride is like a deep bruise: it changes colour and takes time to heal. The late-night whisky was taking me well past midnight. Like most alcoholics, I told myself that strong drink was necessary medication against the stress of a new life. I was easily persuaded.

A month or two passed as I dug deeper into old Paris: sewage on the cobbles, whores at every corner and hovels lining streets narrow enough to throw up a barricade in minutes. This was the city Baudelaire loved; the cafés, brothels, wine shops and cheap restaurants were home to the young poet. This was where he found his poetry. His world was torn apart when the city was reborn with broad boulevards and gracious apartment blocks. Paris became the City of Light, but not for Baudelaire.

●

I went to the Commodore occasionally to have a drink and scan the agency tapes. I enjoyed the place. The bar was always crowded and rowdy, but the agency reports took me out of my solitary life and kept me up to date.

One evening, buried amid news from around the world, I saw a small story about rising opposition to a new nationalist government in Africa. Riot police were breaking up protest marches; arrests and swift extrajudicial trials had jailed the leaders.

I went into the bar and shouldered my way through to get a drink, a pink gin. Patience would be enraged. The new government was using the same tactics of suppression as the old regime. She would have helped organise the marches. She would have been at the front holding a banner. I could hear her shouting, 'Who is to speak for the dead? Did they give their lives for a new tyranny?'

She was sure to have been arrested. They would have dragged her away. The police had not changed. They had merely changed sides. Bram and his agents knew all about Patience Matatu.

I drank the gin and ordered another. A bearded figure wearing a shabby suit and a shirt fraying at the collar and cuffs elbowed his way to the bar beside me. He smelt as if he had not washed for a week. He lit the stub of a small cigar and signalled the barman for a drink. I was about to move away when he said, 'Fancy a snifter, old man?'

'What the hell are you doing here?'

'Same as you, old man, running away.'

I was surprised but not displeased. The dilapidated figure of Chris Raymond would know all about events in the country I still cared for.

He had flown in some weeks earlier on an airfreight flight, after a complicated deal with the pilot, and planned to freelance. He told me his old job had vanished as a new Information Ministry replaced the old.

'Why here?' I asked.

'Plenty of work, old man. This lot need someone to cover for them when they're having fun.' He nodded to the throng behind him.

We fenced around, me asking the usual questions about life under the new government, he giving vague answers.

'They've locked her up,' he said finally.

I had already guessed that.

'I thought she had friends in high places.'

'It's all changed. "Who speaks for the dead?" is her campaign slogan for the protest movement. They hate that.'

'Why?'

'Corruption. That's what she's talking about, and they don't like it.'

•

My routine changed. After a morning's work on the book I drove to the Commodore every day to check the agency reports. It was usually quiet then. Raymond was almost always at the bar. We would lunch at a local café. He had become a fixed part of my day. I enjoyed stumbling out of old Paris into the familiar company of a man unworried by the furious world around him and interested only in good wine and gossip.

I had never paid him much attention apart from our brief exchange when he was Acting Chief Press Officer, a meeting he now preferred to forget. He always wore the same shabby clothes, which he seemed to regard as a uniform. The dark beard was flecked with grey but carefully trimmed. He had a drinker's misty eyes but a welcoming smile. I enjoyed those lunches. He was better informed than the news on the wires and knew in detail what was happening in 'the old country'.

We always talked first about Patience. She had been released by a court order, then immediately detained.

'Bit of push-and-pull in government,' said Raymond. 'They don't know what to do with her. She's a hero to the people but a pain to those in power.'

The authorities were worried. Patience was gaining international support for her 'Who speaks for the dead?' campaign. Human-rights groups inside and outside the country were finding support from the big aid agencies.

I watched every day as the wire agencies reported a story that was climbing up the news schedules. The international media scented a campaign that would sell papers and engage television audiences. Patience was a prisoner of conscience.

She was being held in a high-security jail that had once held nationalist prisoners. News of her hunger strike hardened diplomatic pressure.

I felt powerless and angry as I watched this daily battle between a young woman and a regime intent on destroying her.

I was slowly being pulled out of old Paris. The seductive sorcery of Baudelaire's poetry was still there, but those tortured love poems played with my memories.

I had tried to forget the hard woman with the fast tongue. I had cancelled my old life in Africa. I had a new life. I had a publisher for my book. *The Mad Genius of Charles Baudelaire* was going to be a great success, he said. You have turned a poet into a rock star, stripped him bare and shown the soul of a genius to a new generation of readers, he said. Such seductive words were mere fodder for a book jacket quote and meant nothing.

I had a good apartment in an exciting city. Occasionally a lecturer at the university would join me on the terrace to drink and discuss the latest twist in the mad regional fandango. She taught history and told me her students were enchanted not by the politics of the past but by its unknowable mysteries, great artefacts like the Pyramids, Stonehenge and the ruins of Palmyra.

We didn't become lovers. She said she did not want that. 'All history is gossip' was her favourite saying, and we would gossip over fine wine and local dishes. I liked her enormously.

•

I cannot now remember how I heard the news that morning. It was either a call from Raymond or an item on the radio. In the blur of the day that followed I have forgotten such detail. I do know that I kicked off the bedclothes and drove straight to the city without so much as a cup of coffee. The agency reports in the Commodore confirmed that Patience had been released and expelled. She was variously rumoured to have been flown to Europe by the Red Cross or given sanctuary in a neighbouring country. There were even reports that she had gone to America at the invitation of a women's group.

I went to a travel agent near the hotel and booked a return flight to Geneva the following evening. I did not book an onward flight. I was going to spend a few days walking the hills around the city until I heard further news. In any case I needed a break. It was early autumn, a perfect time.

We lunched as usual that day, and clinked glasses of red. Raymond had become a different person in Beirut. The vagabond clothes were the same, but the wreck of a man who had washed up in Pinks had gone. I began to think it had all been an act. He bent to his food and we ate in silence for a while.

'I'm going to take a break for a few days,' I said.

'Where are you going?'

'Switzerland. Do some walking, look at the mountains.'

'You can walk and look at the mountains here, Richard.'

'I want somewhere different.'

'That travel agent is a crook,' he said suddenly.

'What travel agent?'

'I saw you going in, Richard. He's well known for forging tickets. Show me yours.'

I took out the ticket and handed it to him. He looked at it briefly and tore it in half.

'What the hell are you doing?'

'Saving you a lot of money. It's a fake,' he said. 'Let me handle this.'

'How do you know it's a fake?'

'Never mind how I know.'

I was so stunned I believed him. He told me to go to a proper travel agent. He would get my money back. We were to meet for lunch the following day at a restaurant in the town of Jounieh on the coast about 12 miles north of Beirut. He named the restaurant and said it had a splendid view of the harbour. I was to be there around noon. He issued these instructions, and that is what they were, and left before I could ask any questions.

I watched him walk across the street, his baggy trousers flapping in the breeze. I knew Raymond had been in trouble with the police back in Britain; at least that was the story he had allowed the Pinks regulars to believe. I had seen little of him outside the club and never asked about his time in London.

An unlikely friendship had come about in this city, two lost souls finding comfort in a shared past. That was the way he positioned our relationship. Without friends in the city, I accepted that and trusted him. The tramp-like figure who had been a permanent fixture at the Pinks bar had taken on an entirely new character. It was only now that I began to wonder why he was here and who he worked for.

I went to Jounieh the following morning. I was curious and I wanted my air ticket. Raymond was many things, but I did not think he was a crook. The drive along the coast was pleasant and the restaurant easy to find on a small road below the casino. There was an open kitchen behind a marble bar top and tables and chairs on a large terrace beneath vines trailing across a rattan roof.

It was just past noon. There were a few people at the bar studying menus. I went in, sat down and signalled to the barman. He nodded, came over and began mixing a drink in front of me. The ingredients were familiar, as were his actions with the shaker. He could have been George in the Cancan. He placed a silver bullet in front of me.

'How did you know?' I said.

He shrugged and finished making the second drink, another silver bullet. He set it on the bar beside me.

Someone sat down on the stool next to me and reached for the glass. Yellow finger nails gripped the stem. I turned. She sipped the drink and raised the glass to me.

'Mud in your eye,' she said.

The end

Acknowledgements

Many people go into the making of a book. Even a conversation overheard between two women on a London bus can be a gift to an author. Here are those who have helped me most, with apologies to those I have overlooked.

John Bond and his team at whitefox publishing: Julia Koppitz, Becky Miles, Jess King, Chris Wold, Holly Kyte and Simon Levy, great work all round. Tim Waller, a brilliant and scrupulous editor; Annabel Merullo, my patient, long-suffering agent; the incomparable Dotti Irving; Peter Jordan, Gary Burns, Sue Smart, Paul Harris, George Gordon; Pippa Freer, Louise Gubb, Henrik Ellert, Felicity Green, Karen Robinson, Sally Nicholson, Virginie Roell-Lacaille, Jane Mays, Angus Shaw, Trevor Grundy. To Alex Shulman, Sally Emerson and Jane Thynne, my heartfelt thanks for taking the time and trouble to read and comment on the manuscript. Finally, to my wife, Sally Davies, without whose love and support I would never have got this far, I owe a debt I can never repay.

In memoriam

I dedicate the book to the memory of those departed friends, colleagues and acquaintances in long-ago Africa who still tap me on the shoulder in my dreams.

Godwin Matatu, Roger Horrell, Justin Nyoka, Chris Munnion, Chris "Crazy" Reynolds, John Edlin, Ian Mills, Paul Ellman, Ian Wright, Campbell Page, Marilyn Poole, Neil Davis, Jane Scott Long, Jane Bergerol, Heidi Holland, Stella Day, Sarah Barrel, Wilf Nussey, Patrick Laurence, Deon du Plessis, John and Lola Morkel, Ian and April Piercey, Peter Preston and Martin Woolacott.